CHASING BLOOD

PAUL STANLEY

BALBOA.PRESS

A DIVISION OF HAY HOUSE

Balboa Press books may be ordered through booksellers or by contacting:

Balboa Press
A Division of Hay House
1663 Liberty Drive
Bloomington, IN 47403
www.balboapress.co.uk
UK TFN: 0800 0148647 (Toll Free inside the UK)
UK Local: (02) 0369 56325 (+44 20 3695 6325 from outside the UK)

Because of the dynamic nature of the Internet, any web addresses or links contained in this book may have changed since publication and may no longer be valid. The views expressed in this work are solely those of the author and do not necessarily reflect the views of the publisher, and the publisher hereby disclaims any responsibility for them.

The author of this book does not dispense medical advice or prescribe the use of any technique as a form of treatment for physical, emotional, or medical problems without the advice of a physician, either directly or indirectly. The intent of the author is only to offer information of a general nature to help you in your quest for emotional and spiritual well-being. In the event you use any of the information in this book for yourself, which is your constitutional right, the author and the publisher assume no responsibility for your actions.

Any people depicted in stock imagery provided by Getty Images are models, and such images are being used for illustrative purposes only. Certain stock imagery © Getty Images.

Print information available on the last page.

ISBN: 978-1-9822-8702-3 (sc)
ISBN: 978-1-9822-8704-7 (hc)
ISBN: 978-1-9822-8703-0 (e)

Balboa Press rev. date: 03/09/2023

For my long-suffering wife who has encouraged me throughout this journey; without her positive thinking, this book may not have been written. A thank-you to my friend Dave for his help, his advice, and his very useful knowledge of Belfast. My appreciation also goes to my editor and the team for leading me through the publishing steps and for their help and support.

CHAPTER 1

He stood gazing out at the distant hills. Dawn was breaking, and the brightening sky was the backdrop for the silhouetted mountains still draped in their night colours. The fading moon above was slowly disappearing as the sun peeped over the horizon and prepared to bake the awakening world.

Slowly, his eyes made their way over the brown dusty landscape etched with deep ravines and canyons. Continuing their journey, they came to rest upon the rooftops of the nearby town which lay beyond the compound, the wall topped with barbed wire, the razor-sharp blades glinting menacingly in the morning light.

He looked down to the yard below, which was a hive of activity. Men were busy loading trucks, checking the armoured vehicles, and making the final preparations before beginning their day's work. He was pleased; his men had learned well. They'd had to; not being meticulous or being lax could endanger not only their lives but also the lives of their comrades. Everyone counted on everyone. It was the difference between survival and death. He nodded his approval at what he saw, the results of five years of work, four tours of duty, and strict training. It was a fine balance between being a father figure and accessible and being the boss. He was a hard man to please, but he knew all too well that any deviation from the rules or their focus would, more likely than not, result in death or severe injury. Everyone respected him.

He was suddenly brought back to earth by a sharp knock on the door, which he automatically answered with a loud "Yes, enter."

He turned to see a young corporal standing at the door, saluting his superior. "Sir, your bags and kit have been loaded. We're ready to go when you are."

"Thank you, Corporal. I will be down shortly." The young soldier saluted once more and closed the door.

The officer flinched ever so slightly at the sight of the man standing before him, but his demeanour remained impassive. Slowly, a smile crossed his lips as the intruder stepped forward. "How the hell did you get in, Number 1?" he enquired, keeping his voice level.

"Apologies, Colonel. I didn't mean to startle you." The man continued to come forward. "To answer your question, it was easy; I slipped in about five minutes ago, when Johnson was away getting your kit. The door was ajar. I noticed you were in a different world."

"Well, Major, I certainly think it's time I left this place. If I am so lax as to not hear you coming in, then I shouldn't be here." He smiled and stuck out his hand.

"I just wanted to come and say goodbye and to pass on to you and your family my deepest condolences, Brian. I hope that things settle down for all of you and that the bastards who killed your brother are caught soon."

Colonel Brian Jackson turned back to the window and looked out at the courtyard again. "Thanks. I appreciate you coming. Not sure the police will be able to do anything. You know what they're like— all talk and not much action when it comes to murders like this. I can't be sure, but I feel it was planned, that there is more to it than they're saying." He continued to survey the action below. "Feels like the IRA or one of the affiliate gangs to me. And if that's the case, then the culprits will never be caught."

Major Peter Hollins stood watching his friend in silence. They had gone through training together, had graduated together, and had been posted around the world. The only difference between them was that he had joined the SAS. After all these years, they remained friends—no, brothers, the bond between them stronger than ever. When he had first been sent to Afghanistan five years ago, he had pulled strings to get his close friend to follow and be by his side.

2

"You've done a great job, Brian; the men will miss you, and so will I." He hesitated before continuing. "On another subject, I was wondering whether you could sign my leave papers before you walk out on me. I need a break after six months in this place."

Colonel Brian Jackson shook his head. "Sorry, I am now officially no longer in charge—you know that. You will have to ask the new commander when he arrives."

"Do we know who we're getting?"

"Think it will be a chap by the name of Jones, recently promoted, a pretty smart guy by all accounts. That's what I've been told, anyway. Not much experience in this kind of field, so you'll have to point him in the right direction. I'm sure he is extremely capable, but you know what it's like; things are different out here."

Major Hollins grunted. "That's all we need—a kid, green round the ears, who thinks he knows it all."

"Don't be like that. You don't know him. He may be brilliant and bring some great new ideas. Give him a chance and the benefit of your experience for your sake and that of the lads." He strode forward, hand outstretched. "Time to go, or I'll miss my plane. See you around. And make sure to avoid the bullets and mines."

Peter watched as his friend strode through the door and down the corridor. He went over to the window and watched the man salute the troops who had stopped their tasks to come and wave goodbye to their leader. They all had tremendous respect for him. He had taught them to grow up and to think differently, and in many ways, through his hardness and unrelenting demands, he had helped most of his men survive and stay alive.

With a final salute and a wave, he climbed into the jeep and was driven off.

He walked into the vast cavern of the plane, which was already loaded with crates of equipment and occupied by returning personnel. He walked past the screen of curtains behind which lay beds occupied

3 ·

by wounded soldiers. Farther on, in a special area separated by a makeshift wall, lay four coffins. Making his way to the front, he found a seat and made himself comfortable.

Twenty minutes later, the gigantic plane was rumbling down the runway. After what seemed an eternity, the nose rose and painfully, ever so slowly, the huge aircraft left the ground. Brian closed his eyes. This was the part he dreaded, take-off and landing, the most dangerous times, the slow plane a sitting target for any rockets launched from the hills or the myriad of deep creeks below. His breathing slowed as he felt the vast machine reaching its cruising height, knowing the pilot had set its course for home.

CHAPTER 2

The day was grey with clouds hanging low over the distant hills; the constant drizzle mingled with the mourners' tears. Brian was standing by the grave, his sister-in-law Felicity clinging to his arm, listening to the minister drone on about life after death and how Brian's brother, John, was in a better place. As the coffin was slowly lowered, Brian sighed deeply and felt the woman by his side shake in grief. Instinctively, he tightened his grip on her hand.

No one noticed the two strangers. The first one stood at the back of the gathering, head bowed, hat pulled low. The other stood about a hundred yards away, sheltering under a tree; he had his coat collar turned up high to protect him from the rain, his hands deep in his pockets. He watched the proceedings until the mourners started to drift away. Then he turned and made his way to the gate at the far end of the cemetery.

Brian and Felicity remained by the grave, both deep in their own thoughts and memories, until they were alone. Finally, after dropping a small bouquet onto the coffin, they said their final goodbyes before turning and making their way to the waiting car.

Back at the Horse & Plough, the mourners had arrived and were jostling for a place by the open fire, their conversation no longer hushed. As Brian and Felicity walked in, the voices dropped to a murmur and pitying looks were cast in their direction. It didn't take long before normal chat resumed with laughter and the clinking of glasses.

Felicity started her tour, thanking friends for having come, chatting, and agreeing with most of what people were saying, although half the time she was not listening. Brian automatically set off in the opposite direction, doing the same. He had been collared by a particularly loud woman and was at a loss on how to politely get away when he felt a hand on his shoulder. Relieved, he swung round to face the person who was about to save him. He gaped in shock at the smiling face standing a few inches away. "Number 1! Peter, what the hell are you doing here?" he spluttered.

Peter Hollins turned to the woman and apologised for his intrusion before guiding his friend to a far corner of the room. "Well, unlike you, our new commander signed my leave papers. I have three weeks before I am due back."

"Hey, that's a bit harsh. You know I couldn't do anything. Boy, I am pleased to see you. When did you fly in?"

"Just joking. Landed two days ago and made my way up immediately. Staying in this place, in fact."

"Should have warned me. You could have stayed with us. How long are you planning on staying?"

Peter shrugged. "Not sure. Depends on a few things."

They talked awhile, until they were interrupted by a tall, thin man sporting long sideburns. He introduced himself as Detective Inspector Crawley. Peter was about to leave when his friend held him back. "No, stay. I'm sure DI Crawley won't mind you listening in on what he has to say. DI Crawley, this is my very close friend and battlefield partner Major Hollins. We have fought around the world together for many years, more than I wish to remember. He just came back from Afghanistan the other day to attend the funeral."

The detective nodded. "I was just wondering whether we could have a chat sometime soon. Tomorrow perhaps?" He looked at both men, waiting for an answer. Before either of them could say anything, he added, "Not that I have any real news. Just need to pass a few things by you."

Brian nodded. It was agreed that they should meet in the pub the following day at lunchtime. The detective thanked Brian before making his way out.

"Not sure I really like the little man. He's a bit weaselly and hesitant, and certainly he'd be no use in the field. Too indecisive."

"You are a hard man, Peter. You barely know the chap and have no idea how good he is at his job. You should be more lenient."

Peter Hollins was about to reply when another stranger sidled up, holding a plate laden with canapés. The major looked at the new arrival and instantly took a disliking to him. A thirty-something man with a paunch, which would grow quickly if he continued eating the amount he was holding, and a mop of dishevelled hair matching his shaggy beard stood looking up at them. His clothes were crumpled, and his tie was badly knotted but what really got to Hollins was the state of his shoes. Peter was a stickler for clean, polished footwear, a sign of discipline. The man hesitated before turning to Brian. "You must be John's brother. Am I correct?"

Brian nodded, but before he could say anything, the stranger continued: "My name is Jones, Alwyn Jones, a reporter from the *Daily Echo*. I apologise for intruding on you at this stage, but I was wondering whether you had any clues as to who killed your brother?" With no reaction from either of his listeners, the reporter continued. "Seems strange that the police have not come up with anything yet. Do you have any suspicions? Did he have any enemies?"

Brian looked down at the man in disgust. He hesitated, deciding how to respond. At last, he smiled broadly and stuck out his hand. "Colonel Jackson. Pleased to meet you. No, we have no idea who killed my brother. Nor do the police. But please, I don't wish to talk to anyone except the authorities—and especially not to the press."

"As I said, I'm from the *Daily Echo*, and my job is to report on accidents, muggings, and murders. Seeing as your brother lived in the area, I have been assigned to find out more. I don't want to make trouble. If you hear anything, can you please contact me?" He handed Brian a card. Just then, they were interrupted by a loud burst of laughter from across the room. Looking over, they spotted the source of the mirth. A plump balding man had cornered Felicity and was holding forth about something which, by all signs, was distressing to the widow. The reporter shook his head. "That's Jim. He and that woman with the big black hat spend their time gate-crashing funerals. They go to the services, listen to the eulogies, and then turn up at the wake posing as friends of the deceased. That way they have a day out with free food and booze. They have done it for years. Many people do it."

Peter was about tell the reporter what he could do with himself but quickly changed his plan of action. In a few strides, he had crossed the pub and grabbed the intruder by the scruff of the neck, spilling the large tumbler of whisky down the man's own shirt. Lifting him up, Peter swung round and marched over to the woman, who was looking on, shock etched on her plump face. Her expression turned to horror once he had grabbed her elbow and, mouthing protestations, she found herself being propelled towards the exit. It was all over in a few seconds. Peter ejected the couple into the car park with no finesse and bawled at them to get lost, adding that they'd be wise never to cross his path again. If either of them had thought to reply, it was quickly forgotten.

By the time Peter returned to the main party, Brian was by Felicity's side, consoling her. The other guests had begun to disperse. Peter turned to the journalist. "I hope you will not report what you have seen. In fact, it would be better for your career and your future life prospects if you didn't." The man nodded and slipped away.

CHAPTER 3

Peter Hollins and Brian Jackson were sitting by the fire the next day, nursing a pint, when DI Crawley appeared and sat down across the table from them. He declined the offer of a drink.

"I hear I missed all the fun yesterday," he said with a wide grin. "Never understood people like that or those who go to accidents to gawp at death and carnage. It's a necessity of my job to see gruesome things, but to physically choose to go and look ..." As his voice trailed off, he shook his head.

"Don't tell me that that reporter told you. I warned him to keep quiet!" Peter interjected.

"No, no, not him. He's harmless—just another small-town hack struggling to make a living. No, it was the couple themselves. They came in and reported that they had been assaulted by a large, burly man during a wake." He smiled. "Told them they got what they deserved, that it was one of the dangers of their pastime."

Peter thanked him for his understanding and raised his glass to him.

The detective continued. "Now, about our meeting. I really need to ask you a few questions about what you know. I have spoken to Mrs Jackson, but she was unable to give me much information except that your brother was in the army, stationed in Belfast as an adviser, and that he was due back about now. She said he had no enemies that she knew of and that he got on well with the other officers and soldiers. So, not very much to go by."

Brian shook his head. "As you may be aware, I have been in

Afghanistan for the past six months. The last time I spoke to John was about seven weeks ago, on the day of his birthday. He was enjoying his posting; however, we mostly chatted about his children and Felicity. He was planning to take them to Disney later in the year."

Crawley shook his head slowly and pursed his lips. "I think I will take you up on your offer and have a half pint of lager." Once back at the table and having taken a sip, he continued. "What did your brother do exactly? What was his job all about?"

Brian thought a moment before replying. "He was adviser to the Northern Ireland police in the matter of gangland warfare and was based at the small barracks where he also coordinated the military unit in charge of counterterrorism. The unit was in response to a request by Stormont for intelligence and was established as backup to the local police force. To my understanding, there are no more than twenty to twenty-five men. They are posted on one-year tours, all of them specially selected according to their specific abilities. John had been in his post for ten months and was about to start induction of his successor."

The detective nodded. "Why don't they choose someone from the unit to take over? Why someone new? Could be that one of the men felt spurned and took revenge."

"No, not possible, the MOD in London decides who will be next commander, so it takes that argument out of contention." There was a long pause as all three men worked on their thoughts. Brian was the first to speak, "can I ask you a question? Not being rude, but why are you on the case? I would have thought one of the local Belfast detectives would be sitting where you are."

The DI smiled. "No offence taken. It's a good question. It appears there is a shortage of good inspectors at this moment in time, and they didn't want one of their men away from the city. It seems there has been an explosion of muggings and stabbings in recent weeks and the police are stretched to the limit. As I am the senior DI in this area, they have asked me to investigate matters at this end."

Peter butted in. "What do they think? I'm sure they must have their suspicions and ideas."

"It seems they're discounting it as the work of the IRA or one of the paramilitary groups. No one has admitted responsibility, which confirms this thought. We all know that terrorist groups are quick to claim it is they who have done such deeds. It's good for propaganda and their street cred."

"Fair point and a very valid one. But who then?"

There was another long silence before Crawley spoke. "In my opinion, it points to a random act of violence or to a gang shooting someone by mistake. That being said, your brother may have discovered something, it got out by accident, which resulted in him being targeted and shot."

"I am a free man for a couple of weeks. I could go over and talk to a few of the men and to the detective and see what I can find out," Peter said. "What's your counterpart's name, and where can I find him?"

"Not sure about that, sir," Crawley quickly replied. "I don't think I can allow a civilian to get involved. It's too dangerous; it's against protocol."

"Stuff protocol. And I'm not a civilian. I'm an SAS major on leave and perfectly capable of looking after myself. Now tell me your man's name and where I can find him." He glowered at the DI, his eyes boring into the man sitting across from him.

"As I say, it is against protocol, but I guess you're different from most people," he said hesitantly. "His name is Detective Inspector O'Grady." He fished around in his wallet and pulled out a scrap of paper and scrawled a number and an address on it before passing it over to Peter. "Please don't tell anyone I gave you this or that I told you where to find him—"

"Yes, yes, I know, it's against protocol. I won't say anything if you agree not to warn him of my arrival. I will make contact next week, but I don't want to advertise my visit. Keep it to yourself and we'll get on fine. I promise to keep you updated on anything I find."

"Are you sure you want to do this?" Brian asked. "You're on leave, and I'm sure you have better things to do than to chase ghosts in Belfast. What about I come with you?"

Peter smiled broadly. "Thanks, but no thanks. It's my pleasure. I want to help; I have nothing much planned apart from visiting my aunt in Leeds and a friend in London. As for you coming, I don't think so. Way too obvious. And we certainly don't want another Jackson being shot. No, I will go and see my friend for a couple of days first thing tomorrow, then fly to Belfast, where I'll stay as long as I need before I return to report." He held up his hand as saw Crawley take a breath. "I know, protocol. Don't worry, I won't do anything to upset protocol or get you or your colleague into trouble."

———◆◆———

The next day, Peter hopped onto a train heading for the capital. Once ensconced in his carriage, he rang his aunt, telling her he would come and visit before returning to Afghanistan. She was delighted, her favourite nephew, the warrior with so many stories, would be visiting her. What a thrill. She was already excited at the prospect of telling his tales to her friends during their interminably long weekly lunches. He followed the call by dialling his friend and announcing his imminent arrival. He did not accept the invitation to stay at his flat and told him he was booked into a nearby hotel, adding that he could only stay a couple of days as he was due to go to Belfast before seeing his aunt. He hung up, stretched, and made himself comfortable before dozing off.

CHAPTER 4

London was as dirty and noisy as he remembered. How anyone could live in the place was a mystery. He liked a quick visit, two to three days at the most, before he would begin to feel claustrophobic, his patience running out. All the noise, the bustling, and the shoving—no, not for him. He preferred the wide-open spaces where one could hear silence, hear the wind whispering its secrets.

He hailed a taxi and was driven to his destination by a talkative cabby who had opinions about everything. He sat back listening to the man wittering on, hardly pausing for a breath. It suited Peter as he was thinking of what he was going to ask his friend. After what seemed ages, the cab came to a halt outside a drab-looking grey building. He paid the man and watched the taxi drive off, the driver still talking. Peter looked up at the door and pressed the bell. Instantly, a familiar voice crackled through the intercom and the door lock clicked open. He made his way up the stairs and soon was being welcomed by a large, well-built man with piercing blue eyes, who greeted him with a broad smile and a vicelike handshake.

"Well, I never. You look younger and fitter than ever. Welcome to my humble office. Come on in. Tea, coffee, or a wee dram?"

The Irish lilt was refreshing. Sean had not changed in all the years Peter had known him. "Coffee—strong, black, no sugar—will do. Nice little outfit you have here. When did you move here?"

Sean busied himself making the brew before answering. "Three years. Not mine, as you must have guessed. Paid for and supplied by the Firm to get me out from under their feet," he joked. "Useful, as I can come and go as I like. Don't have to clock in or go through all those security checks. I'm my own man." They clinked their coffee mugs. Sean passed over a packet of biscuits. "What brings you here? I thought you were giving the Taliban a hard time. Causing them major headaches, last time I heard."

"Yep, still trying to do that, but I decided to take some well-earned leave." Peter took a sip of the brew and winced; it was strong. "Aside from that, I came over to attend a funeral. My commander's brother was killed in Belfast a few weeks ago. You might remember Brian, Brian Jackson, my best friend ... apart from you, of course! The brother was also in the army and was stationed up there to help the local boys with counterterrorism."

"For sure, I remember Brian. A big chap, always laughing and joking, but a bloody good soldier. Took no prisoners, just like you."

"That's him, still the same. But as you say, he has a way with people. He has transformed operations out there in Kandahar and whipped everybody into shape, including me." He laughed.

"Not too difficult to do that. You always needed a firm hand. Come to think of it, I'm pretty sure I have met the brother. Name starts with a *J*. Or is it *P*?"

"John. He was shot outside the barracks. Local police don't know who did it, nor do they seem to care. No one has claimed responsibility from what we understand."

There was a pause before Sean spoke. "Doesn't sound as if it's paramilitary. The IRA and all those groups are only too keen to advertise their deeds. Helps promote the cause and their organisation. No, sounds more like a random shooting to me."

Peter sighed and grunted. "Hmm, just bad luck, you mean?" They fell silent again, both men deep in their own thoughts. Peter was the first to talk next. "I'm going over there to see what I can find out. Thought you might give me some pointers as you are a native and from the area."

Sean beamed at his friend. "No problem. You couldn't have come to a better person. Why don't we make our way to a pub and have a few beers? You can ask me as many questions as you like over dinner."

They were on their third pint when conversation returned to the business at hand. Peter Hollins was the first to bring up the subject. "As I was saying earlier, I am flying up to Belfast tomorrow evening, and my idea is to snoop around for a few days, see what I can dig up. I have the name and contact details of the DI in charge, so I'll talk to him as well. You wouldn't know of anyone at the Palace Barracks, would you?"

Sean grimaced and shook his head. "Sorry, no. Since I left four years ago, there has been wholesale change, and all the old guard have either retired or been relocated. I could make enquiries, but I doubt I will have a reply in time."

They ate in silence before Sean resumed speaking. "I do have a contact, a really good chap, ex-army, now undercover and working for the Firm. I could ask him." There was a pause whilst the waiter placed two more pints on the table. "Good chap, very competent and able. He would be good to have on board."

Peter thanked his friend. "How on earth do you put away so much Guinness and not put on weight?"

Sean laughed. "I was thinking just the same thing about you! Guinness is good for you, full of iron or something, but that fizzy foreign crap you call beer is just, well, gassy piss." They finished their meals and swallowed the last of their drinks before asking for the bill. On the way out, Sean looked at his watch before turning to his friend. "Right, it's eleven o'clock. Let's give my mate a ring."

"What, at this time of night? He'll be in bed, fast asleep."

"For sure not. The man never sleeps. And if he is sleeping, well, we'll wake him up, no big deal." With that, he pulled out his mobile and pressed the dial button.

After a couple of rings, a gruff voice bawled, "Yeah, what do you want?"

Sean put the phone on speaker before replying. "Hi, Charly. Sean here." That was as far as he got before the voice at the other end interrupted him.

"Sure, I know who the bloody hell it is. What the hell do you want calling me in the middle of the night? Are you pissed?"

15

Sean winced and shook his head. Turning to Peter, he winked and gave a shrug. "No, just a couple of pints with an old friend, who is listening in. He's planning on visiting Belfast tomorrow for a couple of days, and I was wondering if you could help show him around."

There was a pause before Charly spoke. "Who is your friend? I don't do nursemaid or tour guide. You know that bloody well."

"Now, Charly, don't get all huffy with me. He's a dear friend investigating a murder that took place a couple of weeks ago in your city. A soldier was killed outside the gates of Palace Barracks. The victim is the brother of a commanding officer who was stationed in Afghanistan with him. Both the CO and Peter here are close buddies, and Peter wants to help."

There was another stretch of silence at the other end. Sean could practically hear Charly's brain working. At last, the gruff voice came back on. "Yeah, seem to recollect something like that occurring. Not much was said by the press, and the local bobbies have said even less. Any idea who did it?" he enquired.

Sean shook his head. "No. No one has claimed responsibility, which would point to its not being a terrorist act."

"OK, happy to help an old friend and a friend of his. When's he coming over?"

Peter spoke for the first time, saying, "I was hoping to fly out tomorrow evening. I don't have a reservation yet, but I think there's a flight leaving Heathrow at around a quarter to six."

"Fine. I will be at City Airport to meet you. If you can't get on that flight, take the next one. I'll wait. Make sure you don't go to International, because I'm not traipsing out there, understood? Oh, and tell that bastard Sean not to call me again at this time of night. Unlike him, some of us sleep."

Peter was about to thank Charly, but the phone had gone dead. Peter and Sean chatted awhile before parting company. Sean described Charly Flynn's appearance. The two men agreed to catch up once Peter had returned.

The next day was taken up by making phone calls, doing some errands, and arranging for a present to be sent to Peter's aunt in Leeds before he made his way to the airport. He was in luck: by some miracle he managed to get on the flight, and by 6 p.m. he was watching the lights of Windsor disappear beneath the clouds. An hour later, the plane touched down. As Peter was stepping down from the aircraft, the heavens opened. He jogged to the open door of the airport and stepped inside, brushing himself down. Quickly, he made his way to the exit and emerged into the crowded arrivals hall. He paused and looked around, trying to pinpoint a man who fitted Sean's description of Charly. He soon gave up and was slowly making his way over to the main exit when he heard his name being called out. Turning, he came face to face with a man dressed in jeans, a checked shirt, and an Australian outback hat. A large hand was thrust out. "You must be Peter. Pleased to meet you. Charly, Charly Flynn. Welcome to Belfast. I must point out, just in case you thought otherwise, that it doesn't always rain like this. Well, not all the time. We do have a few sunny days if you get lucky." He chuckled at his joke.

After introducing himself, Peter followed the man to the car. He was amazed at the speed of this chap's walking. Peter himself prided himself on his brisk pace and his being in the SAS was accustomed to moving faster than most, but Charly, well, he practically ran. After a quick dash to the car, they were both soaked. As Charly turned the key, he let out a loud sigh. "Bloody weather. Bet you'll be glad to get back to Kabul. Have you booked a hotel?"

Peter shook his head. "No. I wasn't sure where the best place is. I was relying on you to point me in the right direction." He looked over at the driver queryingly.

"You want fancy or bog standard?" Charly looked over at his passenger and continued, "can't see you doing posh somehow, so I would suggest the Holiday Inn Express on University Street. It's clean, cheerful, and relatively cheap. How does that sound, partner?"

Peter nodded. "Fine by me. Doing anything tonight? If not, the meal is on me. I'm starving."

"Sounds good. I know a good place not too far from the hotel. And there's a great pub just next door."

Peter checked in and made a quick visit to the room to freshen up before meeting Charly in the lobby. The rain had subsided, although a persistent drizzled ensured both men got wet yet again during their short walk to the pub. They ducked out of the rain and made for the bar. Over a couple of pints, they got to know one another, each giving the other a little insight into who they were and what their backgrounds were.

The evening passed quickly, both men enjoying the company. Peter explained in detail his plan and what he hoped to achieve over the next few days. To his surprise, Charly was more than happy to help and be his guide, coming up with several interesting questions. A plan was made, and both men parted company, agreeing to meet up for breakfast the next morning at a small bakery in the centre of town.

CHAPTER 5

Jane was lying on the balcony soaking up the late October sun, her oversized sunglasses covering her sad eyes. She was pretending to be reading, turning pages regularly, but her mind was a million miles away. Glancing over at the man on the sunbed next to her, she saw he was playing with his phone, scrolling through his emails, and scowling. She sighed inwardly.

What had happened, and what had they become, two strangers barely talking? She knew what had happened and how things had gone so wrong.

Her mind wandered back eight years to the day when she had first met the man beside her. She had been persuaded by her friend Emma to go to a party and meet up with some uni. friends, with Emma saying she didn't want to go alone. Jane, having tagged along, had decided to stay only an hour or so before making some excuse and slipping away. It didn't work out that way for her, however. She had just been given a drink when a handsome man in his late thirties, dressed in a loud floral shirt, came up and made a pass. At first, she ignored him, but he persisted, so she decided to be polite and make conversation. It was not long before she warmed to his charms and his humour.

Over the next few months, they courted, and every time they went out, she fell deeper in love. He was witty, attentive, charming—everything a young woman like Jane wanted. He took her to fancy restaurants, bars, and nightclubs, where they were always given special treatment. She liked the attention, and he made sure she got everything she wanted. A year later they married, a lavish affair in a fancy London hotel with several hundred of his family friends. The honeymoon consisted of three weeks on one of his acquaintance's yachts, drifting around the Caribbean.

Back in London, the new flat was far too big for just the two of them but ideal for the round of endless parties and receptions they threw. He didn't seem to go to work but spent hours at his desk in front of a screen or on the telephone. Various last-minute trips were arranged, but Jane was never included, with him saying the trips were too important and he was too busy, and that she wouldn't understand and would get bored, which was his standard reply whenever she asked.

Time went by. They tried for a family, but she never felt he really wanted one, he just seemed content with the life they had. When they made love, she felt as if he were going through the motions with little or no feeling. Not that his caring for her or his attention towards her had changed. No, it was simply that he had neither the need nor the time for children. She had tried to talk him round, but every time the topic of conversation came up, he would find an excuse to change the subject. She had come to realise that they had never spoken about his past or his childhood, or what he did for a living, whereas he knew everything about her. There was no mention of a previous marriage and no mention of illness in the family, just that he had a younger brother who worked as a researcher in an NHS laboratory. From the way he went about charming the ladies, she was sure that he wasn't gay—well, pretty sure, but who could tell these days?

His frequent trips away started to worry her. At first, she accepted them as part of his work, whatever that was, but after a year she began to wonder whether he was having an affair. She started to go through his pockets and his diary, looking for tell-tale signs but finding nothing. She relaxed and admitted she was paranoid; she loved him more than anyone she had ever loved before.

It hit her like a thunderbolt, a day she would never forget, the day things changed forever, leading them to the state they were in now. She was in the kitchen cooking the evening meal when his phone rang.

In no time, the conversation got heated. He blew up. The fractious conversation continued for a while with swearing, threats, and low whispering. It culminated with her husband calling whoever was at the other end all manner of names. He killed the call and went into a deep, dark mood. She hadn't meant to eavesdrop; it just happened. He was shouting so loudly that she couldn't help but hear. And it didn't take a genius to fathom what was going on. For the first time since they had met, Jane understood what kind of business her husband was involved in, and she didn't like what she'd heard—didn't like it one little bit.

The evening was spent in a frosty atmosphere; the man was angry and in a foul mood, snapping at everything, glaring at the TV before eventually going to bed. No kiss, no loving cuddle, but Jane was relieved. She was in shock, her mind, in turmoil.

The next day, he was off at the crack of dawn on one of his business trips, saying he would be back in a few days. For once, she was glad he was going away. It would give her time to think things over and to calm down. Not knowing how to tackle the situation, she needed time to plan, wanting to choose the right moment.

On his return a few days later, he was back to his old self, the assured, level-headed person she knew him to be. He announced they were throwing a party for one of his long-time associate the following day and told her to sort the evening out. She was getting good at last-minute planning and set to work, but it meant she couldn't tackle him and talk about her fears.

The evening was filled with the usual suspects, the young and the old, the pompous and the endless list of hangers-on. At first, Jane had found these parties exciting and fun, but now they were a chore and she hated them. Playing the good wife, she was the perfect hostess, making sure everyone was cared for and plied with copious amounts of food and drink.

She was introduced to the birthday boy, a young handsome Dutchman who exuded charisma and charm. She liked him immediately. In fact, she fell in love with him the minute her eyes met his. The smile, the soft voice, and the pale blue eyes, not to mention the impressive

21

physique and firm muscles—it took a lot to tear herself away from his company and mingle.

The following day, her anxiety returned with a vengeance, and she decided to approach her husband head-on. He was lying sprawled on the sofa when she broke the silence. She told him that she had overheard the heated conversation the other night and that she was shocked to learn what he did for a living, imploring him to stop and change.

He leapt out of his seat and grabbed her by the throat, pinning her against the wall. With his eyes bulging, he ranted and raved, threatening her, and warning her never to tell anyone on pain of death.

She turned over and closed her eyes. That was the day things had changed, when her love for her husband had vanished and their lives were no longer united. She told herself that the current situation was her fault; she was to blame, having been too weak or insecure to walk out. Or was it that she had gotten used to the easy life, the flats, the flashy cars, and the money and didn't want to lose any of it? She felt ashamed of her weakness. By not walking out and turning her back on the life she so despised and abhorred, she was as guilty as he was. She was a criminal, no better than the scum who was lying on the lounger next to her. She started to weep, not from pity but for all the pain that he and, indirectly, she was inflicting on strangers.

She lay there a long while, silently planning her new life. She would leave him and make a new start with the handsome Hans, but not before she had covered all bases and seen her husband put in jail.

CHAPTER 6

Ron Stokes was going through his messages, checking to see that his empire was running smoothly, a large whisky within easy reach. He was aware that his wife was upset. She seemed to be like that most of the time these days, never content, seldom smiling, and certainly not the fun-loving girl she used to be.

He could pinpoint when things had started to go wrong, but he blamed her and her ridiculous idea of wanting a family. No way did he want to be burdened with screaming brats or demanding children; he was too busy, and anyway, it would hinder their partying and socialising. Then there was the day when she'd overheard his furious conversation with one of his main henchmen; the bloody fool had just cocked up one of the biggest deals Ron had put together after months of negotiations, costing the organisation a small fortune.

Yes, that was probably the day when things really took a nosedive in his relationship with Jane. The stupid little bitch had twigged and gotten all uppity and righteous. Where had she thought all the money came from for the clothes, jewels, fast cars, and parties she so enjoyed? He tried to explain, but she would have none of it, refusing to understand and accusing him of being a criminal. He had told her to get out, to leave, if she disliked what he did so much, but no: she knew which side her bread was buttered on and didn't want to lose the easy life or all those perks the hated husband brought in.

He took a large gulp from the glass and slyly glanced over. She was lying on her front, those large glasses hiding her eyes. Did he still love her? No, not really. In fact, apart from her figure, which was still fantastic, there was very little else he liked about her. Yes, those breasts were something else, and her slim endless legs and her doll-like figure were excellent attributes, but you couldn't base a marriage on just looks. She lacked brains. In the beginning, when they were courting, he had thought that with some guidance she would make a good business partner, but now he knew that was never going to happen.

He got up and went over to pour himself another drink, figuring it was pointless to ask her, as she would just shake her head. She used to be happy to join him, although she could never take much before getting giggly and moody. Back on the balcony, he looked out over the town to the shimmering sea speckled with yachts and small fishing boats. There and then he made up his mind: things had to change. He had to free himself of her. She had refused a divorce, turning down what he thought was a more than generous payoff and the promise of the flat in London. He didn't understand her, didn't understand women. One minute they were moaning and complaining, causing everyone grief, and the next they were refusing to move out. *What does Jane want?* he wondered. He decided to try to talk to her again, to make her see sense and cut a deal. If she wouldn't play ball, well, then perhaps it was time to take more drastic measures. He would see how she reacted, but he certainly wasn't going to accept life as it was now.

Wondering what his father would do, he quickly dismissed that thought. The family had a humble background. His father was a bank clerk in a provincial town, and his mother worked as a milliner in the local store. Neither was glamourous, and both were deeply religious. Ron remembered on Sundays that he and his brother had to dress in their best clothes and were dragged to church. They were paraded in front of all the local gentry, and his mother endlessly showed them off as if they were some special treasures. Neither he nor his brother was spoilt; to the contrary, their father kept them on a short leash. Unlike his mother, his father had no aspirations for himself or his children. Ron well remembered the day his elder brother announced that he was going to study to become a physicist and had gotten a place at Cambridge; his mother was over the moon and wouldn't stop gloating and clucking. His father simply nodded and asked why anyone would waste their time with such a useless job. From that day on, both brothers were cast out and left to fend for themselves.

Ron had decided from the moment his brother left home for his studies that he would make a life for himself. His mother was besotted by her eldest son and virtually abandoned her second boy. All she could talk about was number one, how brilliant he was, how far he would go, what a credit he was to the family. Well, if only she could see them now.

The brainy one, still festering in some laboratory, working all hours of the day for a pittance, had married into a similar family to theirs with no ambition, no drive. The young woman he'd married was nice enough, although she was plain and boring. Both were content with a middle-class suburban life.

Ron, by contrast, was a multimillionaire, running a worldwide business operation with hundreds of people relying on him and his decisions. He owned a flat in Chelsea, another flat in Mayfair, a villa in Spain, and this place overlooking Nice in the South of France. He had a chauffeur but preferred to drive the Ferrari himself, leaving the driver and Rolls-Royce to ferry Jane around.

It had not been easy, having taken a lot of hard work, much arm-twisting, and even a few killings, but he eventually imposed himself and carved out a niche business. Any muscling in was met with force. He had learned from an early age that intimidation went a long way towards imposing one's own will and keeping rivals away. He had started by selling fags to his classmates which he had nicked from his parents. Both their parents were heavy smokers, and cigarettes could be found everywhere in their house. He made sure to take only a few so as not to arouse suspicion. Soon he went on to shoplifting and for a couple of years managed an impressive haul, only picking the items his friends wanted. At an older age, he diversified into booze to sell to the younger boys. Things developed quickly after that, and it wasn't long before he was ruling the area and controlling a workforce of half a dozen. It was at this stage that he learned to rule with a fist of iron—no cheating, no side deals, and no messing up. Woe betide to any of his minions who thought otherwise, a couple of whom soon discovered that messing with Ron Stokes was not a good idea.

Ron was shaken out of his dream by the shrill sound of the doorbell. He looked over to Jane, who remained where she was, and shook his head, his anger returning. The young postboy would be disappointed. It was obvious for all to see that the lad was mesmerised by madame, especially when she went to the door dressed in her skimpy bikini. The poor lad could hardly speak, his eye taking in the sight of her curvaceous body and long legs.

Ron opened the door and signed for the package, noting the disappointed look. A quick glance at the package and he was satisfied. He went over to the fake Renoir and pressed a small button, causing the painting to swing out as an opening door. Ron placed the unopened package in the safe, carefully closed the door and went back onto the terrace.

He had barely sat down when his mobile rang, which he answered with a grunt. A long conversation took place, punctuated by Ron's asking some vague question and insisting on clearer replies. When the call ended, he turned to Jane, who had been pretending to be asleep. "I'm going to Athens tomorrow. Not sure how long I'll be gone."

There was a stony silence, no reaction. Jane had heard but decided to ignore her husband. She knew better than to ask what the purpose was and whom he was meeting. He wouldn't tell her anyway, so why waste her breath?

Later that evening, over a silent dinner, Jane told Ron that since he was going away, she was going to go back to London. She had a few things to do, including checking on the smooth running of her interior decorating business. She had started the company three years ago after several of her friends had asked for advice and liked what she had come up with. Through their contacts, she had developed a wide clientele, taking her business to the point where she decided to employ a couple of real professionals with proper training. The business was growing fast, and nowadays her only input was to sit on the board and pretend to run the company. At the beginning she was enthusiastic and worked hard, but all that had changed when she inadvertently learned what Ron had done.

She was sure that she had managed to arrange the financing herself and was hurt when she learned the truth. Ron had gone, unbeknown to her, and arranged the overdraft, giving his personal guarantee and signing the documents, indicating that he would underwrite any losses. From that day Jane had lost interest and took a back seat; it was no longer her business.

He had never told her the truth and was happy in thinking that she didn't know. He was keeping the news as a surprise, a card up his sleeve for when he needed it. That time was soon approaching.

CHAPTER 7

Peter Hollins had arrived at the bakery-cum-cafe early; he had slept badly and was certainly not a man to stay in bed if not sleeping. He had ordered breakfast and a strong coffee. Just after 8 a.m., Charly Flynn walked in, a wide smile on his face. "How are things with you this morning?" he exclaimed as he sat down. "Big improvement in the weather. It's not raining."

A surly young waitress shuffled over to take Charly's order of bacon, egg, sausage, and beans. She looked at him as if he had come from outer space and shook her head. Charly could not resist making a comment in a louder than usual voice. "Don't you love it when people enjoy their work and smile?" The young woman shuffled off, ignoring him. He shook his head and raised his eyes to the ceiling. "I pity the lass—in fact, anyone who goes through life with that attitude. She won't live long. Die of grumpy disease if you ask me."

Peter was eager to get started but checked his impatience. The two men made small talk as they waited for the order to appear. Before long, the "happy" waitress returned and, in her usual charming self, enquired if they wanted more coffee. She sighed deeply as the answer was a firm yes. Once they had been served the extra cup and she was gone, Peter looked up. "I would very much like to talk to DI O'Grady before perhaps making our way over to the barracks."

Charly nodded between mouthfuls and wiped his hands before replying. "Yes, that was my thought. First the DI, and then I'll check in with a friend of mine. I phoned him first thing this morning. He used to

28

be stationed at the Palace and will try to find out if anyone he knows is still there. It's a long shot and probably won't help, but it's worth a try."

The sky was still heavy with clouds by the time they walked out into the street and headed for police headquarters. As they walked up to the desk, a young sergeant in her twenties greeted them, smiled sweetly, and asked how she could help. She took a few notes and pointed to a couple of chairs. "Please take a seat. I will see what I can do."

Detective Inspector O'Grady was finishing a report on yet another serious attack and mugging, the ninth in as many days, and still they had no real clues. His hunch was that it was some type of gang warfare; these attacks all took place in the same area and the victims were all young, in their twenties and thirties. The style of attack was similar each time, with varying degrees of harm meted out. Only two had ended in death; one had died in hospital, the other instantly at the scene of the crime. DI O'Grady was getting grief from his superiors and was under pressure, so he was not too pleased to be told that a couple of gentlemen were waiting in reception. He sat for a long time, debating what to do. His first reaction was to tell the desk sergeant to get rid of them. However, his professional training and instincts kicked in and he reluctantly agreed to see them. *Who knows, they may have something of interest to tell me.* He doubted that, however. They might just admit to the crimes he was investigating and were there to turn themselves in, which he doubted even more. He got up, put on his jacket, and followed the young woman to reception, briefly stopping to hand the names of his two guests to his assistant.

His trained eye immediately picked up that these two men were military, with their physiques, the way they stood, and their quiet confidence indicating that they had been through serious training. O'Grady's brother had the same look, and he was serving in the navy, floating around somewhere in the Pacific. Yes, DI O'Grady knew a soldier when he saw one.

He greeted the two strangers and pointed to a door leading to a private interview room. Once seated, he introduced himself and, despite already knowing the information, asked the men for their names. Peter didn't let on that he was a major, just giving his name as Peter Hollins with a home address in North London. When Charly introduced himself, it didn't take a genius to know he was local. Picking up his pen, O'Grady looked across the table. "So, can you gentlemen tell me what you do in life—your profession?"

Peter hesitated a second, something the detective picked up immediately, before speaking. "I'm in the military, in Afghanistan, but currently on three weeks' leave."

O'Grady nodded. "Thought you were military. The way you dress, the way you stand, and those polished shoes—a dead giveaway. What regiment?"

"I'm stationed in a small place forty miles outside Kandahar. Colonel Jackson is a very close friend of mine. We've been all round the world together, fighting wars and trying to make a difference. I got leave to come over to his brother's funeral the other day. He was shot dead here in Belfast, outside the Palace Barracks, a few weeks ago. I'm over here to see what I can find out. That's why I asked to see you. Your colleague DI Crawley spoke to us and kindly gave me your contact details."

"Did he now?! Breaking protocol. I'll have to have a word with him. What's your rank?" The detective inspector grimaced slightly. "You still don't look like a normal soldier. There's something about you."

Peter acknowledged that the man was good and was, for a policeman, a nice enough sort of man. He knew he would have to come clean at some point soon, so he smiled. "I'm an SAS major in a small unit. Our job is to help the main regiment pick off any targets they and intelligence identify. Quick in and out, no fuss."

O'Grady nodded. "That makes sense now. So, you're over here to help your pal the colonel find out who killed his brother. It's not going to be easy. I have six men on the case, and I admit they're struggling to find any leads." He looked over to Charly. "And you, what is your involvement in all this?"

"Ach! I'm only here to show Peter around and to be his guide. I'm not army, police, or anything, just a good Belfast citizen helping a long-lost friend." Seeing the DI's questioning look, he quickly added,

"I knew Peter when I studied in England twenty-five years ago. We used to play rugby together. Became good pals. Lost touch when I came back to work on the shipyard as a manager and he went off fighting the baddies. We always exchanged Christmas cards and vaguely kept in touch, until the other day when I got a call telling me he was visiting and asking me to be his guide. So here I am, doing my chaperoning."

The detective looked at the man and, overall, believed him. It was all very plausible, so he moved on. "What did Crawley tell you? And why is the colonel not with you?"

"Crawley didn't tell me a lot. In fact, nothing. That's why I have come. Brian wanted to accompany me, but I dissuaded him, not wanting to put him through the ordeal or make it obvious that he or his family is looking for answers. And anyway, one Jackson killed is enough." He looked at the DI. "Do you think it's the IRA or one of the dissident groups?"

O'Grady shook his head. "No, none of the para groups. If it had been any of them, they would have very quickly admitted responsibility. It's good for their street cred. No, we'll keep looking, but I very much doubt we'll get a result. I'm sorry I can't be of more use." He closed his notebook and put his pen away, indicating that the meeting was over. "What is your next move?"

Peter shook his head and sighed. "See if anyone at the barracks can help. It's all I can think of."

The two men stood up. O'Grady showed them to the door. "Good luck. Let me know if you find anything out. I can do with some help."

Outside, Peter turned to his new friend. "What was all that about, us being old friends and playing rugby? You never told me that you worked at a shipyard."

Charly looked sheepish and started to walk down the street. "Well, I wasn't about to tell our DI my real job. Not my style to publicise that I'm a spook working undercover for the Firm and have been doing so for the past twenty-five years. My job is to keep tabs on the IRA and all the splinter dissident groups in town. Having said that, I did work, and still am working, in the shipyard as my cover story.

It's a hive for all kinds of dissent, trafficking, and mob rule. You'd be surprised what goes on. Must say, I have been off on 'annual leave' for the past two months; they, the Firm, needed me down in Cork. Only came back last week."

Peter was trying to keep up with Charly. "So, that's how you know Sean, from working together? How long have you known him for?"

"Not all that long really. We met when he was stationed here as an army officer. You know he is a Native? Well, near the end of his last tour, he was selected as a potential spy, so he went to England to get trained before being sent back here to keep track of our friends. We met then and have worked closely ever since."

It all made sense to Peter now, the way the two of them had spoken on the phone, the ribbing and remarks, all signs of a good friendship. "What's he doing in London? Any idea?"

Charly shrugged and mumbled something about working drugs and the Triads, but he didn't really know.

They turned the corner and headed to the car park, their heads bent against the rain, which had started up again.

CHAPTER 8

DI Patrick O'Grady had hardly entered the main office room when his assistant, a young man in his mid-twenties, handed him a file. "Think you should take a look at this, sir."

Back at his desk, DI O'Grady read through the pages he had just been handed. He let out a loud noise resembling that of a steam engine before starting to swear. "Shit, shit, shit. In the name of the wee man, what have I done to deserve this!" He tossed the papers in front of him and looked at the young assistant. Holding up his hand, he controlled his voice, "no, not your fault. You have done a great job. Relax." He swore again. Sitting for some time in a trance, his mind racing, he knew deep down that he should go and tell his boss, but no, that would mean a whole lot of questions and recriminations and an uproar. He could do without all that for the time being.

Waving his aide away and pointing him to the door, the detective inspector picked up the phone and dialled. After a couple of rings, he heard a gruff voice at the other end. "DI Crawley, good day to you," O'Grady said. "Just had two gentlemen in, the two you gave my contact details to, asking me if I could help them with the Jackson murder." Crawley's jaw tightened. He was about to speak when the caller continued, saying, "Thanks for warning me. Over here, it is customary for people in our position to give one another notice of such visits. I don't like surprises sprung on me."

Crawley winced. "Very sorry, Patrick. I didn't mean to put you on the spot. You said two men. I only know of one, a Major Hollins." There was no answer, so he continued, saying, "Major Hollins was present when I was interviewing the victim's brother. They—Colonel Jackson and this major—seem very close, so when the major said he wanted to go over to Belfast and dig around, I did try to dissuade him, but he was very insistent."

"Even so, Detective Inspector, why the hell did you give him my details? You know it's against protocol."

"Yes, yes, very sorry. I did try, but he wouldn't take no for an answer. You said there was a second man? Nothing was mentioned about that."

There was a snort at the other end. "Yeah, well, one is bad enough, but two is another thing. You will never guess what we have just found out. This other chap is not only a so-called old friend but also a bloody spy, for Christ's sake! Works for MI6 and has been employed there for years." There was a gasp from the other end and a gurgling sound emanating from Crawley.

"Oh shit, when did you find out?"

"Shit indeed. It has really hit the fan. All I need is some bloody spook sticking his nose into this affair and stirring things up. I'm going to have to tell the boss, and God knows what he's going do. Probably string me up and eat me for breakfast. It's well known that he hates anything resembling a spy."

A long silence followed as Crawley was trying to find something to say. Eventually he croaked an apology and asked what he could do to help.

"Apology accepted, but don't, whatever you do, get involved or try to put things right. I will deal with it in my way and in my own time, understand?"

DI Crawley thanked DI O'Grady for his understanding before replacing the receiver. Cold sweat trickled down his shirt.

Sighing, O'Grady called his small team in and gave his orders. His main priority now was to keep tabs on this Flynn chap. He didn't want a spy messing up his investigation or causing trouble. He had enough problems already without having to contend with a nosy, volatile, and unpredictable spook. Yes, they were all the same, had to be to get into that business. He instilled more urgency into his team and gave the two senior members responsibility, instructing them to double their efforts and find the person or people behind the murder of Brian Jackson and the recent spate of muggings and assaults.

O'Grady chose a couple of the younger members, giving them orders to follow Flynn and not to let him out of their sight. He wanted to know every movement the man made, every place the bastard went, and every person the prying snoop met. He expected a full report by the end of each day. Anything the slightest bit suspicious or out of the ordinary, they had to call him and keep him posted.

Once the teams had left, DI O'Grady sat back and went over the conversation he had had earlier with his guests. He analysed and made notes, mulling over his options, wondering what the two were doing.

———————◆◆———————

Peter and Charly arrived at the barrack gates and went up to the duty guard. The man greeted them with suspicion and was unconvinced by their story. He looked even more sceptical after hearing they wanted to meet his boss, the commanding officer. Charly Flynn flashed his fake ID card. This didn't faze the soldier, who told the visitors to wait outside the gate before he entered his hut and called his superior.

The two men waited patiently for twenty minutes. Just as Charly had decided to go up and ask what the delay was, the guard emerged. He nodded to both men to come forward, pointing at a soldier marching towards them, before handing back the ID card. "Follow that soldier. He will escort you to the main building." He saluted and left them. The soldier simply nodded before taking them towards a large door across the quadrangle. As they approached the imposing building, the large door opened and they were greeted by a young subaltern, who showed them up a flight of stairs and into a sparse, cold meeting room.

Another fifteen minutes were spent cooling their heels, until suddenly the door burst open and a middle-aged man, dressed in battle fatigues, marched over, introducing himself as Captain Jordan. He gestured towards two wooden chairs and took a seat across the table.

Peter introduced himself, stressing his rank and saying that he was in the SAS. Charly simply gave his name and told his host that he worked as an operations manager at the docks, explaining that he was there as a guide to his friend.

The meeting lasted well over an hour. The captain asked questions and replied to his guests' queries as best he could. The long and short of it was that he didn't know much; the killing had taken place before he had taken over, and most of, if not all, the men there now had only recently taken up their postings. He promised to ask around and to contact Peter if he found anything out.

Outside the gate, Peter turned to his friend and looked despondent. "Well, that was a total waste of time. Do you think he was telling the truth when he said he knew nothing?"

Charly nodded. "Most definitely. He didn't hesitate, nor did he look shifty, so my guess is that he knows diddly-squat. A good enough man, but without much flair or drive—hence his position after a lifetime of service."

Peter had to agree. The man seemed genuine but lacked the sparkle required of a good leader. "Not sure what to do now. We have hit the buffers before we've even started."

"Don't get despondent. The war has just started. We have lost the battle, but we're in for the long haul. You'll see, things will get better. You should know that better than most. I do think that your time in Belfast has come to an end, at least for now. I suggest you go back to Leeds or wherever and enjoy the rest of your leave. I will make some enquiries and talk to a few contacts. If I find out anything, you will be the first to know. So, for now, I suggest we go and have a bite to eat, and then I'll take you to the airport in time for the last flight. Hopefully you can get on it."

Peter had to admit that he had no better plan. Accepting that his friend was making sense, he reasoned that he had to rely on this man, a professional who knew the city, and give him time and space. He was sure Charly would do as much as he could to help. Peter also knew deep down that it would be easier for him to operate on his own. He nodded his agreement and thanked Charly for his help and advice.

CHAPTER 9

Ron Stokes was first to get off the plane, one of the main reasons he liked first class, apart from the luxury of being isolated from the screaming brats and noisy holidaymakers. He made his way quickly to passport control before heading to the nearest taxi rank.

As the taxi drove through the suburbs of Athens, he stared out the window. The drizzle and low clouds meant daylight was fading fast, making the city even greyer than usual. He watched as tourists, dressed in anoraks and taking shelter under umbrellas, traipsed around the city, sightseeing. Most were not interested, but it was the thing to do, to boast one had been—a topic of conversation back home or in the pub. He smiled to himself at the locals all dressed as if in the Arctic. Anything below fifteen degrees and they were frozen, wearing layer over layer of knitwear with furry boots, bonnets, and gloves.

The drive to the hotel was interminable. Although Greece was experiencing a dramatic financial crisis with soaring prices, it seemed to Ron that everyone had taken to the streets or was in a car; perhaps it was cheaper than living at home. Finally, after what seemed an eternity, the taxi pulled up in front of the ornate hotel, and a liveried doorman came bounding towards it.

Once in his room, Ron made a beeline for the bathroom—first things first. He had to have a shower and get rid of the stale smell of human sweat mixed with cheap cigarettes. He stood in there a long time, enjoying the hot water as it beat down on his body. Once clean, he lay on the bed and went through his messages. Nothing bad, just the usual problems, which none of his team seemed to be able to sort out without asking him for his help. OK, he had always made a point of checking and taking decisions. More often than not, he would instruct whomever it was on what to say or do. He realised that his mistrust in people had made a rod for his own back, but he couldn't help himself. The last time he had left a decision to someone else, it cost him a fortune. Satisfied everything had been dealt with, he called room service and went over to the minibar to pour himself a large scotch.

He wanted to be alone because he had lots to think about. Firstly, most pressing, was how he would deal with the two meetings scheduled for tomorrow. Much depended on these negotiations, and both could prove a life-changer, turning him from being a wealthy and powerful man into one of the megarich, someone everyone would be in awe of. Secondly, he had to decide what to do with Jane. It was a tricky problem as she was seeing his main henchman, not that that bothered him at all. It was better that she was seeing a trusted colleague who knew all aspects of his business empire and was financially reliant on his position rather than a stranger. If she blabbed to Hans about her concerns and how unhappy she was about her husband's business, then he would gently steer her away from her thoughts and tell her not to worry, saying it was none of her concern. His second-in-command would report back to his boss, and Ron would encourage Hans to keep his wife happy.

That was one aspect. The other was that Ron no longer wanted to have Jane in his life. He was bored with her nagging and irritated that she hadn't gotten 100 per cent behind him. Now he wanted to be alone so he could fully concentrate on his future as one of *the* megarich of this world.

Back to tomorrow. His first meeting was with his associate in Cairo, a slimy, slippery customer with shifty eyes, someone Ron disliked but needed. For all his faults, the man had fantastic contacts. In addition to that, he was ruthless, but above all, he knew his business and never failed to come up with a way to supply the goods. Over the past two years they had been working together, both parties had made a small fortune and this man had only one idea in mind, namely making money, which suited Ron just fine.

The second contact was a different kettle of fish altogether, a cold, calculating client whom Ron had tried to make a partner but was turned down. Both men respected each other, but the Turk had his own ideas and agenda and was not prepared to get into bed with a Westerner.

Ron awoke early the next morning, having slept badly. It was not often that he felt nervous about a meeting, but he felt nervous today, knowing full well the pressure that lay ahead of him. He would need all his negotiating skills, tact, and charm if he was going to pull off these deals.

After dressing, he made his way down to the lobby and selected a sofa situated in the corner of the vast hall, well away from the other seats but in view of the revolving doors. He picked up a copy of the *USA Today* and sat back to wait for his first guest.

The man arrived just after 9 a.m., dressed in a crumpled suit, a creased shirt, and a garish tie. His shoes were as scruffy as he was. Ron greeted him with a smile and a warm handshake. He ordered two Turkish coffees, and they chatted aimlessly until the waiter returned with the order and a plate of sweets. The little man's eye gleamed at the sight of food. He was soon stuffing some in his mouth.

A short, balding man with a two-day stubble, Ron's associate was only forty but was going to seed rapidly. Married with two children, the man had grown up in the sprawling suburbs of Cairo, and his youth reflected Ron's. He was a self-made crook but had never reached the heights of his Western counterpart.

After cramming a third sweet into his mouth and licking his fingers, the man delved into his tatty briefcase and pulled out a slim folder. With eyes gleaming, he proudly handed over the file with a magician's flourish. "Mr Ron, you will be very pleased. I managed to get a much better deal from that crook in Aswan. It will make us much more than originally thought." He watched Ron take the file and then sat back, pleased with himself.

The file was thin, containing several pages, the first with columns of figures and a final total highlighted at the bottom The others were a detailed description of the deal, along with precise instructions and the timescale. Ron took his time reading through the figures carefully, trying to hide his excitement. The man had certainly excelled, but he was weary, not believing everything he'd read, thinking it was too good to be true. The contract and the suggestions on how the operation was to proceed all looked fine. He looked up just as his man was stuffing the last of the food into his fat mouth.

"Very impressive. At first sight, it seems you have done well. I do, however, have some questions." For the next hour, Ron grilled his associate, digging, probing, and double-checking the figures and the man's answers. Finally satisfied that things were as they looked, he placed the file on the table and nodded. "You certainly have done well. Thank you. Of course, you will get your usual commission on the difference. I will ensure it is paid as usual once the goods have arrived."

The little man's eyes twinkled as he bowed his head slightly. "I am pleased you are happy. As the deal is much more profitable for you, I was hoping you would consider increasing my commission on the extra to"—he paused—"perhaps 20 per cent?"

Ron had expected such a request but feigned surprise. "Twenty per cent! That's a very big cut you're asking for. No, no, far too much. I was thinking seven and a half."

Little beady eyes stared back expressionlessly. "Mr Ron, we have worked much together. I have done much for you, and I have three boys, a wife, and a mistress to take care of. What do you say to seventeen and a half?"

The thought of the little man having a wife, let alone a mistress, shocked Ron. What on earth did they see in this creep? He shook his head and looked thoughtful. "I agree you have done well, but please don't take me for a fool. How much did your supplier give you, 10, 15 per cent?"

The man looked hurt. "Mr Ron, you know it's not like that. I would never take anything without telling you. No, it is me who had to bribe my supplier and push for such a good deal. My friend, trust me, I have worked many days for this opportunity, but because it is you, I will accept 10 per cent." He held out a plump, sticky hand.

Ron sighed and reluctantly shook the man's hand. Inwardly, he was pleased at the cheap price. He would have gladly paid the man what he initially wanted.

The Egyptian beamed with pleasure and looked longingly at the empty plate. "Mr Ron, perhaps we could have another coffee and some more sweets to celebrate?" He looked over and beckoned a waiter. After placing their order, he turned and continued. "I have another surprise for you. I'm sure you will be most happy." He pulled out a second folder, which he passed over.

Ron quickly flipped through the few pages before starting to read again. He looked up at the man sitting across the table from him. "What's this?" he enquired. "You have never mentioned anything about it."

"A second deal from the same supplier, a much bigger one and very urgent. That's why the price is better. You see, when I was down to finalise the first one, my contact offered me this. I couldn't refuse. I had to trade some of the profit from the first deal to get this one, but as you see, it is twice as big. And the potential is incredible."

Ron reread through the figures before speaking. "It sure is big, probably too big for us. And the timescale is very tight. You know I don't like to rush things, that I like to plan and cover all angles."

"This is no problem. You can work the two together. There is only a week in between, and the logistics are the same," was the enthusiastic reply.

There was a long silence during which Ron thought things through. Yes, the little man was right, it was possible. They could use the same channels, the same setup as for the first deal. Financing was not a problem for such a big deal; he could arrange that easily. "When does your contact need to know by?"

The shifty little man fidgeted in his chair. "Mr Ron, this is not to be missed. You know what it's like; you must take decisions at the time. So, I agreed. We shook hands on it."

Ron winced. "You what? When in heaven's name have I ever given you permission to close a deal without my approval first? Who the hell do you think you are?" He feigned rage, no matter that it was a dream deal; he couldn't be seen to let such a thing pass without playing hell and showing who was boss. He fell silent and slumped in his seat. The little man was about to speak but was immediately interrupted; Ron had been waiting for this very moment. "No. Before you say anything, the answer is no." He looked up and saw the man's shoulders slump slightly. "Just because you went behind my back and didn't get my agreement first, I will pay you no more. You understand? It's the standard 10 per cent and nothing more. If you don't like it, do the deal on your own." He knew his associate couldn't afford to argue; by being tough, he showed his displeasure and asserted his authority. The Egyptian's shoulders slumped further, he recognised he had played his cards wrong and accepted he had to shake hands on the deal offered.

"You are a very good friend. Thank you. You'll see, the deal is very good for us. And my contact has promised more if we are happy."

Not long after they rose and shook hands a final time, Ron accompanied his associate to the main door and ushered him out into the cold winter day. Checking his watch, he made his way back to his room, needing to regroup before his next meeting. So far it had been an excellent day.

Just before 2 p.m., Ron's watched pinged, reminding him it was time for the second meeting. He took his time; the next contact was always late, and Ron didn't want to look too eager. He waited ten minutes before heading down to the lobby, at which time he was shown to the same seats; he had tipped the waiter well and asked him to reserve the place. Unsurprisingly, his next visitor had not yet arrived.

Twenty minutes had elapsed before a tall, bearded man came through the rotating doors. He glanced round and immediately spotting the Englishman, marched over. Immaculately dressed in an expensive suit with his hair sleekly combed back and a neat, well-trimmed beard, the Turk oozed confidence with a firm handshake and cold, sharp eyes. With the niceties out of the way and coffee ordered, the man wasted no time in beginning to talk business.

He thanked Ron for coming at short notice and, after handing a file over, went through the figures and contract in a precise way. He answered Ron's questions with no hesitation and in turned quizzed his client in depth on how his side of the operation would be carried out. Ron felt intimidated—he always did in front of this man—but tried to hide his anxieties. He was impressed at the detail and professionalism of the man and still wished he could make him a partner, but he knew better than to ask again.

"I think, Mr Stokes, we have covered everything. I am very happy about how you are planning to continue your side of the deal. It is most important to me to know I can trust my clients. Any troubles or problems on their end can affect my business." He smiled for the first time. "I'm also happy at the financial arrangement; you have been excellent in the past, and I'm sure it will be the same now."

Ron started to relax just a little. If the last deal or deals were big, this one was huge, promising to propel him into a new world. He had calculated that if all went to plan, it would net him just over twenty million pounds sterling. Not only would it give him status in his world, but also it would open even more doors and lead to even bigger deals.

The two men chatted politely for a few more minutes before shaking hands and making their way through the lobby. Before parting, the Turk turned and spoke in his usual business-like manner. "Mr Stokes, may I say it is a pleasure? Let us hope this all goes well. We have many more to come. I will not be contacting you until the delivery has been finished. You have all the instructions in the file. We will talk in a month or two." He turned and made his exit.

Ron let out of a long, slow sigh of relief; he was drained but still had lots to sort out. He quickly made his way up to his room and helped himself to a large celebratory whisky.

Work for the day wasn't over though; he had much to do and organise. He picked up his mobile and phoned his favourite hotel in Zurich to book a room. Then he called Hans and told him to meet him in Switzerland the day after next. He was about to speak to his man in Belfast when he received a call from another contact, an Indian living in Qatar. He didn't like the man one little bit—someone with whom it was impossible to discuss things or suggest any alternatives. It was either the man's way or nothing. He was a shrewd operator, having been in the business a long time, and treated Ron neither any better nor any worse than any other of his clients. For him clients were clients, all of them equal, all of them expected to pay up on time and to uphold a deal no matter what. Anyone who reneged or tried to wriggle out of a contract was swiftly discarded and was either found dead or prevented from doing any future business, finding all doors had been closed. He wanted an urgent meeting to discuss a possible deal; time was of the essence. They settled on a meeting in Zurich Airport the following day.

Ron was not looking forward to this one. He always found it difficult to keep his cool and be polite but needs must.

CHAPTER 10

After dropping Peter off at the airport, Charly Flynn had thought long and hard about checking in at work. He hesitated, but with further consideration he finally made up his mind, no give it a couple of days. After such a long absence he didn't want to go back to the office and ask for more time off. He decided to wait a week. He drove back to his semi on the outskirts of the city, where he made a couple of calls before stepping out and making his way to the nearest bus stop.

As he looked out of the window at the racing clouds scurrying over the distant hills, the thought of moving to warmer climes returned once again. At the ripe old age of fifty-five, it was time for him to retire, settle down to a more normal life, move to a place where there was more sun, and marry the woman he had always loved. The idea was appealing, certainly the moving and marriage part, but he was not sure about retirement. Apart from rifle shooting, he had no real interests. Travel was all very well, but he had done that all his career, so it wasn't all that exciting a prospect. No, he'd give it a few more years and reconsider when he hit sixty. Lorna was happy with things as they were, never asking questions, never making demands, just accepting that his work entailed a nomadic lifestyle. She was content to wait and enjoyed the times they spent together; in that way he was lucky, and he knew it.

He got off at May Street and headed leisurely towards Castle Court Shopping Centre. He stopped to look in the window of a shoe shop, not that he was interested in buying a new pair. He waited until a young man had walked by before turning and following him. He had noticed a car trailling him earlier from the airport and stopping a little way down his home street.

Once in his home, Charly had peeked out the bedroom window. There were two passengers in the car, a young man and a woman. After boarding the bus, they went to sit at the back, acting as if they were lovers. He had then noticed them getting off behind him, so had decided to check them out. He looked for the woman, but she had disappeared. Needing to get a look at the man close up, he quickened his pace and soon caught up with him at a pedestrian crossing, the man looked anxious and seemed to be talking to himself. As the pedestrian light turned to green, Charly stepped backwards and the collied into the young man. Turning to apologise, he made eye contact. Once across the street, Charly slowed his pace again and decided to take a different route. It was not long before he noticed the young man had been re-joined by the woman. He smiled to himself: *Let the game begin.*

He allowed them to tail him for a few hundred yards before quickening his stride. They soon fell behind; at which time he took the opportunity to dart down a side street and take cover in a doorway. Peering round the corner, he saw them walk past, looking worried. He waited a few minutes before returning to the main street, carefully checking if he could see them. They had disappeared, so he hurriedly made his way back to the crossing and took a left. His pace ensured him he was putting distance between himself and the two pursuers. Happy he had lost them, he pulled out his phone and made a couple of calls, needing to change meeting point. Satisfied, he headed for Victoria Park.

The two young officers were frantically searching for their target. Their man certainly could walk fast. How did he know they were following him? They decided to split up and search the area. They had initially separated to make it less obvious, but the young man started panicking and had called his colleague to join him; it was soon after that that they'd lost him. For more than an hour they searched, before admitting defeat. They made their way back to the station to confront the boss, DI O'Grady.

Patrick O'Grady was not a happy man, and he made it be known. The simple task of following an unsuspecting target and they had blown it. What did they teach recruits these days? he wondered. He still wanted Flynn followed, needing to know what he was up to and who he was meeting, as sure as hell his boss would ask. He called in his second-in-command and told him what he wanted and ordered him to take over from the youngsters. The man nodded, taking a few notes before departing.

Looking at his watch, O'Grady groaned and got ready to go and see his boss. On his way, he prayed he would still have a job by the end of the day.

———————◆◆◆———————

Charly Flynn, having made good time, soon walked into the park. He checked the area carefully before making his way down one of the paths to a bench situated against a wall. Not long after he'd sat down, a woman dressed in a heavy tweed coat came up and sat beside him. No introductions were needed, no niceties exchanged; the second she sat down, Charly turned and told her what he wanted. She remained silent and nodded before getting up and leaving. He watched her walk away, soon disappearing in the distance.

He remained seated for a while before spotting a figure walking along the same path he had. Checking his watch, Charly smiled, having never known this contact to be late, the man always timing his arrival to the second. Charly had worked with this man for many years. A retired bomb disposal expert, he was a man of few words, but what he lacked in verbal skills, he made up for with his professionalism. An expert in his field, he had become tired of the stress of his job. With age, he had developed arthritis in his hands and was no longer able to continue the delicate work of defusing explosive devices. He had met Charly soon after retiring and initially had helped him to do some surveillance. Having took up the offer of special training and following a few intensive months training in a remote part of England, he had returned to take up his new career.

Charly liked the man and trusted him implicitly. He would have liked to be close friends, but in this business, one didn't make close friends. It never paid to get close; people one worked with were just colleagues. The man sat down at the far end of the bench and stared into the distance. He listened intently, then asked a couple of questions before getting up and confirming he would be in touch very soon.

Charly rose and walked in the opposite direction. He walked round the corner and entered his home street, immediately spotting a car halfway down the road ahead of him. Persistent bastards, he thought, shaking his head. He walked past, noticing that the occupants were two older men, and continued a few yards before stopping. Returning, he made a sign for the passenger to wind down the window. Both men looked suspicious and a little worried. Once the window was down, Charly greeted them. "Good day, gentlemen. My name is Charly Flynn, as I'm sure you know. How can I help you?"

Both looked on in surprise. "Nothing, sir. We're here just having a chat and waiting for a friend," the older one spluttered.

"Now, boys, I know perfectly well what you're doing here. Guess you're replacing the two youngsters who lost me earlier. Am I not right? Well, I'll save you a lot of trouble and spare you wasted time. You go and tell your boss, DI O'Grady, that he has far more important things to do than to tail me. I have nothing to hide and am doing nothing untoward, merely trying to help him and my friend. You just go back and tell him I will be in contact the minute I hear or learn of something of interest. We're all on the same side. Now go, before I call and make a fuss." He smiled politely, patting the car as he left them and waving them on.

There was a moment of hesitation, but eventually the driver took the decision to leave. It was a waste of time staying there, as the man knew they were watching him. They could certainly be doing something more useful. Once they had reached the end of the street, the passenger spoke, "what are you going to say to the boss? Think you were a bit too quick to leave."

The driver shrugged. "No point. Flynn knows he's being tailed, and we have no idea of the lay of the land. We may have been sitting there for hours. He could easily have slipped out by a back lane for all we know. No, either we need a full squad, or we rely on him. It's not as if he's a dangerous criminal. He may even be of help."

Charly watched as the car turn the corner, able to imagine the conversation being carried out and the excuses the policemen would be concocting. He shook his head, what a bunch of amateurs. No wonder they can't solve anything. Ah well, life needed people like Charly, people who knew their jobs and took pride in their work.

CHAPTER 11

Jane had left the same day as her estranged husband. Once her plane had landed at Gatwick, she made her way to her parents'. It had been months since she'd last seen them. She felt guilty, but that wasn't the main reason he was making this visit. Most of all, she needed to feel their love.

Her father was a sprightly seventy-five-year-old, but he suffered from failing eyesight, something which was getting to him. He loved to tie flies and repair clocks, but with his condition worsening and with frustration setting in, he was becoming grumpier and grumpier. His mood was not helped by the fact that he had recently been diagnosed with advanced-onset dementia. His wife took his moods and illness well and tried to make light of the situation, although she knew the prognosis was not good and nothing would help. His eyesight could be seen to, but she had resigned herself to the difficult times ahead. She was worried about her only child—not that Jane had mentioned anything, but by the tone of her letters and phone calls, she knew something was wrong.

For Jane, it was good to be home, to be surrounded by real people and real things. She loved the smell of home, the warmth of the things she had known all her life, and the reassuring nature of her parents' love. She had none of these in her married life now.

Her mother fussed over her whilst her father quizzed her on "that husband of yours", as he put it. He had never taken to Ron, had never trusted him—much too smooth and slippery. He had tried to warn his daughter, but she told him he was wrong, that he didn't understand—and anyway, she was in love. Her mother had also fallen for Ron's charms and loved the attention he had given her.

As the three of them sat down for dinner that evening, Jane hinted at her problems but fell short of telling her parents the truth or about any of her concerns and what she knew. Seeing the expression on her mother's face change and cutting her father short before he had the chance to lecture her, she steered the conversation swiftly to her business and its success, suggesting that she would send her top designer to oversee the makeover of the bungalow. Her mother clucked with excitement, whilst her father simply asked how much of their pension this unnecessary work would eat up.

The following few days were spent in the office, going through the ongoing projects, checking the accounts and bank balances, and planning for the next few months . All that had been done by Jane's team, but she felt it was her duty to double-check and give her input. She arranged for the head designer to visit her parents and to transform the living room and the two bedrooms; she would pay.

Jane had been in London a couple of days when her mobile rang one afternoon. It was Hans. He was in town on business and hoped she would be free to spend the evening with him. Her heart skipped a beat at the sound of his voice. They agreed that he would pick her up at 7 p.m. and they would go to the Ivy for a meal before moving on to a club. Like a young girl on a first date, she spent hours deciding what to wear, finally choosing a red clingy dress with a low-cut front which showed off her cleavage. She decided on no bra and chose the smallest of thongs. Looking at herself in the mirror, she liked what she saw. The sight of her hair loose over her shoulders and of her short skirt, along with the sensation of the soft fabric against her skin, made her feel sexy. She was looking forward to her date.

The evening went too quickly and passed as if in a haze. Jane soaked up the attention, the compliments, the conversation, and yes, the love Hans showed her. At the club, she couldn't keep her hands off him, getting him to dance and holding him tight, feeling his strong muscular body close to hers. As he kissed her, she shivered, a tingling sensation running down her spine. Her body ached for him. The idyllic evening came to an end all too soon, only to be punctuated by disappointment. Outside her flat, she had suggested he come up and spend the night with her, but he declined. He had to be at Heathrow by 6 a.m. to leave town. He kissed her and held her tight before ushering her up the steps and into her hallway. Before leaving, he promised her that he would make it up to her and that they'd spend time together soon, probably in a couple of weeks, at his place in the South of France.

Once Hans had driven off, Jane's tears came in a flood, streaming down her face. Not having looked back, Hans didn't see her distress or waving and blowing a kiss.

Before flying back to Nice, Jane returned to see her parents. She had to tell her mother. Since the evening she had spent with Hans, her mind had been in a turmoil, and she craved her parents' love. She took her mother out for lunch and had a long heart-to-heart, telling her everything except how Ron made his living. After she had opened up about the problems and had told her mother about the breakdown of her marriage and her love for Hans, she felt a calmness come over her, a weight having been lifted from her shoulders. Her mother tut-tutted and patted her hand, at a loss for what to say except that all would be OK and that she was confident her daughter would take the right decisions when the time came. Jane made her mother promise not to say anything to her father, knowing all too well what his reaction would be and how disappointed in her he would be. Plus, in his condition, she didn't want to cause him any unnecessary worry.

The next day, Jane flew back to the apartment outside Nice. She was feeling much happier and was looking forward to her time with Hans, whenever it would come.

CHAPTER 12

As Swiss flight LX1843 started its descent into Zurich Airport in Kloten, Ron started to feel uneasy; he was dreading the meeting with the Indian and regretted agreeing to it. He never liked sudden, out-of-the-blue discussions, especially when he had no idea what was on offer. He kicked himself for having been so impetuous; he hadn't been thinking straight, still euphoric after his two other deals, and hadn't thought things through. Too late now. He had to go and make the effort. Who knew what it might bring.

As he walked into the executive lounge, he spotted his man seated in a corner, staring at a laptop. The greetings were forced, as was small talk, whilst an attentive waitress served them coffee. Once they were alone, the Indian took out a file and looked over to Ron.

"Mr Stokes, I have a most very interesting deal to propose, not quite in your area of expertise, but I feel most confident you will be up to it. It is a very, very delicate matter which requires much discretion on your part. And rewards will be huge." The fixed gaze unnerved Ron, who felt as if he were being talked to as a child. He nodded to the man to continue.

His contact continued in a hushed tone, spending the next twenty minutes carefully explaining what was required and the sums involved. Ron's mind was racing. Had he heard right? It was certainly a field he knew nothing about, but the rewards were unimaginable. But so were the dangers. Questions came flooding out, each clearly answered by the man opposite him, who remained calm and patient. Ron excused himself and made his way to the toilet, feeling the need to be alone so he could think calmly and rationally. He felt sick and exhilarated at the same time; the thought of his contact thinking of him for the job and trusting him enough to offer him a deal like this blew his mind. He figured the man must think highly of him, which boosted his ego and his confidence. That being said, the deal to his mind was too big and too dangerous, especially seeing as he had no contacts in that world and would have to rely on the Indian. No, be sensible, Ron. Don't let yourself be sucked into something you will regret later. Stick with what you know. That has always been your mantra, so don't deviate from it now.

He took a deep breath and was about to tell the man he was not interested, when his contact spoke first. "Mr Stokes, I am very much aware that this is outside your comfort zone, but I must tell you that now you have been told about the deal, there is no going back." He looked over at Ron, whose face had drained of all colour. "You see, my superiors don't like people not obeying their orders, and once someone is put in the know, that person is expected to come on board. I would very much suggest you agree to this deal. It is a very big honour to have been chosen. It proves they trust you very much."

Ron was silent for a long while. His throat was dry, his mind in a turmoil. "What happens if I turn it down?" he croaked.

The little man looked at him straight in the eye. "Mr Stokes, for your sake, I suggest you not turn this down. Most truly, if I were you, I would agree. The financial benefits outweigh any negatives. Your future will be guaranteed."

Ron realised the threat of being cut off or worse. The double-crooked bastard had him by the balls, and he had no way out unless he was happy to give up everything, including probably his life, something he was not going to do. He slowly nodded his agreement, then signed the papers placed in front of him. The little Indian beamed and grinned widely. "I'm so very happy. You are very astute. My superiors will be most satisfied." He handed the file to Ron. "Now, you are expected in Boston on Friday. I will send you details later today. I must go now. I don't wish to miss my plane. Good day to you." With that, he got up, leaving Ron slumped in his chair.

It was a long time before Ron himself got up and made his way out of the airport. He was feeling glum and was furious at the way the meeting had gone and at his own naivety. What an absolute idiot he had been; all his principles, from the start, had been thrown away. He had agreed to a meeting without hesitation, not having asked what sort of deal to expect, and had been duped—no, sucked into something he knew nothing about. He hadn't seen the net as it was enveloping him. He had been too mesmerised by the thought of easy money. Making his way over to the taxi rank, he spat out curses.

By the time the taxi pulled up to the hotel and beneath the large awning that covered the entrance, Ron had calmed down. No use in crying over spilt milk. He had to make the best of a bad situation and turn it to his advantage, something he was good at doing.

Walking through the doors of the Baur au Lac, his most favourite hotel, Ron's mood changed instantly. Just being surrounded by class and opulence made him feel better. He was greeted at the desk by the deputy manager, who welcomed him warmly and immediately showed him up to his suite. Ron had long understood that if you wanted service and attention, you asked for a suite and tipped well. Once on his own, he made a beeline for the decanter placed on a silver tray with eight crystal tumblers and poured himself a stiff drink. Making his way over to the window, he looked out over the garden, where he was just able to see the lake with a few white boats bobbing at their moorings. He let out a long sigh and closed his eyes. What had he let himself in for? He gulped the drink down and took out his phone.

Firstly, he called Credit Suisse and made an appointment to see the private banking manager that afternoon. Secondly, he called Herr Straub in Vaduz to tell him he would be visiting the next day. He spoke to Hans, giving him an update on the two deals finalised in Athens and provided him with some precise instructions. He had decided not to tell his trusted aide about his latest meeting; that could wait until they met face to face. He rescheduled their meeting for after his return from Boston. Before ringing off, he confirmed that he was happy that Hans had a few days off, especially since he would be seeing Jane. Ron was about to leave the room for the bank when he decided to text his wife, simply telling her he had to fly to the States and that he didn't know when he would be back.

Ron was ushered into a large modern meeting room. A grey oval table surrounded by ten chairs stood in the middle; a computer hummed across from him. He declined the offer of coffee and waited patiently. The door burst open, and a short tubby man, dressed immaculately in a blue suit and a tie emblazoned with the bank's crest, strode over. The greeting was effusive but cold, something the man had done hundreds of times before with people he didn't know or those he didn't particularly care for. He sat himself down in front of the computer whilst enquiring if his client had had a good day so far.

Ron simply nodded and immediately got down to business. Firstly, he wanted to know if a large deposit had been received. If so, he wanted confirmation of the exact amount. He then instructed the banker to make an internal transfer to another of the bank's clients. He gave the name of the Egyptian and his bank details. The financier knew both Ron and this man, so he asked no questions. Secondly, Ron asked the man to make a transfer of three million Swiss francs to a bank in Vaduz, giving him the details. The man never batted an eye; it was part of his job to move large amounts around the world with no questions asked—well, almost no questions.

Having completed his two transactions, Ron thanked the man and left. He was happy; his associate had been paid the first tranche of his commission, and Ron had moved some of his own cash to a safer location. Swiss banks were fine and once were the place to keep one's money, but over the past few years, things had changed. Under pressure from world governments, and for the purpose of putting an end to money laundering, especially from terrorist groups, the Swiss government had become fussier and tightened up the rules. Although Swiss banks were still a safe place to deposit one's money, things weren't what they used to be. However, the small principality of Liechtenstein had resisted such changes and quickly found its banks being used by the wealthy instead. Ron was one of those wealthy people who had moved his money to Liechtenstein. So was the Turk.

Ron awoke the next morning to a bright sunny day. He walked the short distance to the train station and boarded the 9 a.m. to Vaduz, having chosen to sit on the left side, which offered him a wonderful view of the lake and the snow-capped mountains beyond. Two hours later, he was making his way to Herr Straub's private bank, where he was warmly welcomed and well looked after. Once his business was completed, he killed the time until his return trip to Zurich by having a late lunch, washed down with a bottle of local wine. He was a happy man, relaxed in the knowledge that his money was in safe hands and being well looked after.

His next stage was not going to be so pleasant. Boston was calling, and he had no idea what to expect.

CHAPTER 13

Peter Hollins arrived back in London. One of the first things he did was to call his friend Brian. He tried to paint a good picture of the visit to Belfast and concentrated on his meeting with Charly Flynn, telling Brian that he was absolutely sure the man was going to come up with an answer; he could feel it in his bones. Brian was not convinced but refrained from saying anything apart from thanking his friend for his time and effort.

The second call was to Sean, which was brief, Sean having made it clear to Peter that he was on business in Amsterdam and couldn't really talk, suggesting they should meet up at the weekend to catch up and perhaps take in one of the rugby internationals. There was no mention of Charly and no questions about Peter's visit to Northern Ireland or how it had gone. Disappointed, Peter decided to take the first train up to Leeds. He had hoped to find an excuse not to visit his aunt, but, well, that was life. On the train, he called his regiment headquarters and spoke to the commander in chief, a man he knew and got on well with. After the usual niceties, he came to the point and asked outright for an extension of his leave. He explained the reasons for his request, stressing that the investigation into John's death was not as easy as he had first hoped, then saying that nevertheless good progress was being made. He thanked his lucky stars that the boss liked him and knew he wouldn't be requesting more time off unless it was for something important. He was assured all formalities would be completed by the end of the day. Would an extra three weeks be sufficient?

Three days with Aunt Edith was enough for any man. She meant no harm, but she simply went over the top. A delightful woman in her late seventies, she was on the go nonstop. When excited, she talked incessantly. Peter had always been her favourite, the boy wonder, the soldier who fought in faraway lands, facing daily dangers whilst defending land and country. She liked his intelligence and his simplicity; he was not vain or conceited, just a down-to-earth, hard-working man who loved the military life. He had always had a vivid imagination and was a wonderful raconteur.

Once at Aunt Edith's, in between being fed and fussed over, Peter regaled his aunt with tales from his latest posting, embellishing when it suited, omitting the more gruesome moments. Not too soon, it was time for him to leave. That morning she fussed over him more than ever and insisted on driving him to the station. He tried to dissuade her, but to no avail. As he put it, being driven by Aunt Edith was more dangerous than facing a Taliban attack. She took the comment well and roared with laughter, saying she would have to tell her friends.

Peter had just checked in to his hotel when his phone buzzed. It was Sean calling. He had gotten back earlier that day and suggested they have a night out.

Sean marched into the hotel lobby and greeted his friend with a gripping handshake and a slap on the back. "How was your visit to Leeds?" he enquired.

"Fine, fine. She is a lovely person—means well—but boy, does she talk. Guess it's being on your own. I'm just sorry for her friends."

Sean laughed. "Drink and something to eat?"

Peter nodded. "Sounds good, so long as it's not tea or scones. I've had enough of those in three days to feed the whole regiment for a month. Talking of regiments, I have an extra three weeks' leave. I asked the other day. The chief had no problem with it."

They strolled down the bustling street until they found a decent-looking pub. "Any news from Belfast?" Sean asked.

"No. Charly said he would call if he had anything. So far, he has been conspicuous by his silence. What were you doing in Amsterdam?"

"Working on something big. Not sure if I told you last time. I'm looking into links between the Taliban and the Chinese Triads. Looks as if they're working together in drug running, and there may be a link also with dealers in Holland and over here. I've been trying to infiltrate these organisations for some time now, but it ain't easy."

"Sounds bloody dangerous if you ask me. Sure, opium production is booming in Afghanistan, probably the main crop they have. The government over there says they're getting on top of it and that it's under control, but it's not. Every farmer grows the stuff and sells it openly in the markets or privately to an intermediary."

Sean grunted. "Yeah, that's the bloody problem. It seems there is a massive trade between them and the Chinese Triads. Most of the stuff goes out east before being shipped to Europe or the United States. Sometimes it's shipped directly here through Pakistan. I was in Holland meeting my counterpart; we're working on a joint operation. They're keen to crack that route as their government is under pressure from the EU to curb such trade. Not that it will stop the guys. They'll simply find a new way, and it'll simply be a token gesture."

"Thought the South Americans were big players also."

"They are, but for the moment they haven't linked up. Doesn't mean they're not dumping stuff in Europe. It's easier and cheaper for them to use the US."

The rest of the evening was spent talking about past years, their various postings, and the merits of doing a job they both loved. It was late when Peter finally made it to bed, his head spinning from the copious amount of alcohol he'd consumed. He was amazed at the quantity Sean could knock back with seemingly little effect.

They met up the next morning, both slightly jaded, and made their way to Twickenham. Sean had managed, through a contact, to get a couple of tickets for one of the internationals. The fresh air cleared their heads, and it wasn't long before they started discussing the topic of Belfast. They called Charly, who still had no news, although he did assure them that his team were working round the clock. During the conversation, he mentioned that he had heard rumours that one of the local terrorist groups was involved in a major drug smuggling operation. He was wondering whether the murder had anything to do with that. Promising to call the minute he had anything new, he ended the call just as the referee blew the kick-off.

Back in Belfast, Charly had been looking out the window and watching two plain-clothes policemen sitting in a car. Having known that his suggestion they leave him alone would fall on deaf ears, he shook his head. What a waste of man-hours and money, two men being paid to watch an innocent civilian who was working on the same side. Trust did not figure high up on DI O' Grady's list of priorities, nor on that of his boss. Charly returned to the sofa and settled down to watch Ireland take on Japan.

He had returned to the office a couple of days ago, reporting back to work. His colleagues and the women in HR were happy to see that he was back, as he was one of their favourites. They all soon brought him up to speed. No longer had he settled down to read a couple of files when he was summoned up to see the boss. Returning to his seat fifteen minutes later, he began clearing his desk. He had been told that his extended absence was no longer acceptable. Although he was excellent at his job, the company could no longer warrant employing him.

Before leaving, he stopped by one of the desks and handed a young man a Manila envelope, asking him to read it once he was home.

Charly was in a reflective mood as he watched an Irish player dive between the posts. Did he really care about the desk job? It had only been a cover story, perfectly understood by his old boss, who had now retired, but the new generation didn't, or didn't want to. The new forty-something CEO was from a different world and a different era. Old Jimmy Burns was ex-army and had understood the situation well, giving Charly all the leeway needed, and not being averse to pulling a few strings in higher quarters if required. In contrast, this Brad chap was simply a number-cruncher and had no clue, nor did he care, what his employees did outside work. Charly clearly remembered the first time he tried to explain what his real job was; a blank expression came over the man's face, causing him to tell his director of planning that he didn't care a stuff, that he was paid to work for the company and gave not two hoots about national security.

Well, too bad. He didn't need the job anyway and enjoyed being a spy far more, chasing down the bad guys was what he loved. He'd been about to call his two contacts when Sean had called.

DI O'Grady had decided he had to inform the boss about Charly Flynn. Not looking forward to the meeting, he had postponed it as long as he could. Eventually he had run out of excuses and could not delay his going upstairs.

As he waited at the door, he felt a bead of sweat slowly tracing a path down his back. The door swung open, causing him to jump, startling him out of his daydream. A secretary showed him through and tapped on a door marked "Chief Constable", opening it immediately. A tall, lanky man in his fifties was sitting behind a large desk, his blue eyes peering out from beneath a pair of bushy eyebrows. He remained seated and waved the secretary away. Patrick O'Grady knew things were not going to be easy because he was made to stand, no chair, no offer of tea or coffee, just a stare from those icy eyes.

"What news have you for me, Patrick? Hope your visit means you have put whoever is responsible for all these muggings behind bars." The voice was monotone and flat.

"Well, sir, not exactly. In fact, we have been treading water despite having my full team on the case." He looked at the man across the table, the bead of sweat now feeling more like a stream. "Of course, we're looking into every possibility, and I feel it is only a matter of time before we make a breakthrough."

His boss's demeanour darkened; the man was about to speak, but Patrick interrupted him. "Sir, we had a visit the other day from a Major Hollins, a friend of the first victim's brother. He was trying to find out how the investigation was going and asked if we had any leads. I managed to pacify him. He is now back in England."

"Who is this Major Hollins, and why did Mr Jackson's brother not come himself? I hear that there were two men. Who was this second person?"

"Sir, Major Hollins thought it would be unwise for Colonel Jackson to come over. As he put it, one dead Jackson is sufficient. The second gave his name as Charles Flynn, a local and a long-time friend of Major Hollins. He was here to help the major and guide him around the city."

The chief constable looked at his DI and frowned. "Continue. I can see from your looks that there is more. Come on, spit it out."

Patrick O'Grady swallowed hard; his mouth felt dry as sandpaper. "Sir, we subsequently found out that this Charly Flynn works for MI6 and has been there for years."

The chief leapt out of his chair, his cheeks flushing and his cold eyes bulging. "What! A fucking spy here, in this station, snooping around?! How the hell did you not suss it out?" He started to pace the room. O'Grady could see that he was working himself up. "You know how I hate—no, abhor—the thought of spies. They are the scum of this world, double-crossing creeps with no morals and no interest in anyone else. You bloody idiot, I should sack you here and now." He paced some more before sitting down. "What's he wanting? What the hell can he do except put the bloody cats among the bloody pigeons? What did you tell him? Come on, what did you tell him?"

Patrick watched in silence as his boss literally spat out the last words. "Nothing, sir. We—sorry, I—told him that the police were well into their investigations and that everything was under control."

The chief constable looked at his detective for a long while before speaking in a hushed voice. "Make sure you put more men on the case. Ensure you keep round-the-clock watch on this creep of a spy. I want to have a report every day on what he has done, where he has been, and whom he has spoken to. Understand? Do you read my lips, Detective Inspector?"

"Yes, sir, fully. We already have a couple of men keeping an eye on him, but we're stretched to the limit, and as you know, it's not easy; we're short-staffed as it is." He did not mention that Flynn had lost the two rookies in record time, nor did he say anything about the spy warning his men off.

"O'Grady, make sure you get this case wrapped up quickly. I already have the people above me on my back. Just make sure this bloody snoop is kept out of it all, understand? If I hear he has given you the slip or is causing trouble, I will have your balls and will feed them to the sharks myself. Now get out and catch whoever is behind this mess."

CHAPTER 14

Charly awoke with a start to the buzzing of his phone beside him. He peered bleary-eyed at the clock: 7 a.m. Who the hell would call at this time of day, on a Sunday of all days? He looked at the number and immediately recognised it as belonging to one of his contacts. He decided not to reply, needing time to gather his thoughts and clear his head.

After the game, Charly had celebrated with a couple of Guinness's and stupidly followed that up by sipping a few whiskies, which, on an empty stomach, he realised was not the wisest of decisions. He lay in bed a few minutes, yawned, and then gave a final stretch, getting up and making his way to the bathroom. A cold shower had always been his cure for hangovers. After a shave and a good brushing of his teeth, he felt much better equipped to face life. He made himself one of his strong black coffees, wincing as the brew burnt the back of his throat. He considered making himself a fry-up, but his stomach rebelled at the thought of greasy food.

Crossing over to the window, he peered out. The car with its passengers was still there. He shook his head. *Poor sods.* However, that was their decision; he had told them not to waste their time, but he also knew that orders were orders and had to be followed. He called his contact, who answered after a couple of rings, and proceeded to lecture him about the merits of rising early and not partaking of too much amber nectar. He was a teetotaller and a health freak who never understood people hoping to compensate for their weakness by going to the gym. Diatribe finished, he went on to tell Charly that he had some interesting news. They arranged to meet at the park in two hours. The man then suggested asking the woman to come along, which Charly agreed to.

For the first time, Charly felt excited. Like all good operators, he never gave a thought to saying anything over the phone. One never knew who would be listening in.

An hour later, Charly Flynn left the house and made his way over to the car. The driver's-side window was lowered. He greeted the two men. "Good morning to you, gentlemen. I trust you had a decent night, not too cold. I'm going to meet a friend for coffee on Donegall Place. Should be back in a couple of hours." He tapped the bonnet of the car as he left, then made his way to the bus stop. As the bus left, he noticed the car was close behind.

He got off a stop early and marched along the quiet pavement before turning right and proceeding up a one-way street. The car that had been following him stopped, the two men deciding what their next move would be. Charly turned into a side alley and quickened his pace before making for his destination. He kept to small side streets and mixing his directions, knowing that neither the car nor either of the men could keep up with him. An hour later he entered the park and headed for the bench. As he sat waiting, his mind turned to the poor coppers. He felt sorry them. They were nice guys, no doubt, but were totally out their depth when it came to keeping tabs on him.

A man and a woman came ambling over and sat down on the bench beside Charly. He listened intently and asked a few questions, nodding before he gave his instructions. The next few days were going to be interesting and could prove to be a turning point. He thanked the pair for the excellent work before heading off home. He was a happy man.

As he turned the corner leading into his street, he noticed the car. He walked up and knocked on the window. The startled driver opened the window. Charly handed him a bag. "Here, brought these for you. Hope you like bagels and doughnuts." He left before either man could say anything, soon disappearing through the front door.

He rose early the next day and left the house by way of the rear door; it was business time, so no more playing games or being nice to the local police force. He made his way swiftly through the playground and joined the main road, where he caught the first bus heading west. He got off well short of his destination and entered a coffee shop. Sitting next to the window, he surveyed the passing traffic, watching the passers-by going about their business. He checked his watch before leaving, then crossed the street to buy a paper. Half an hour later, a man holding a plastic bag and dressed in jeans, a T-shirt, and a woollen beanie, with a newspaper stuck in his back pocket, limping down the road. As the man neared the pub, he noticed a beggar seated by the door. Before entering, he fished around in his pocket and tossed a coin into the woman's plastic pot. She looked up at the stranger and nodded. Reaching out to retrieve the donation, she showed three fingers.

The pub wasn't busy, with only a handful of hardened locals as patrons. The man limped over to the bar and ordered a half pint, then went and sat at a table not far away from a table of three mean-looking individuals. As he sat down, he nodded and took out his paper. The three strangers ignored him and continued their conversation. They were all young, in their early to mid-thirties. Two were dressed in casual clothes, whilst the third member sported a suit but no tie. They were discussing the rugby game, each giving his opinion on how he would have played. The conversation soon turned more serious and became business like. The well-dressed individual did most of the talking and was clearly the boss or their leader. The man pretending to read his paper listened intently, not missing a word, remembering everything. Just before the conversation concluded, the man rose and limped out into the street. He crossed the road and slipped up a nearby alley, from where he watched the group emerge from the pub. As they came out, one of the men looked down at the beggar and kicked her plastic cup into the gutter. They all laughed. The leader spat in the woman's direction and called out some obscenity.

None of them noticed the man who had come from nowhere and followed them as they crossed the road. Now standing at the bus stop, he lit a cigarette, watching as the group split up. He started to follow the well-dressed leader; he was not to lose sight of him for the rest of the day.

Charly Flynn, who had been watching from a doorway, emerged from his hiding spot as the two younger men headed in the opposite direction. He had changed, having put on a bomber jacket, swapped his beanie for a cap, and placed a pair of dark glasses on his nose. He doubted either of the men would recognise him; they had barely glanced up when he sat down a couple of feet away in the bar. He followed at a safe distance and, like the other man, would never let them out of his sight. They headed towards the south side of the city.

It was well past midnight when Charly let himself in by the back door. The car and its occupants were still there. A pang of guilt passed over him but soon disappeared. He sat down and made notes of what he had seen and heard. It had been a long, busy day, but he was used to it; it was his job.

For the next couple of days, he and his two companions, helped by a fourth contact, trailed the three men, none of whom suspected anything. Most people, if they're not a spy and haven't been trained, never think of looking around at their surroundings. They live in their little world, oblivious of their surroundings and of the people who populate their space.

By the end of the third day, the spooks had learned all they wanted about the habits and business of the three men. They had overheard discussions, had eavesdropped on phone calls, and had built a picture of the men's lives. None of the information was particularly nice. In fact, in Charly's words, these people were scum of the tallest order. Two additional contacts had been called in, which had allowed him and the woman to delve deeper into the trio's past and backgrounds. Surveillance was continuous.

Taking pity on the two men in the car, Charly went out and spoke to them on the fourth morning. He told them he had been ill and had been confined to bed. They believed him and wished him a prompt recovery. Guilt briefly swamped over him once again.

That night, he rang Sean and Peter and gave them a sketchy outline of what he had found out. They agreed to meet up in London the following evening. He then called DI O'Grady and asked to meet him the next morning. The detective was not entirely pleased but felt he had no choice but to agree. His men had reported nothing out of the ordinary apart from saying the spy had been ill and hadn't left the house. Progress on the murder and muggings had stalled big time.

CHAPTER 15

O'Grady remained seated as Charly was shown in and marched over to the policeman. The detective nodded to a chair across from his desk and motioned for his guest to take a seat. Coffee or tea wasn't offered, he didn't want the spy to feel too welcome or at ease.

The cool reception didn't faze Charly, who was used to people acting aloof and distant towards him, especially when they knew he had gotten the better of them. He greeted the detective with a broad smile and a chirpy voice, continuing before O'Grady could say anything. "Thanks for seeing me at such short notice. I appreciate that you are very busy, so I'll cut to the chase." He then explained what he and his colleagues had found out over the past few days, being careful not to tell him the whole story, at no point divulging too much—keep the man guessing. He kept his report simple but included sufficient detail that the detective felt he was being told everything.

Patrick O'Grady sat listening intently. He was pleased with what he heard but was annoyed that this man had managed to find so much out in such a short time. Why the hell were his boys so useless? Why was he having to have a spook, of all people, do their job? Still, he was puzzled at how this man had found out so much when in bed ill. He decided to ask the question bluntly.

"As you appreciate, Detective," Charly began in reply, "surveillance of this kind is very delicate and must be done discreetly. No offence to your men, but I couldn't have people following me or my people when we, in turn, were keeping a close eye on these individuals. I did suggest to your boys—who, may I suggest, should get some better training—that they leave off their attempts at watching me, but my suggestion was ignored. I also told you I would report back as soon as I had news. You should trust me, Detective. We're on the same side, and we both want the same thing. Leave me to do my job and deploy your resources in a better way."

O'Grady bristled at the lecture and was about to reply when he was interrupted again. "Patrick. I can call you Patrick, can't I? It seems to me and my team that this may turn out to be a very big operation which will need to be handled very delicately. When the time comes, we will require your support and manpower, but for the moment I would appreciate it if you left this operation to us. Call off the two lads who are ensconced outside my house. I promise I will keep you updated."

DI O'Grady looked glum. Deep down he knew that Charly Flynn was right, that his team were not up to the job. The simple fact that they had been duped for the past four days proved that they were no match for Flynn. How would he tell the boss? He could just imagine the reaction when he talked to the chief constable. It was even odds he may lose his job or worse in his mind, be demoted. Who knew. After a long silence, he reluctantly conceded that the suggestion—or was it an order?—was a wise one. He wasn't sure either way, he nodded his agreement.

"Well, that's just fine. I appreciate your full support, and I'm convinced we'll crack this case." Charly rose from the chair and stuck his hand out. The detective simply looked at him with a resigned expression, remaining seated.

Patrick O'Grady was working out what to tell his superior when he was summoned to the man's office. His heart sank. He slowly got up and made his way to the floor above. As he entered the lion's den, he was struck by the brightness of the reception.

"Ah! Patrick, thanks for coming so quickly. This case, the murder of the soldier and all these recent muggings, any news?" He looked at his DI and returned to his chair. "Just had an interesting call. Not sure I like it, but it may be a blessing in disguise." He looked up at the worried man standing in front of him. "Seems MI6 want to take this one on. Pretty much ordered me to tell you to pull your men from the investigation. This Flynn chap, your spook, will be taking over and doesn't want us poking our noses around, the conceited bastard! What do you say?"

O'Grady looked at his boss, wondering how his recent guest had gained so much power. But he had to give it to the man, he acted fast, so he must be holding some clout within his organisation. It had been, what, forty minutes since Flynn had left his office.

O'Grady hesitated before answering. "It's up to you, sir. I just follow orders. I must admit, the man came to see me about an hour ago and gave me some sketchy information, but I'm sure he was holding back. Never mentioned anything about having us taken off the case."

The chief constable pursed his lips. "Yes, well, I'm surprised the two men you had keeping tabs on this Flynn chap didn't tell you anything. He must have been out and about, so why haven't they reported anything?"

The detective gulped but was spared having to answer by his superior continuing. "All in all, I think it's for the best. You know I hate spies and the thought that they are taking over a police case. The fact remains that we have found nothing out in three weeks. Your team is clearly incompetent. I had no other option but to agree. So, DI O'Grady, I order you to immediately call your men off this case. We'll review your section's performance at a later date."

The detective mumbled his apologies and his thanks. "Sir, does this mean we are to stop investigating the muggings as well?"

"Yes, the lot. Let's see how good this man really is. I can't wait to hear the excuses he makes when he comes cap in hand, begging for our help." He chuckled. The meeting had ended.

———◆———

After leaving the police station, Charly Flynn made his way to the airport and boarded a plane to Heathrow. First thing that morning, he had contacted his superior in London and reported what he and the team had found out; he had also expressed his concerns about the competence of the local police and suggested they be taken off the case. The phone call to O'Grady's boss was timed to coincide roughly with when Flynn would be finished with his meeting. Charly had nothing against the DI, whom he regarded as a good honest cop working under financial pressure with a team of well-intentioned but not particularly bright or resourceful men under him. He hoped the chief constable would be understanding and go softly on him.

Once in town, Charly made his way to the huge building beside the Thames which was headquarters. He brought his superior up to speed and told him his plan. Although on a secure line, he had kept his earlier explanations purposely sketchy and had asked for the meeting to be a full-blown case report. This meant the involvement of several high-ranking members. He stressed that the matter was of the utmost emergency.

The meeting lasted several hours, during which time Charly give a detailed account of what he and his team had uncovered. All agreed the matter was serious and would need some close cooperation between sections and desks. By the end, everyone knew what they were expected to do. A special dedicated team had been set up, to be led by Flynn.

Charly entered the small Italian restaurant in Soho and greeted Sean and Peter with a warm handshake, apologising for being so late. He quickly explained the reason for his delay before they ordered. Conversation was free flowing and the banter excellent. None of them mentioned the real reason they were meeting until they got outside, Sean suggesting they go back to his office. They talked long into the night, consuming much coffee. They divided their tasks, each taking on a specific role. Charly would return to Belfast and continue to monitor the three men and their organisation. Sean would concentrate on Holland and the Far East, whilst Peter was to take up surveillance of events in England. This would mean Peter would have to ask for another extension of leave if things did not go to plan; with MI6's help, that would not be a problem. Things were going to be tricky as they had three, if not four, different operations to keep tabs on, all of which could or were interrelated. Timing and coordination was going to be crucial.

CHAPTER 16

Ron Stokes had arrived in Boston, still apprehensive about the meeting the next day. Why had he accepted? Again, why had he not thought things through properly? Even though he hadn't known what the deal entailed or what his involvement was going to be, he should have taken more time. He knew now that it was not going to be easy. He had a bad feeling; his gut instinct told him to be cautious and not to agree to the first offer made. He doubted he could get out of this one—that had been made plain to him—but at least he would put up a fight and make sure to limit his involvement.

He awoke to a cold, grey day, just like his mood. His head was thumping from too much of that free wine he had had on the plane. His stomach was in knots, and he noticed that his hands were shaking. He tried to get a grip, but even a couple of strong coffees failed to calm him down, instead adding the unpleasant side effect of making him rush to the toilet.

The morning had dragged by, but at last it was time. He jumped into a cab and headed north to the suburb of Somerville, one of the up-and-coming areas of the city. The old, traditional-looking buildings lining the bustling streets were a far cry from the concrete and glass towers which made up most US cities. Ron hadn't ever visited Boston before. He liked what he saw.

The taxi stopped all too soon outside a large redbrick building. As Ron got out, his guts contorted once again as his hands began to shake.

He was greeted at the door by a massive doorman, more like a bouncer at a nightclub, and was ushered towards an old-style lift. The man pushed the button, closed the gate, and watched the cage move up. Not a word had been uttered. The lift creaked and rattled its way up to the third floor. Ron eventually alighted into a brightly lit hallway with a double glass door, which opened as he approached, allowing him to enter the modern reception area. The woman behind the desk was expecting him. Rising, she greeted him with a smile and led him immediately down a short corridor and into the conference room. As the door closed, Ron found himself standing alone. He selected a chair with its back to the window and sat down. His palms were sweaty; his breathing quickened. He tried to breathe slowly to calm down, but still his inner self was in turmoil.

After what seemed an age, the door swung open and three well-dressed men breezed into room. They greeted their guest with firm handshakes, each introducing himself. Ron nodded at every handshake, immediately forgetting the names. The three looked foreign, although their accents didn't seem to be. Introductions were done by the slightly portlier man, who was immaculately dressed. Once he took a seat, he motioned to everyone to do the same. Meticulously, he took out a pen from his top pocket, put on his specs, and opened a file, which he then slowly read through. Looking up, he addressed Ron in a low, deep voice. "Mr Stokes, welcome to Boston. Thank you for coming at such short notice. I'm not sure how much you have been told but let me bring you up to speed. After I have finished, you may ask any questions you have." He inclined his head and gave a thin smile.

For the next half hour, the main man spoke, explaining in detail the proposed deal and what he expected his guest to do. Ron sat silently, listening, digesting what they wanted of him, his alarm and disbelief growing by the minute. Even if he had wanted to be part of such a proposition, he doubted very much that he had the skilled manpower or the know-how to get the job done. The more his host went on, the more Ron was convinced he had to get out the situation. But how? They all spoke as if it was a fait accompli, which he knew was the case. He didn't like what he heard, didn't like it one little bit.

The man finished up at last. Closing the file, he looked up at Ron, sitting back contently.

There was a long silence whilst Ron considered the best way of turning down the deal. He could neither find the right words nor muster the courage. He looked at the three men in turn. All three staring back with impassive expressions. Ron gulped and took a deep breath.

"Thank you for such a clear and precise explanation. It is, as you suggest, a massive enterprise, and I must point out that I am only a small operator with a small team. I really don't think this is for me, nor do I think you would be best served by having my organisation as partner." He paused but quickly began speaking again, saying, "Not that I don't appreciate you considering me, but I really and sincerely believe you would be better off finding a larger outfit which has better contacts and is used to such important deals."

One of the sidekicks, a tall, thin man sporting a long, bushy beard, looked over at Ron with a pitying expression. "Mr Stokes, you don't seem to understand; you have no choice. Our superiors have selected you and your organisation to work for us, and that's final."

Ron looked surprised and became emboldened. "I thought I was talking to the top brass. That's why I flew over. Had I known you weren't the main people, I wouldn't have wasted my time." He made to get up but was immediately told in no uncertain terms to sit down again.

"You have not been listening, Mr Stokes. We are the main people in America. We are the ones who chose you, and we are the people you will report to. Our superiors are our partners. We represent them here in the West. What we say reflects what they and we have agreed to. So, you see, Mr Stokes, you have no choice. You are indeed speaking to the top of the hierarchy." His dark eyes bore into into his guest.

Ron was not going to succumb without a fight. He looked at the three men sitting impassively in front of him, deciding how he would continue. At last, he shook his head. "Not good enough, gentlemen. I was given the impression that you, and you alone, were heading this operation. Nothing was said about partners and you acting on their behalf, which, let's be frank, is what you are doing. No, I am very dissatisfied and will not agree to anything unless it is with your superiors or partners, whoever they are. What is this organisation anyway?"

The three men continued to stare at him with steely eyes. The silence was deafening. The first man cleared his throat and put on a smooth, smarmy voice. "Mr Stokes, as my colleague here has just told you, we are the main people. The organisation, like many companies, has offices across the world. Here in Boston is the headquarters. All our directors are involved. Some are based in South America, others, in the Far and Middle East. I can assure you, you are talking to the highest people in the organisation. As for what we do or who we are, this has nothing to do with you and is none of your concern. You are, I am sorry to say, simply a small cog in a large wheel, here to obey orders and to execute them to our requirements. I repeat, you have no choice." He smiled a sickly smile before continuing. "May I suggest you think carefully about your next comment and your next move? We don't want to set out on the wrong footing." He unclasped his hands and sat back.

Ron couldn't think of anything to say. The man had made it more than clear that there was no negotiating, no choice. He nodded.

The three men rose. As they reached the door, the little one turned. "May I suggest that you not try anything funny, Mr Stokes? We'll be watching you, and we won't hesitate to take the appropriate action." They left without a further word.

The secretary appeared and led Ron to the lift, where the bouncer was waiting to escort him to the street. Unsure of the geography, Ron made his way up the wide, busy road. His legs were weak; he felt sick. He could feel the bouncer's eyes following him penetrating him like a bullet; it sent a shiver down his spine. He spotted a bar across the street and made a beeline for it. Taking a seat at the bar, he ordered a large whisky and gulped it down, ordering another immediately. He then asked the impassive bartender to call a cab. He had to get out of the area and return to the relative safety of his hotel room; he had to think.

His feeling of nausea and foreboding were still with him as he let himself into his room. Making for the minibar, he poured himself another large drink and went to lie on the bed, his mind racing and in turmoil. No matter how he looked at his situation, the answer screamed at him: he had been a total fool, and now he was in big danger. He had no way out except to go along with what these people wanted and hope for the best, hope that his wits and the trusty Hans would see him through this terrible ordeal.

It was dark when he awoke, his temples thumping, his mouth tasting of sandpaper. Feeling better after a shower, he decided to call Hans to give him the bad news. His aide kept his feelings to himself and remained upbeat. He was sure it was not as bad as Ron was imagining and that their experience and guile would see them through. A meeting in Paris was scheduled for the day after next, when Ron and Hans would discuss their options.

The following afternoon, on the way to the airport, Ron kept looking behind himself, checking that no one was following. He had a feeling whilst he was paying his hotel bill that someone was watching, but he didn't see any of the men from the previous day. Still, the feeling wouldn't leave him. It was only when he boarded the plane that he started to relax.

CHAPTER 17

Following the London meeting, Sean, Charly, and Peter all went their separate ways. Sean left immediately for Amsterdam. After agreeing and getting support from his Dutch counterpart, he organised twenty-four-hour surveillance on several individuals they had pinpointed as being involved in their case. As with the British, the Dutch had highly trained professionals who were accustomed to following suspects and keeping constant contact with them without being picked up. Within a couple of hours of Sean's finalising the details, five operatives had started trailing the suspects, noting every movement, checking any contacts, and listening in on phone calls and other conversations.

One person of special interest was a tall, well-built man going by the name of Hans van der Brawn. Well dressed and apparently enjoying a fine lifestyle, Mr van der Brawn made many calls to people known to be dubious characters, both in Holland and England, who were involved in the murky world of smuggling. He lived in an upmarket area of the city centre overlooking one of the main canals. His flat was situated on the fourth floor of a building that was slightly set back from the main street and was guarded by a security guard posted at the gated entrance. Access to his flat in normal circumstances was not easy, but for the likes of the secret service, it was child's play.

One day when Mr van der Brawn was away on one of his frequent business trips, his home was visited by two men. They entered unseen by the guard or any neighbour and quickly got to work bugging the apartment before carefully going through the place with a fine-tooth comb. They discovered a treasure trove of names, contact details, and information, meticulously photographing it all. They left a few hours later, leaving no trace of themselves and not a hint of their presence.

Later that afternoon, a large pleasure boat slowly glided into a mooring just below the row of houses. The occupants quickly got to work setting up the radios and listening devices before settling down. It was going to be a long surveillance operation, but they were used to it; it was their job.

Sean took up residence in a small hotel not far from one of the AIVD (the General Intelligence and Security Centre of the Netherlands) offices and began to sieve through the information that had been collected from the flat. It made interesting reading to say the least. With his counterpart, the two men built up a comprehensive picture of the man and the operation he ran. They learned that he had a boss, a man living part-time in the South of France and part-time in London. Exactly what the connection was and how much freedom van der Brawn had, was not yet clear.

A couple of days later, the target returned home. It seemed he had visited Switzerland, presumably to take care of his stashed fortune. He had received a phone call from the States, Boston precisely, from a man called Ron. By the tone of the conversation, this Ron was extremely concerned, his voice shaking as if he were scared out of his wits. A meeting had been scheduled in Paris in a couple of days' time, at the Hôtel du Louvre. The conversation revealed that Mr van der Brawn also had a place in the South of France and that he would be making his way there from Paris to see his girlfriend who, by all accounts, seemed to be Ron's wife.

Sean and his Dutch counterpart tried to piece together all the information. Although much of it made sense, there was still plenty they were not sure about. Did this Ron know that his closest aide was seeing his wife? What was the connection, and was she involved? Sean decided to return to London and investigate this Ron chap, who could be the key. Determined to find out who he was and what his involvement was in all this business, he felt things would quickly become clear.

Thanking his partner, Sean left to return to London that evening.

He would be kept updated on developments and promised to do the same.

⟶◆◂━━

Peter felt guilty. He hadn't been in contact with his friend Brian or, for that matter, DI Crawley. He didn't mind the latter so much, but to ignore his close friend was different.

He called Brian on the way to the station and arranged to meet him later that afternoon at Felicity's place. He immediately followed that up with a brief call to his aunt, telling her that he was on his way back to Afghanistan. Saying that he looked forward to visiting again the next time he was on leave, he thanked her for all she had done. As much as he loved her, the thought of spending another day with her was enough to justify telling her a white lie.

He jumped into a taxi and gave the driver the address he had been given. The house was situated on the outskirts of the small town and surrounded by woods and fields. As the taxi approached, he noticed a couple of cars. One was Brian's for sure, but the other one? Well, he would soon find out.

Peter was greeted at the door by Felicity, who gave him a warm hug and a kiss. She was in her forties with a fine figure and shoulder-length dark hair. Dressed in jeans and a checked blouse, she smiled brightly. Peter couldn't help but notice the sadness in her big, dark eyes. As much as she tried to hide her feelings, he couldn't but help see the pain she was going through. She led him to the lounge, where Brian was sitting deep in conversation with DI Crawley. Both men jumped up to greet the new arrival. Brian clasped his friend warmly. "Not very soldierly, Brian," Peter said, grinning and nudging his friend before turning to shake hands with the policeman.

"Tea, coffee, or something stronger?" Felicity asked.

Noticing that Brian was nursing a dram, Peter nodded towards his friend. "That looks just what the doctor ordered, thank you."

Peter waited until Felicity had returned and sat down next to her brother-in-law before he started his report. "I'm afraid there isn't all that much to say. I visited Belfast as you know but didn't get very far. That being said, a friend of mine had put me in contact with a chap over there who was very helpful. He has taken it upon himself to investigate and try to find out what happened. Apparently, he has some good contacts. Only time will tell."

There was a sniff and what sounded like a snort from the detective, who fidgeted uncomfortably in his chair. "Yes, I heard from my colleague DI O'Grady that you paid him a visit. Seems that not long after your meeting, a couple of days later in fact, his boss received a call from MI6 requesting that his men step down from the case. What is that all about?"

Peter's expression was blank. "I have no idea. Are you sure? I left the next day to visit my aunt. I have no knowledge. This is certainly the first time I have heard that MI6 is involved," he lied. "The only thing I know is that this man works for a company somewhere on the docks, but he did say he had some good connections."

Crawley looked at the man through squinted eyes. He didn't believe him for one minute and wondered what he was hiding. Peter quickly continued to apologise for not having more good news, saying that it had been much more complicated than he had expected. He looked over at Brian and Felicity, who both seemed to be a bit downcast. "Have you any news, Detective?"

"No, sir. I did have a conversation with O'Grady and was told all was in hand, but then I heard he had been taken off the case. I must say, I was rather upset with you. I thought I asked you to keep the whole thing low-key, but then I hear you went to meet him with this man. How long have you known him?"

Peter looked over at the detective and fixed him with a look in the eyes. "As I said, I met him through a friend I have known for a long time and who's done some business with him in the past. He certainly seemed a very affable person and very helpful. If he can help, then surely that's a good thing."

The detective shook his head slowly but decided not to pursue the matter further. The conversation moved on to other matters, and Peter learned that Brian was returning to Afghanistan the following week. He was feeling restless and helpless just hanging around so had asked his commanding officer to send him back to Kandahar and assist his replacement.

When, at last, the detective had left, Peter told them that he had not given up and that he was now helping his friend and this new contact, both of whom were secret service, in the investigation. It was unclear if John's death was directly related to the case they were working on, or if it was a totally different matter. "The DI was correct when he said that MI6 has taken over, but there was no way I could admit I knew. It is all very delicate, and we think it's related to drug running. I'm not sure why they don't want police involvement, but I've been asked to help here in England."

Brian grunted and Felicity gaped in horror at the new development. "Thought you were going back east shortly," Brian said once he had recovered.

"I managed, with a little help from my friend, to get my leave extended. He pulled some strings."

Felicity got up to replenish their drinks. "Your friend must be quite high up and important to get the brass to extend your time over here. I know from experience how difficult it is to get leave extensions." She handed each of the two men a well-filled tumbler and smiled. "I'm not upset with you, Peter. I know you have done your utmost, and I appreciate everything you have done. You certainly didn't have to offer. I just hope all this has not led you into danger or caused you problems."

Brian raised his glass to his friend. "The same here. I know you've done your best, and I, too, must thank you. Who knows what this investigation you have been roped into will lead to? Just make sure you don't get yourself killed."

Peter declined the invitation to stay for dinner, saying he had several calls to make, one of them being to Sean.

As Brian pulled into the pub's car park, Peter turned to his friend and patted him on the arm. "Don't worry about me. I'll be fine. I can assure you that I will do everything in my power to find the person or people who killed John and make them pay. Make sure you focus on your job when you get out there. Felicity needs you more than ever, and in one piece when you get back home."

Lying on his bed, Peter made a couple of calls, the first one to Charly, followed by a call to DI Crawley. The inspector did not sound amused at being disturbed, but he quickly changed his tone when Peter suggested they talk. Forty minutes later, both men were sitting at a table, pints in hand, looking at menus.

The detective was the first to speak. "What's all this about then?" he enquired.

"I owe you an apology, Detective Inspector. I didn't want to give too many details back at the cottage. Not that I don't trust Brian and Felicity, but I just didn't want to upset them any more than I had to." He looked over to the man and waited until they ordered before continuing. "I was telling you the truth when I said I didn't know this contact in Belfast. I had met a friend in London who is well connected, and he made the arrangement for me to meet this chap."

"Does he work for MI6?"

"I didn't know that at the time, but now I do. Yes, both do. I must tell you that since then, I have been roped in to help, and no, I am not secret service. They managed to pull a few strings and get my leave extended, but please, keep all this confidential. Protocol is what you call it, no?"

Crawley sighed and nodded. "I promise to stick to protocol better than you did. Certainly, this whole thing seems to be far bigger and more complex than I first thought. Have you spoken to O'Grady? I have basically been banned from contacting him after your and your friend's visit."

"I appreciate your help and trust. I promise I will keep you posted and keep you updated regularly. You never know, we may need your help at some point."

After they finished their meal, DI Crawley left. He felt happier now that he understood more. He had to admit to himself that he quite liked the soldier. At least he'd had the honesty and decency to come clean and tell the truth.

Charly Flynn had flown back directly after the London meeting; he had a whole load of things to do and much to prepare. Back at home, he got down to work. Firstly, he called his team leader and arranged to meet him in an hour for a full update. Next, he rang his boss and requested more men, saying that things had turned out to be more complicated than expected, adding that he wanted specific people with the specific skills required for the job. He asked for two women and a man, all three of whom he knew and trusted implicitly. Although relatively young, they were experienced, hard-working, dedicated agents, not afraid to get into a scrap and unafraid of hardship. People often had the idea that agents were like James Bond, but the reality was very different. Spying, going undercover, was a dirty, gruelling business carried out mainly in harsh conditions and surroundings. Hours turned into days that could turn into weeks. You were, more often than not, left on your own, reliant on your training and ingenuity, and on your physical and mental strength. The selection process was long and hard with only a small percentage making the cut. It was not glamourous, and the rewards, if there were any at all, were few.

After some persistence and persuasion, Charly had the people he wanted. He promised to keep costs to a minimum but couldn't guarantee the time frame, saying that that would be decided by the criminals they were fighting.

He met his team leader in a noisy pub and brought him up to speed. The operation had grown very large and was now thought to involve several different suspects. No one yet knew if they were linked, but instincts pointed to a large organisation with several shipments. No one was sure what these were, but they suspected drugs.

The team leader made mental notes, asked questions, and was delighted to hear his boss had managed to get the three new operatives enrolled in the operation. Having known them and worked with them before, he had total confidence in them. He rubbed his hands in glee at the thought of what was to come. Having been in the Firm for thirty-five years, starting within the lower ranks and making rapid progress and being promoted, he was a shrewd man, one who always had the ability to think quickly and, on his feet, to make the right call. His glinting, smiling eyes and fatherly manner hid a cold, calculating persona unafraid of hard graft, someone who would not hesitate to take drastic action. He never hesitated, and his motto to shoot first and ask questions after was well known within the service.

Charly and his team leader planned the next few days carefully, deciding how to deploy their team to the best advantage. Surveillance would be stepped up and would be 24/7. Reports would be received every two hours unless developments dictated otherwise. Charly looked over to the man opposite him. "Make sure you have all ferries covered and get your pals at the terminal to keep their eyes and ears open. I also want the airports to be on the alert for any suspect on our radar. At the slightest suggestion that someone looks suspicious, I want to hear about it." They parted, having agreed to meet again the next day.

Just speaking to his team leader and planning the operation gave Charly a buzz; he was on a high and 100 per cent up for the fight. He would get those sick slimy bastards. They would pay, especially if they had shot that soldier outside the barracks. Although fewer, the muggings had not stopped. Charly was becoming more and more sure of who was behind them.

On his way home, he had thought about dropping by O'Grady's office to bring him into the picture, but he quickly put that idea out of his mind. He didn't need any more complications and was sure that his visit wouldn't be welcomed.

He spent the next few hours in deep thought, planning every eventuality depending on the contents of the reports he was about to receive. He liked to be prepared, to be one step ahead. His main concern was how best to use Major Peter Hollins; he was adamant the man would come in useful and be an asset, but how? For now, he had no plan, but one would come. Unlike Sean, Charly was not convinced the final act would happen in his home territory. No, in his opinion it would be in England. But where?

CHAPTER 18

Hans was getting ready to fly to Paris. With his meeting with Ron scheduled for the next day, he would spend the night there before taking the TGV down to the South of France, where he'd stay a couple of days, making up with Jane, before returning to what he foresaw as a couple of very busy weeks. The hard work would be worth it; the deals his boss had set up assured them both a more than comfortable life. Yes, with his share, he would probably retire, buy a place in the Caribbean, and settle down, hopefully with Jane. Ron wouldn't be pleased at losing his right-hand man. For sure, he would pressure, threaten, and cajole, but in the end, he would have to accept it, seeing as he had no other choice. Over ten years of loyal service, doing the dirty work and most of the organising, had entitled him to a free life. It wouldn't worry his boss to see his wife leave him. In fact, it would probably be a blessing. He knew Ron wanted to be rid of her, and he, Hans van der Brawn, would be only too pleased and happy to have a beautiful, sexy woman taking care of him.

The afternoon was spent making phone calls to his contacts in northern France and in England. Hans was prepping them and ensuring everyone knew what to do and was ready. This was no time for foul-ups, no time for misunderstandings; the three operations had to go like clockwork. As in the past, everyone would be paid handsomely, and any dissent would be acted upon swiftly. Ron Stokes did not abide inefficient or greedy associates. Anyone who asked for more or who failed to fully toe the line was swiftly dealt with. The few who had dared question him or go behind his back were no longer in this world, serving a reminder to anyone who had similar ideas. Satisfied that everything was in place, Hans poured himself a drink and toasted his future life.

He may not have been so happy had he known that every conversation he had had, every word he had spoken, over the past few hours had been recorded. He would be even unhappier to know that the men in the boat moored below his apartment even knew what he was drinking. The cameras that had been installed relayed pictures of him as he went about his daily life throughout the flat. The target couldn't even go to the bathroom without someone two hundred meters away knowing about it.

Fully equipped with the knowledge of Hans's itinerary, the Dutch secret police made plans to ensure the target would not be let out of sight.

A taxi pulled up and Hans got in. The journey to the airport didn't take long. As he alighted from the first cab, a second one pulled up behind. Hans made his way into the vast check-in hall and through to the gates, stopping at the kiosk before buying a coffee. He felt great and was relaxed, looking forward to the few days after Paris. On the plane, a middle-aged woman came to sit next him. He barely looked up and continued to read his paper. Not a word was uttered during the short flight. He didn't like getting into conversations, especially with old women. He had no time and no interest in hearing them rabbiting on about grandchildren, friends, or how lovely their cats were. Had it been a young woman, perhaps he would have engaged, but even then, he liked to keep himself to himself.

He closed his eyes and simulated sleep, his mind wandering back to Ron's phone call from Boston, the fear in the man's voice. Hans, having never heard his boss sound like that before, tried to make sense of it all. What on earth had spooked him to such a degree? Why had he been sucked into a deal which he clearly wanted no part of? It wasn't like him; something had happened. Well, Hans would find out soon enough but ultimately, he was certain all would be fine in the end. Anyway, he would be away, retired, when all this went through, so it wasn't his problem. Yes, he liked Ron. Well, not really.

Respected him? Yes. And yes, Ron was the one who had taught Hans all he knew, having nurtured him from a petty criminal making a living stealing cars and shoplifting to one of the most feared criminals in Holland, in Europe even. He had taught the little Dutch kid all the tricks of the trade and how not to be noticed; how to get others to do the dirty work; and most of all, how not to get caught. He had shown him how to hide his money and the spoils of their operations whilst enjoying the fruits of their labour. Yes, he respected Ron and, in a way, was concerned at the latest development and the state his boss was currently in.

———◆◆———

Ron checked into the hotel. It was nice enough, but he wouldn't have chosen it if he weren't meeting Hans. He liked much grander establishments, which gave him a good feeling. And it never failed to impress the clients. But this one was good enough, perfect for the job—and it sent out the right message to his subordinate.

He made a beeline for his room. The jet lag was taking its toll; he felt awful. He had tried to sleep on the plane and resorted to take a couple of sleeping pills and probably drinking one or two glasses of wine too many. Despite all that, he couldn't settle and had only managed to doze fitfully. His mind kept going back to the meeting of the day before and the final threat. He was convinced someone had been following him and wondered if they would continue to tail him in Paris.

Hans was not due until later that afternoon, so Ron lay on the bed and soon drifted off. He awoke soaked in sweat, his heart thumping hard in his chest. He had dreamt that a two-headed dragon was chasing him, flames gushing from its mouth. The creature had features resembling those of the little man who seemed to be the leader and the bouncer in Boston. It pursued Ron through dark alleys, in cellars and finally cornering him against a cliff face. Fires were being lit all round him by the flames coming from the monster's nostrils. Through the flames emerged a figure, grinning, laughing, taunting him. It was the little man from Boston dressed as the Devil; he had caught up with Ron and was about to take him to the bowels of the earth, to his final destination.

Ron sat up in bed, his mind in turmoil, his breathing heavy, and tried to calm himself. It was only a dream, just like those he used to have when he was a little boy. His mother had told him he had an active mind and said he should stop reading those silly comic books; dreams were nothing and should be treated as such. He never really agreed with her, but he liked the idea. She used to give him a glass of water and a fruit gum, then stroke his cheek and give him a kiss before leaving him in the dark. The dreams never went away; they would always linger. He tried to analyse them but, at the tender age of ten, never found an answer.

Willing himself into action, Ron went to have a shower. Whilst standing there, hot water beating down on his shoulders, he started to wonder, was he such a bad person? Did he deserve to be consumed by the Devil's fire? He was just trying to make a living, to give people jobs. OK, it wasn't your usual type of employment, but it provided him with a good life, in fact a very good life, better than he had ever imagined. No, he was a good, hard-working man with a too vivid imagination, just like his mother had said. The fact that he didn't like, one little bit, this last deal must prove he was a good person. Just how he would get out of it was another matter.

Hans was seated at the bar nursing a beer when his boss walked in. Waving, he got up to greet him. He hid his shock at seeing Ron looking so haggard; the man must have aged ten years since they had last met a month ago. They went and sat on a sofa in the corner of the dark room, well away from the half dozen businessmen and the young couple who made up the other patrons of the bar. After ordering a round of drinks, Hans turned to the worried-looking man. "Boss, what's going on? You're looking terrible. I don't want to be rude, but I have never seen you like this."

Ron remained silent for a while, until the waiter had placed the drinks in from of them and left. "I'm OK, just feeling the pressure a bit. This deal I was in Boston for, well, it's complicated, and I'm not sure we can handle it." He fell silent once more, his eyes gazing into space. Suddenly, he jumped, looking around him, watching the other patrons. "I think I'm being followed. I don't recognise anyone, but I'm sure I'm being followed." He took a large gulp from his glass.

"Why don't you tell me about this deal? I'm sure it's not as bad or as difficult as you're thinking. As for people following you," Hans said, looking round the room, "I really don't see anyone suspicious."

Ron smiled a weak grin and sniffed. He sighed deeply. "You're right. I'm being stupid and paranoid." He finished his drink and signalled the waiter to bring two more. "Before I tell you about the American deal, I want to bring you up to speed on the others. We are working on a very tight schedule."

They waited again until the server had left. "The first deal is taking place in a week's time. Shipment is leaving Cairo and will head for the port of Bari in Italy. We still have our contacts there, don't we?" Hans nodded, so Ron quickly continued. "We'll need six trucks ready and waiting to take the containers up through Italy and into France. Once there, the team will split into two groups and head towards Boulogne and Dieppe. Before they reach their respective destinations, our French contacts will take over, probably on the outskirts of Lyon. Any questions?"

Hans shook his head. It was the same plan as usual; he had dealt with this many times, and the contact and his men knew what to do. Timing and communications were the most important parts. "No problem. Everything will be in place. I just need to be kept informed of their progress so that the boys are not hanging around too much. You will transfer the funds as usual?"

Ron nodded. "The second shipment will take place a week later. Same route, but it'll involve eight trucks."

The Dutchman gave out a low whistle. "That is big. Not sure we have sufficient drivers and backup for that number. With that number of trucks, is it not too risky to use just the two staging points? It may be wise to split the convoy into three and perhaps send one up to Antwerp. I have a contact there who could help."

Ron thought about the idea and nodded his agreement. Inwardly, he was pleased he had a man like Hans, a sharp, astute operator who had learned his trade well—from an expert, of course! "As you know, the key to a successful trip is having good people, so make sure your contact has trustworthy extra drivers, and ensure they have done similar jobs before."

"No problem. As you know, we've used the guy before. He's fine and not expensive." He grinned.

"Good. I will leave you to sort out the details. Thanks. Now, the Turk. His deal is due to be shipped in ten days' time. It will arrive in Liverpool by the end of the month; the exact date is not known yet. Trans-shipment should happen quickly and in time to leave for Belfast within four days. It's really, really important that our men there have everything prepared and that the operation runs smoothly. You know what our Irish clients are like."

Hans gave a knowing smile. "When will we get the paperwork? And have we set up everything for payment?" he questioned.

Ron assured him everything was ready and said that their clients had been notified. "I just hope this time things go smoother than the last. I'm confident we can deliver, but I'm not so sure about that lot." He looked at Hans with questioning eyes. "Would it be too much to ask you to be there and make sure the handover goes smoothly? I really don't want any more foul-ups. And make sure they don't get into any further scraps. I want them to stop their war games and keep a low profile."

"No problem, Ron. Provided the second deal is completed, I am only too happy to fly out and oversee things, teach them how real pros work." Grinning, he raised his glass. "Cheers to a very successful few weeks."

Ron took a long drink of his beer and shifted in his seat; as he looked round the room, his unease returned. He tried to delay the inevitable but knew he would feel better after telling his aide. Taking a deep breath, he began explaining in minute detail the complicated transaction he had been forced to enter in Boston, making sure to inform Hans of every angle, every danger, and every nasty possibility just in case things should go wrong. He stressed to his confidant the enormous rewards it would bring to both.

In a hushed voice, he related how the meeting had ended, mentioning the threats and his feeling of being watched.

Both men sat in silence for a long while, Hans digesting what he had been told, Ron feeling drained, but relieved that he was no longer the only one in the know. At last, Hans let out a long, low whistle. He felt slightly numb after hearing his boss explain what he had been sucked into. He felt sorry for the man. Yes, the payoff would be enormous, but the consequences would also be huge if things were to go wrong. What was being asked of them was way out of their league, way too big even for any criminals aspiring for world renown. This was something for an organisation like the Mafia, not operators like them.

Suddenly, relief flooded over Hans. The thought that he, Hans van der Brawn, would, by the time things came to a head, be relaxing by the side of a pool in the Caribbean made the problem seem unimportant. Yes, he was sorry for his boss, but the man had brought it on himself, having been too greedy and too interested in hitting the big time. No, it was not Hans's problem, so he could relax. He looked at Ron and soothingly told him things would be fine, saying not to worry, it would all work out.

They ordered another round of drinks and chatted about other things before deciding to retire to their respective rooms. As they rose, Ron looked around. Most of the guests had left; only the young couple remained, and they were clearly enjoying each other's company. As the two men crossed the vast lobby, the couple got up and unhurriedly made their way out of the bar.

Back in his room, Hans immediately made a couple of phone calls. Although he would be gone within a month, he still had work to do, things to organise; he had a reputation to uphold and a future to ensure. Before he finished the day, he texted Jane, telling her of a change of plans. He would not be making his way down to see her tomorrow, saying he would be returning to Amsterdam and stay there for a few days to finalise arrangements on a couple of deals.

He promised her that he would be there as soon as he could, saying he'd let her know once he knew. He also told her that he missed her and loved her.

Exhausted, Ron fell onto the bed and was relieved he had told Hans of all his concerns. He was pleased his second-in-command seemed confident they would get through the problem. He trusted Hans implicitly and knew that if his friend had had any doubts, he would have told him. He thought about phoning Jane but decided against the idea: she wouldn't listen, nor would she be interested or believe him. He would fly back to London in the morning and immerse himself in the imminent deals with the Egyptian and the Turk. There was a lot of planning still to be done on his side. Hans was sorting the supply route; Ron had the clients and the finances to deal with. Once he was satisfied that he had everything under control, he decided that he would get his lawyer to start divorce proceedings as soon as possible. Feeling more relaxed, he drifted off into a fitful sleep.

The next morning, Hans decided to take the train back to Amsterdam, which was just as quick, if not quicker than flying. As the express slowly pulled out of the station, a young woman sat herself on the seat diagonally across from him. He looked up automatically, his mind going into overdrive. He recognised the face—or did he? Was it the young women who was with the man in the bar the night before? He glanced over again, unsure. She looked similar, but no, her hair was different, and she appeared to be older. He relaxed and picked up his newspaper. She did the same. It was an English paper, and he was sure he had heard the couple from last night speaking French. This caused him to relax even more. Smiling inwardly at himself, he wondered what the heck had Ron done. His story of being followed had gotten to Hans, and now he was getting to be as bad as his boss. He concentrated on reading the news, occasionally looking over towards the woman. She continued her own reading and ignored him. He closed his eyes and went through the list of things he had to do once he got back to his apartment.

CHAPTER 19

Charly Flynn was sitting in his car watching the house fifty yards down the street. He had checked for back entrances or gates but had found none. Surveillance was a tedious business, something he usually left to the more junior members of his team, but today he had decided to go back to basics; they were stretched enough as it was, so everyone was expected to step up. Being in charge and a hands-on sort of fellow, he never hesitated to get his hands grubby and do the dirty work. "Lead by example" was his motto.

He had been following the well-dressed dude whom the team had called Mr X. It was policy not to call any suspects by their names just in case the lawmen were accidently overheard. Mr X had been very busy of late talking to the two thugs, as well as to several known dubious characters involved in drug dealing. One particularly unsavoury chap was known to be heavily involved in controlling the market in the city and for being ruthless. It seemed the recent spate of muggings and the two killings were turf war related and the man's way of imposing his organisation. Mafia tactics of brutal beatings, murder, and intimidation was the standard way of controlling his territory.

The team had also found out that Mr X had close contacts with a similar organisation in the south and were cooking up something big. It was not clear what was planned, but they would find out soon enough. They always did.

Charly was jolted out of his thoughts by his phone buzzing; he picked it up and was pleased to see it was Peter. The Englishman sounded very chirpy and excited and was about to tell him his news when Charly interrupted him. "Don't say a word. Whatever you have to tell me must, by the sound of your voice, be important. We must never speak about delicate matters over the phone." He stopped briefly but picked back up quickly. "Sorry, I may have come across wrong and a bit harsh. Didn't mean to. If you have news concerning our friends, then I suggest you get Sean to send it via his encrypted line. Or you come over and see me."

Peter was taken aback by the severity of the tone but soon realised the reason for it. He had a lot to learn in this alien world he had joined. Upon reflection, he saw that it was not all that different from his; secrecy and discretion were the mainstays. He acknowledged the apology and told Charly he fully understood. Sean was away in Holland. Peter hadn't heard from him in a while, so he'd decided to give his Irish friend a call. He'd been contacted by that reporter chap Alwyn Jones, who asked if there had been any developments in the case. He also learned that, through a friend of the reporter's, something big was brewing, but he couldn't be sure what. This friend of Alwyn's was heading for the South Coast to dig around.

Charly smiled to himself. Reporters, always sticking their noses into things and rarely coming up with anything concrete. They got snippets from here and there, made assumptions, and wrote an article. It did not matter if the facts were wrong or if they had misunderstood, once they had an outline of a story, they would make up the rest. Never mind if it hurt people in the process, and never mind if it hindered an investigation and weeks or months of hard work. No, so long as it sold newspapers and that their bosses took notice of them, that was all that counted. "Did he tell you what it was about and when this big thing will happen? Why did he tell you? What did he think you could do? No offence meant," Charly said, half joking.

"No, just that his mate had suggested he join him so they could snoop around together. No idea why he told me, and he never asked for anything. Just thought you may be interested. Anyway, my main reason for calling was to ask if you have any news and whether you had heard from Sean."

A sound on Charly's phone indicated another caller had just rung;

he made his excuses and promised Peter he would get to back to him very soon.

Surprised to hear Sean's voice, Charly said, "Hey, just been talking about you. Your ears must have been burning."

"For sure, telepathy is one of my things. Who were you talking to? Apart from me, I didn't know you had any friends." He chuckled.

"Peter rang, wondering if we had any news. I get the distinct impression he is feeling a bit left out. Told me some reporter chap who had spoken to him and Brian at the funeral was asking for a progress report. For some reason, this Alwyn bloke said he was heading for the South Coast to do some snooping. Had a tip-off something big may happen. Typical bloody reporters."

"I wonder what this big thing is and how he came to learn about it? The reason I'm calling is that there are some big developments. Something is brewing, but we're not sure what it is exactly. Anything on your end, or are you just staring at your navel?"

Charly ignored the last comment. He knew Sean well enough. Sean wasn't known for his jokes, and when he did try to make one, it normally came out wrong or, as in this case, rude. "Aye, we've certainly learned a lot in the past week, and we now have a good idea who's behind many of the muggings and troubles in this city."

"As I said, we have wind of some major developments. I suggest we meet up sooner rather than later. I have a lot to tell you guys."

"Sounds intriguing. I can be with you within twelve hours."

"Good. Why don't we meet tomorrow in Birmingham? There's a flight leaving Schiphol first thing in the morning. There's bound to be the same from Belfast. Meet in the lobby of the Novotel, eleven-thirty in the morning?"

"Great. Perfect. I'll phone Peter and get him to join us. See you in the morning."

The three men were sitting round a large table in the corner of the hotel's bar lounge, all of them dressed in casual clothes, just three friends meeting up. Once coffees had been served, Sean was the first to speak. "Some big developments over the past few days. Not sure if they're connected to anything you two are working on, but my gut tells me they are." He then proceeded to tell them about the meeting in Paris between Ron and Hans. He and the Dutch service had quickly discovered that the two were partners, with Ron as the boss. The Dutch boys had been trailing Hans and had his flat bugged and under twenty-four-hour surveillance. The two men had met in Paris three days previously, although their conversations couldn't be overheard. Back in Amsterdam, Hans had made numerous calls to various people. From what was gathered, there were going to be two large shipments being made very soon. The exact nature of these deliveries was still unknown; however, the destination was known. Each shipment would be coming from Italy on a fleet of trucks through France. Somewhere near Lyon, they would split into two convoys. The first would head for Boulogne for a crossing to Folkestone, and the other would sail from Dieppe to Newhaven.

"How come with all the listening in, no one knows what these shipments contain?" Charly looked puzzled.

"The target was like an open book. It seems he has used the same donkeys before, and they're all in the know. Our guess is it could be the same type of shipment as previous ones. One thing we can say for certain: it's not narcotics."

"What the hell is it? There's nothing that comes to my mind. Coming from Italy, the only thing worth the effort would be gold or wine, but even then, that's a large number of trucks! I'm surprised."

Sean continued to tell them about the second, larger shipment. This would follow the same pattern and head from the same two French ports. Given the number of lorries involved, it seemed that it had been decided to split the group into three with the third convoy heading for Antwerp. The Dutch were currently alerting both the French and Belgian authorities and making plans. Sean then went on to tell Charly and Peter about the second deal. "Now, this is drugs for sure; our friends haven't taken many precautions when talking over the phone. The shipment is being loaded onto a container ship in Karachi and most likely originates from either north Pakistan or Afghanistan. My bet is the latter. As I said earlier, it is due to dock in Liverpool before being sent on to Belfast. Seems the gang have done this for a previous shipment and have close ties with people over your way, Charly."

Charly agreed that it made sense and explained the increased activity of the group he and his men had been following; it all tied in with what they had learned. Mr X had been busy lately, presumably in preparation. "Do we have any idea how big this delivery is?" he enquired.

Sean shook his head. "We have some idea, but it's not small, that's guaranteed. Rumours have it that well over half will go south, so it's vital we intercept it before it crosses the border."

Peter had remained silent all through the briefing, having decided from the onset that the last shipment was the bigger and most important of the three. He suggested that they hand the truck convoys off to the border control and concentrate on the drugs. He didn't like narcotics and was certain that these had come from Afghanistan. Having spent more time there than he would have wished, he could well imagine that all those farmers who were peddling their crops in the markets would be only too delighted to supply one big buyer, saving them many days and weeks of work.

Sean had not been happy at the thought of handing one of his tasks over to a third party, but he agreed it made sense; he and the others just didn't have the time, or the manpower, to be involved in all three operations. He would talk to his boss and ask him to do the brief and hand over the truckloads of whatever.

A buoyant Peter suggested that he return to Belfast with Charly to help him try to find out more about operations at that end. All three separated and went their own ways. Peter headed into town to purchase some clothes and a few necessities before joining Charly back to Belfast. Both men were excited and minds racing, they knew what had to be done. Sean took the train to London, where he went straight to his boss, using his influence to get a priority meeting. Following that, he would return to Amsterdam and set out his plan to his Dutch counterparts.

CHAPTER 20

The head of customs at the port of Bari gazed out the window, watching the rusty ship dock. As it was being tied up, he made his way over to the vessel. He watched as a tatty gangway was lowered. Once it was secured, he made his way on board, where he was greeted by the bearded captain, who was so scruffily dressed that he looked like a deck hand. The man mocked a salute and handed the customs officer a dossier containing the ship's papers and a list of the containers it was carrying. The official scanned through the file and nodded—only six containers containing fruit and vegetables, the usual for this small ship. He placed the file under his arm and made his way down the swaying gangplank. Once on firm ground, he barked an order to the head docker, who immediately radioed up to the crane operator to start unloading.

Within two hours, the six trucks had been loaded onto trailers and the trucks were rumbling towards the huge metal gates. The convoy quickly made for the main road but, before reaching the motorway, turned off and headed down a deserted grit lane, stopping well out of sight. The drivers got out, each going to the rear of his vehicle. An hour later they were all making their way up Italy, heading for Turin.

The customs official stood watching the operation from his office window before returning to his desk, where he opened the manifest. He took out a brown envelope, which he stuffed in his breast pocket before locking the papers in his filing cabinet. As he was heading for his car, he glanced over to the freighter that had just slipped its moorings heading for home.

The convoy trundled upcountry, regularly stopping in deserted places. The drivers spoke little and concentrated on the backs of the trucks, working fast and efficiently; the cargo was precious. As they neared the outskirts of Turin, the lorries detoured around the city and continued their way north-west towards the frontier. An hour out from the border, they veered off onto a little-used side road and parked up. Only after checking the rears of their vehicles did the drivers settle down for the remainder of the night. It was still dark with a thin drizzle falling when the convoy started off once again, soon approaching the border post. A young customs official stepped out of the booth and waved them on. They made the short distance to the French post, where a couple of tired douaniers stepped up and held up their hands. The older official ambled over to the lead driver, who handed him the papers, made a few comments, and answered a couple of questions before offering to open the back of his truck. The man flipped through the papers and shook his head. It was 6.30 in the morning, half an hour from the end of their shift, and he was in no mood to delay matters. Anyway, the douanier knew the drivers and the company; they used the route frequently, so there was likely nothing untoward. Before pulling away, the driver mentioned that next time, in about a week, they would have eight or nine trucks, a big job, and suggested the two men called in a couple of more volunteers. They joked together, before the douaniers wished the trucker a good journey, along with his friends.

After having negotiated the tortuous winding road down to the valley below, the drivers once more pulled over into a quiet lay-by. This time, in addition to checking the containers, they set to work changing the number plates, replacing the Italian ones for a French set. It was routine; everyone knew what to do. The switch was done quickly and efficiently. Satisfied, they drove off, heading for Lyon.

They had the trip down to a fine art. Timings were kept to schedule and, as usual, the journey was boringly routine. The lead driver checked his watch and smiled broadly: forty minutes to go before he and his fellow drivers were relieved by a new crew. He, and they, needed a shower and some good sleep.

They pulled into a lorry park on the outskirts of Lyon and parked in a secluded area. As they got down from their cabs, they were met by five men and a woman. Keys were handed over. A few words were spoken before the new crew got in and slowly took their trucks over to the pumps. The six tired men headed over to a waiting minibus and slumped into the tatty seats. Their shift was over, no hitches, no problems, and on time. The pay cheque would be good.

The convoy once again set off and headed north. Half an hour into their journey, the three lead trucks took to a slip road and left the motorway. The two groups, heading for their destination, would need another twelve hours, then the first part of the operation would be complete.

CHAPTER 21

Hans was awakened by the buzz of his phone. He opened a bleary eye and looked at the clock; it was half past one in morning. Who the hell could that be? Reaching over to take the call, he sat up immediately and focussed. He listened, nodding to himself before killing the call. Then he jumped out of bed and made his way to the kitchen, where he made himself a coffee and debated as to whether he should call his boss. He knew Ron didn't like to be disturbed at night, but on the other hand, he had to know.

Taking a deep breath, he made the call. A sleepy voice quickly answered. "Hi, Ron, it's Hans. I've just had a call from our man in Boulogne. One of the convoys has arrived safe and sound. All went smoothly. They are currently parked up in the usual place, waiting for daylight before proceeding to the port." He paused to see if the boss would make any comment. "That's the good news. The bad news is that the second half has had a problem. All was fine until after the split, but the number two lead found major damage when checking the goods halfway to Dieppe. He wants to know what to do."

There was a long silence. Hans winced inwardly. He could practically hear the boss's mind working and his anger mounting. When the voice came back on, it was icy cold. "What kind of problem? What kind of damage? How bad?"

"I am told all was fine when they checked after the split, but somewhere south of Le Mans, they discovered on a routine check that one of the trucks had a problem. The other two are fine."

"What kind of a problem? Where are they now? How much damage? Spit it out."

Hans grimaced to himself and took time before replying; his mind raced and was working overtime. Whatever the decision they took and the outcome, he knew the situation wasn't good. It would affect them financially, but most of all Ron's reputation would take a severe hit. Hans was just relieved that he had decided to cut loose and retire to the Caribbean, away from it all.

"Seems most of the goods have suffered badly and are not usable. The contact didn't go into details, but from what I gather, it is pretty much a write-off. The emergency plan has been set in motion. The two other trucks are nearing the destination and will arrive on time."

Ron swore loudly; he was gutted. He never liked losing a shipment. In fact, he had never had such a loss. He understood very well what the consequences would be, and he didn't like that at all. "Make bloody sure all the rest goes smoothly. We don't want any more cockups. Make sure you make the contact pay for this, financially and otherwise, and that he knows his name is blackened forever and that he will never work for us again." He paused for effect and to give himself time to think. "There's only one person to blame in all this, and that's you, Hans. You are the one who found this incompetent idiot. You, who have overseen the shipment—you are the one I'm blaming."

Hans had expected something like this and decided to ignore the threats and accusations. Yes, he had a lot to do with it, but if it had been his choice, he would never have entered into such a deal. "I will make sure the man pays a high price, boss; don't you worry. Do you want to cancel the second shipment?"

An apoplectic voice exploded from the other end of the phone. Hans had to hold the phone away from his ear as he winced. "What the fuck has gotten into you, Hans? What is the frigging matter with you? Have you completely lost your bloody sense?" Ron yelled. "What in the name of God makes you think we can cancel the second shipment at this late date? The bloody thing is about to set sail; you know that fucking well." Heavy breathing and snorting came down the airwaves.

Hans realised that what he had just said was not the most intelligent question he had ever asked; no, he knew pulling out now was impossible, as Ron said, the ship was about to set sail and most likely the trucks' drivers were heading south to meet it, just as they had done a week or so ago. No, they had to see the whole contract through. He changed subject.

"Any news on the Turk's shipment, boss?"

"Don't bloody change the subject. We haven't finished discussing our problem. What is going to be done with the dud load? Will we have enough drivers and vehicles for the second shipment?"

"I will take care of the problematic load, and yes, all is set for the second. I promise, all will go smoothly this time. We have done it often before, and this is the only trouble we've ever had. We're good at what we do."

Ron had calmed down slightly. "Yeah, make bloody sure something like this never happens again. Deal with it and make sure it can't be traced back, or we're both in the shit."

Hans mumbled a weak apology and promised all would go smoothly from now on. He knew this was a major hiccup but was more concerned about the delivery from Pakistan; that was a big payday, the deal he was relying on to fund his retirement. He and Ron continued to talk for a short while before he hung up. He picked up his cold cup of coffee and took a sip, then sat a long while thinking what to do before going back to bed. He knew what he had to do, but that could wait until morning.

Down in the barge moored across from the flat, three men had been listening in on the conversation and making notes. Clearly something was afoot. The spies were careful so as not to miss a word. As the call was cut, they sat back and took off their headphones, all three looking slightly shell-shocked. They were experienced men, having seen and witnessed many gruesome and delicate things in their careers. All three were fully aware that what they had just

105

heard was vital information, a turning point in the case they were on. They discussed the possibilities and consequences of what they had learned, analysing every possibility, before compiling an extensive report setting out the two possibilities they had concluded could happen. With the task completed, the senior of the three called over the fourth team member, a junior who had picked up the listening post, and instructed him to take the file immediately to headquarters. His orders were to ensure he handed it over, in person, to the head of department and only to him. The three men stressed the urgency of the matter and impressed on the youngster not to return until he had obeyed orders. After he left, they took turns on the headphones and the radio. It was natural; twenty-four-hour surveillance meant twenty-four hours, no matter how tiring or boring.

CHAPTER 22

Peter had decided to take the ferry across to Belfast. He needed a vehicle and didn't like relying on Charly to move about. The crossing was smooth with the ferry slowly making its way towards the jetty when Peter decided to call his friend and ask for directions. They agreed to meet up at the hotel on Titanic Quay before making their way over to Charly's house.

After taking a couple of wrong turns, Peter found himself driving round the basin, then headed towards the airport. It was easy when you got things right. As he parked outside the hotel, he recognised the dark blue car left at the door. Making his way into the reception area, he was greeted by a buoyant Charly Flynn.

"Where the hell have you been?" a loud voice from behind him bawled. "It takes twenty minutes, twenty-five tops, but I've been waiting forty. You call yourself an army man, SAS, but you can't find your way from the docks. No wonder the Taliban have given you so much grief," he joked.

"Took a wrong turn and ended up somewhere north of the city. But point taken. I'd like to see you navigate in Kabul with no signposts and thousands of carts and bikes. Bet you would be as bad as me."

After checking in, Charly suggested it would be easier and quicker if he drove them to his house; they had lots to talk about, and he didn't want more of his precious time wasted. On the drive through town, Charly told Peter that Sean had indicated that things had developed rapidly and taken off on all fronts; it was now a case of working as a unit and working fast. A pang of excitement went through Peter. Just like normal times, he thought. The battle was developing fast.

They were sitting in Charly's flat enjoying a can of Guinness, talking about the various possible scenarios, when Charly's phone buzzed. "How do I get to your place?" Sean's voice came over loud and clear. "I'm at the airport but realised I don't know your address."

The two men looked startled. "You never told me you were coming. What's the rush?"

"Sorry to bother you, indeed. Now, are you going to tell me your address, or am I going to have to call your boss?" Sean jotted down the details. "OK, I'll be with you in a jiffy. Hope you have some of your delightful local stout. I'm gagging for a drink."

An hour later, the three men were sitting comfortably in their deep chairs, each with a can in hand. Sean took a long swig before speaking. "Right. A lot has happened since we last met four days ago. Firstly, it has now been confirmed without a doubt that the guy in Holland, a certain Hans van der Brawn, is in cahoots with an Englishman called Ron Stokes. In fact, this Ron is Hans's boss, and between them they run a very unsavoury smuggling organisation which is partly based in London and partly in Amsterdam. They seem to be into all kinds of stuff, and this time it's drugs and something else which is still unclear. Could be gold, arms, cigarettes, or the like." He paused to open the second can which was being handed to him.

Charly was going to say something, but Sean raised his hand. "Let me finish, and then you can ask as many questions as you like. So, we first got our breakthrough the night before last, when the Dutch intercepted a phone call made to this Hans. It seems that one of their shipments coming from Italy had a problem and had to be jettisoned or abandoned somewhere in France. We don't know where or what it is. Our Dutch friends have contacted the French, who are looking into it. It seems two other truckloads—there were three in all—have made it to Boulogne and are heading for the UK sometime soon. It appears that a similar but larger shipment will be setting out from Italy very soon. Interpol and all border controls have been alerted." He looked up at Peter. "Did you not say that a reporter chap had a tip-off and was off to Kent or somewhere on the South Coast?"

Peter nodded. "That's right. He has no idea what it was all about, but he and his mate should be down there now, ferreting around as reporters do."

"Have you got a contact number for him? If so, get onto him right now and tell him not to poke his nose in too deep. We want border control and local police to take care of this. We definitely don't want these guys spooked in any way." He nodded in the direction of Peter's phone, indicating he had to call his reporter friend immediately.

Sean and Charly waited until Peter had finished speaking to Alwyn Jones, impressing on him not to interfere in the case. He and his friend would get first scoop of the story, but only on the condition that they stay well away. Any funny business and they would both find themselves in deep trouble and out of a job. The reporter gave his assurances and was in no doubt the threat was real and would be implemented.

"Good work, Peter. The plan is to keep track of the shipment and hopefully delay it until the second consignment is intercepted at the French border. Only then will the police swoop and hopefully get everyone involved put behind bars. Fingers crossed it won't be long. We understand the trucks with the second shipment should be presenting themselves at either the French or Swiss border sometime by the end of next week."

Sean took a long drink from the can and shook his head. "The bastards are good but, if the French police will find the abandoned load soon, then, we'll know what we're dealing with. Now, for the second problem. We're pretty sure, again from phone interception, that the same gang is waiting for a large shipment from Pakistan; in our mind, it's drugs. This delivery is being trans-shipped in Liverpool and is due here in Belfast sometime within the next two weeks. It's up to you guys to stop it from reaching its destination or destinations."

Charly was the first to react. "Certainly, that ties in very nicely with what I have found out. Indeed, it seems the guys we've been tailing are expecting a large delivery, plans seemingly are being made to break the load up and send it to various destinations. Not sure where this will take place, but like your Dutch mates, we've been listening in on phone calls and conversations. And with every day, more and more is being gleaned. It seems that the boys who are involved here are now wholly independent but take orders from someone in London. Could be this same Ron chap."

He was about to continue when he was interrupted by his phone buzzing. He picked up, listened, nodded, and smiled, then thanked the caller. "Well, what a coincidence! That was one of my boys reporting that he just listened in on a conversation with a gentleman with a strong Dutch accent who requested that 'Dicky' start getting the rendezvous site prepared. Then, this Dicky made a couple of calls. It seemed preparations will start sometime next week."

Peter, excited, offered his services. "I'm used to checking out things like this and would be more than happy to take on the task. I know you're short-staffed, and it's my guess you'll need as many people as you can find. Count me in."

There was a buzz of anticipation in the room as a long session of planning began. Night had fallen by the time everything had been set in place. Each of the three men knew exactly what his role was. Whilst waiting for their takeout to be delivered, they discussed at length the possible contents of the first two shipments and what could have possibly gone wrong. Charly phoned his men and gave precise instructions, ensuring each member was clear on what his task was. Sean contacted his Dutch counterpart and explained what he would like them to do, then followed up by ringing a contact in Liverpool, a long-standing friend and operator whom he knew well. Little explanation was required, just a couple of requests to check something out, so matters were agreed quickly. Peter, meanwhile, made a list of what he would require for his surveillance and for working in a country he knew little of. With Charly's help, he jotted names and addresses of possible suppliers; what he could not find, Charly's headquarters would procure.

The rest of the evening was spent in conversation, the three men continuing to plan and consuming rather more Guinness than any of them intended. Not to worry, from now on all three would be teetotallers until the end of the operation. Well, that was what they hoped.

CHAPTER 23

Darkness had fallen when Ron stirred from his thoughts, gloom hanging over him like a heavy cloak. His stomach was in knots. He hadn't felt like that since his first big deal, upon which so much had depended, but ever since then he always kept cool and relaxed. The feeling of nausea continued, so he went over and poured himself a stiff drink, hoping the alcohol would numb his feelings and fears. He had had a conversation with Hans, who sounded different, not the concerned associate but cooler, more aloof. Ron couldn't put his finger on it, but deep down he knew something was troubling the man. They had gone over the two deals, agreeing what still had to be done and discussing at length the ramifications of the recent problem in France. After hanging up, Ron sat a long while, considering his options. Finally, he called a local contact he had dealt with a few times before and asked him to investigate quietly and discreetly. He needed to know what had happened to the cargo and what its precise location was. Only then could he decide what course of action to take. The jettisoned load was not the only problem; the two other trucks had parked up outside Boulogne, waiting for a ferry slot. Typically, the French suddenly came out on strike, and there was concern that the delay would cause the remaining loads to deteriorate.

To compound Ron's problems, the second convoy was about to leave from Southern Italy earlier than expected. All the trucks and drivers were ready, but the team which was supposed to take over outside Lyon was not doing as they had agreed. They were demanding more money after the recent problems and required assurances that matters would run smoother. After a heated discussion, Hans had agreed to pay a bonus, but only if all the goods were delivered on time and in good condition. He had discussed this with Ron prior to negotiating with the contact, and both had agreed it was the only course they could take. Ron was furious. The thought of firstly losing a large percentage of the initial shipment, and now of paying more, which would dent his profits considerably, enraged him. Things were not going well.

He did not like or appreciate disobedience. His whole business empire was based on discipline and on people doing what they should do, no questions asked. Any dissent was dealt with. Once the second shipment had been safely delivered, Ron would teach the French contact a lesson.

He turned his mind to the second deal. That, at least, seemed to be going well. The vessel had left on time and was making excellent progress. In fact, it seemed that it would be docking early. That was good news, but the early docking would also cause a few problems. Getting the right people to be in place at the right time was crucial. Ron had discussed this with Hans, and both had agreed that a visit to Northern Ireland was necessary to ensure everything was ready in time.

Hans had told him he would go to Belfast within the next few days and from there would fly down to the South of France for a couple of days. Jane had been giving him a hard time and was pestering him, saying he had promised to come see her. He pacified his boss, explaining that he had not seen her in a while, adding that she was getting fidgety and had begun asking questions. It would be a quick visit, two or three days at the most, but not to worry: he would be back in time for the big event. Ron was not pleased but had to agree. The last thing they needed was for his estranged wife to start being difficult and poking her nose into their affairs. Reluctantly agreeing, he made a mental note to contact his lawyer as soon as all this was over. He got up and poured himself another drink, gulping it down in a oner. He was not a happy man.

A couple of days later, a taxi pulled up at the door of the flat overlooking the canal. Hans jumped in and asked the driver to take him to the airport. He sat back and texted Jane a brief note telling her he was on his way to Belfast but saying that he would be seeing her in a couple of days—"Looking forward to it"—and promising to make their short time together unforgettable. He got three heart emoji and a row of kisses as a reply.

Prior to leaving the apartment, Hans had had called his bank in Switzerland and requested a large transfer to be made to his account in their Nassau branch. No questions were asked once he had identified himself. The banker at the other end, being satisfied, gave instructions in a prearranged code no one else would be able to understand. Checking he had taken all he needed, Hans had locked up and made his way out. He was oblivious of the car parked up the street, its engine silently running, the passengers in deep conversation. The car pulled out and followed the taxi at a safe distance, the passengers knowing where it was heading, so no panic—just routine to ensure there was no last-minute change of plan.

On the way, Hans went over his plans; everything had been organised meticulously and methodically. Go to Liverpool, meet up with the contacts at the dock and make sure everyone was ready for the early arrival of the ship, then hop over to Belfast to check their people were ready and had followed orders and that the warehouse was prepared. That should take a couple of days at the most. During that time, he had to impress on the contacts how important organisation was, no room for slip-ups or any other misunderstandings, and no more shootings like last time. No, this had to go smoothly, or they would pay dearly. No more blame games. They had cocked up big time a few months ago, thinking they knew better, and ended up killing an innocent soldier. Then, there was the turf war. At least that had ended when Ron ordered the execution of the rival gang's leader. With no brains behind them, the rest had come meekly and settled for peace. Well, it would last until this operation was over. After that, he knew what was in store for all of them. He was happy to be getting out, figuring that he was getting too old for all this and knowing that he didn't really need the money. He was brought out of his dream by the driver telling him they had arrived. He checked in and made his way to the gate.

A car had pulled up behind the cab, and a bearded gentleman got out, following Hans to the check-in desk and watching discreetly from a distance. As the Dutchman headed for passport control, the man nodded to a middle-aged woman, who fell in behind the target. As they boarded the flight, the woman settled in a seat a couple of rows behind and across the aisle, ensuring she had a clear view.

In Liverpool, as they passed through border control, the woman was greeted by a tall, fair-haired young man. The two had a brief exchange before she headed to the far end of the building and checked in for her flight back. The young man kept his distance and watched as Hans was met by a couple of men and escorted to a car.

Hans knew his two hosts and followed them with a minimum of conversation. He jumped into the back of the front car and settled down. He didn't like the driver, a creepy, skinny man with piercings and bad teeth. Picking up a paper, Hans pretended to read intently. As they drove out of the airport compound, he knew the second man was hard on their tail as an escort, but both vehicles were oblivious of the private taxi that was following them. Keeping at a safe distance, the white Ford trailed the two vehicles through the suburbs of Liverpool. They headed north-west, passing the football grounds in the distance, then taking the Kingsway Runnel under the Mersey. Hans didn't know the city too well, but he knew it well enough to realise they had taken a long detour. He desisted from asking why and kept on pretending to read. Just before entering the tunnel, a black Honda cut in front of the trailing car and took over. It followed the two vehicles through the tunnel. As they emerged, all three headed south, eventually arriving at a large industrial estate on the perimeter of Stena Shipping Line dock. As the front car, followed by the escort, pulled into a small warehouse, the black vehicle passed by unnoticed, stopping a hundred yards further on.

The skinny driver grunted, announcing they had arrived. As Hans was about to get out, he was greeted by a large man, his head shaved and covered with tattoos. The man nodded for Hans to follow, which

115

he did, keeping a safe distance from the body odour emanating from the individual. They entered a modern reception area, and Hans was shown into an airy reception room with a view of more ugly buildings. A stained table with six chairs was the only furniture; he chose to sit in a chair facing the door and offering the protection of the wall behind him. As much as he was the boss and employer; he didn't trust them an inch. They were all help and smiles provided they smelt money, but it wouldn't take much for their joviality and loyalty to turn. He had to tread carefully, cajole and nurture them, make them feel important. He hated playing games but needs must.

The door suddenly opened, and a huge man with arms as big as hams covered in tattoos, a huge overflowing belly and a face covered in stubble, burst in. He was panting heavily as he took a seat across from Hans; beads of sweat dripped onto the table. He was accompanied by the shaven-headed minder, who stood at the door, arms folded menacingly. It took Hans a huge effort to hide his feeling of nausea from the smell of sweat and stale beer emanating from both men. He sat back, ignoring the giant hand that had been stuck out, and smiled politely. He decided to speak first. "Gentlemen, good of you to see me at such short notice. I realise you must be busy." Both men stared back blankly.

"As you know, the shipment is well on its way, somewhere fast approaching the Strait of Gibraltar, which means that it should be docking here most probably next Thursday. As the last time, it is a small vessel, and I understand it's carrying some thirty other containers. Ours will be the first to be taken out, the usual yellow and red markings, so we're counting on you to ensure it is put on a truck and loaded onto the Belfast ferry as quickly as possible." He looked across at each of the men.

The huge boss man wheezed and sniffed. "Just like last time, boss. Everything is in place. Our guys know exactly what to do. Our man at customs has been primed and paid well, so no problem there."

"Excellent. Sounds good. As usual, we knew we could count on your professionalism and expertise. Just to remind you, if the shipment is on the ferry within twenty-four hours of arrival, we will transfer the

116

fifteen-thousand-pound bonus as agreed." He had argued with Ron about that point at length; however, the boss was adamant it was a small price to pay. The shorter time the goods spent being transferred, the less risk of their being found or checked. Still, Hans thought that fifteen thousand was too much and that they could have negotiated harder.

The huge man wiped his face with a filthy handkerchief and let out a grunt. "Sounds fine to me, mate. I can guarantee that you will not be disappointed." He hesitated a short while before continuing. "As I said, my men are all ready and primed. I just hope your contacts across the water do a better job than last time."

Hans picked up on the hint of reproach and nodded. "Yes, so do I. We have sorted a few things out since then, and I'm on my way over there this afternoon. You can rest assured that it will all run smoothly."

Hans wanted to get more details about how things were going to proceed. He never trusted people who guaranteed things, and he liked to be in control, making sure every *t* was crossed and every *i* was dotted. He wondered how and why they'd ever chosen such an awful, disgusting man in the first place. He had to admit that Jimmy Cut-throat Shand was good at his job, and he was in no doubt how he had gotten his name. Like Ron, and in a way like Hans himself, a person had to have a ruthless streak if he wanted to survive and rise to the top in this business. Show weakness and a man would be quickly swallowed up.

Once Hans was satisfied every angle had been thought of, he leant back and allowed himself a thin smile. He coughed. "Well, gentlemen, you seem to have covered all bases, and I'm confident everything will run smoothly." He glanced at his watch before continuing. "I must now make my way over to Belfast, and hopefully things there will be as well organised as here." He rose, indicating the meeting was over.

Jimmy Cut-throat Shand proffered a clammy hand, which Hans hesitatingly shook. "My men will escort you to the ferry. Don't want anything happening to you on the way!" He laughed at his joke.

Once out in the open air, Hans breathed in deeply. With the stench of body odour clinging to him, he wondered whether he would ever get rid of it. He thanked his host and wished him well before quickly getting into the car. As they drove off, a black Audi came round the corner and fell in behind for the short journey to the ferry terminal. The skinny man dropped Hans off and departed without uttering a word, heading back to base. The black car dropped off a passenger before finding a nearby parking space.

Hans went straight to the gents', where he splashed water on his face and washed his hands in the vein hope of getting rid of the smell. Everywhere he went, he smelt the rancid aroma of stale sweat and beer. He boarded the ferry as quickly as possible and found himself a lone seat, far away from anyone else.

The passenger of the black Audi watched as his man walked on to the boat and remained in the departure lounge until the vessel had set sail.

The crossing was routine, the sea calm. Hans spent the time going over what he had to do on arrival. First things first: he would check in at the hotel and take a long shower before handing his clothes in to be express dry-cleaned. He shuddered at the thought of living with such people as those he'd recently parted ways with. *Do any of them have wives or girlfriends?* he wondered shuddering involuntary.

CHAPTER 24

Belfast was sunny with a cool north-easterly breeze when the ferry docked. Hans was one of the first passengers to descend the gangplank. Heading straight for the taxi rank, he entered one of the cabs and instructed the driver to take him to the Fitzwilliam on Great Victoria Street. He opened the window slightly and sat back. As they left the ferry compound, a couple of Charly Flynn's men pulled out from the car park and followed discreetly. The expert driver kept in touch with the cab, burning a couple of red lights. As the taxi stopped outside the impressive hotel, the two men pulled up behind it and watched Hans make his way to reception.

Once in his room, he called housekeeping and requested express dry-cleaning and told them he would leave the clothes outside his door. He stood under the shower for a long time, soaping himself down twice and washing his hair. As he stepped into the room, he felt a different man, clean and no longer smelling like a chimpanzee's backside. He made his way to the minibar and poured himself a stiff drink before calling his contact and arranging a meeting for the following day. Then he ordered a light room service meal, which he devoured, realising that he had not eaten since breakfast. Next, he called Ron and confirmed everything was in place in Liverpool, saying that he was going to check out the plans and the warehouse first thing next day. He enquired if there was news of the lost shipment and was told that nothing had been discovered. The French police were still looking and crawling all over the area, which meant their people were unable to nose around much. The good news was that the main consignment, or what was left of it, was due to arrive in the UK within the next couple of days; the second shipment was about to leave the port in Italy and make its way to northern France.

The silver 4 × 4 pulled up outside the hotel at 9.30 precisely. A young man got out of the passenger seat. He was elegantly dressed in a dark suit which was covered with a Burberry raincoat and a tweed cap. He was about to mount the steps when Hans appeared and strode towards him. The young man took off his cap and thrust out a hand deferentially, which was ignored. Hans made for the open rear door and settled himself into the rear seat, leaving the young man to make his way round to the opposite side, a thin drizzle started to fall. Immediately the car pulled out and headed south. The young man stuck out his hand once more and needlessly introduced himself. Hans nodded and uttered a few words of greeting, then enquired whether it ever stopped raining.

Charly had detailed two of his best surveillance men to tail the 4 × 4 and to report back once they knew where it was headed. His phone pinged, his men messaging that they were heading south of the city on the A24 in the direction of Ballynahinch . Charly immediately contacted base, and a few minutes later an army helicopter took off, rising rapidly into the grey sky.

The two vehicles travelled on into the countryside, passing the small town of Carryduff. The journey was slow because of roadworks, but at last the lead car turned right into a narrow country lane that was flanked on either side by a tall hedge. The following car slowed and took the same road, keeping a good distance from its target. The driver was anxious, not wanting to be spotted and certainly not wanting to catch up with the front vehicle. The tension was relieved when they heard the low throb of an engine overhead. The phone pinged with a short cryptic message advising that the airborne surveillance team had picked up the target, which was a couple of miles ahead. Suddenly, yet another message came through, this one indicating that the front car had turned off up a narrow lane and was heading towards a farm building with a large warehouse. The helicopter veered off and disappeared into the distance. The two surveillance officers turned on to the small country road keeping their distance. They drove past the farm entrance just in time to see the front car heading up towards the farm. As they did so, they had a perfect view of the farm and outbuildings. They parked on the verge a few hundred yards farther on and watched through binoculars as the 4 × 4 came to a halt and three men got out. One of the surveillance members raised his camera and began taking photos of the three men standing looking at the warehouse. Two of them headed inside. Unable to see anything more, the surveyance team turned and parked the car out of sight.

Conversation was minimal on the drive to the warehouse. Hans did not trust the young man and certainly did not like his cocky, self-assured way. He had never seen the driver before so had kept the talk to banal subjects and had sidestepped the young man's questions. Losing patience with the incessant interrogation, he simply told him that nothing was going to be said until they were alone.

They stepped inside the vast farm building and headed to the far end before Hans rounded on the young man. "You talk too much; I would have thought after the last fiasco that you would have learned your lesson. Loose tongues cause problems."

The young man was about to reply but thought better of it. He paused, composing himself. "Fly is a trusted associate. He would never say anything. He has been with me for a long time. I have full confidence in him."

"That's what you said last time," Hans replied, snorting. "Look at what happened then." He started to pace up and down. "I hope you have sorted the opposition out. I know you said you had, but I'm not sure that I, we, can trust you. That mess nearly finished us. What assurance can you give us that it's not going to happen again and there won't be more shootings?"

The young man looked defiant and was clearly hurt. "I told you; we have dealt with the matter. Dealt with it! They ain't going to come back. No more turf war. We are in total command of the entire province."

Hans looked at him hard and long. It certainly seemed that he was speaking the truth. And from his enquiries, Hans believed the man had indeed cleaned up the mess. As for being in control of the province, he had to admit that was true. Ron had tried to find someone else, with no result. All he'd gotten back was the same sort of answer: "Not for us. Too big by far," "We value our future", etc. Ron and Hans knew that the man was ruthless and had wiped out all opposition by severely maiming or killing.

Convinced that things were now fine, Hans signalled for the young man to sit down, then went through all the details with a fine-tooth comb. He questioned, interrogated, and questioned again until he was satisfied that every last possibility had been covered. He liked that the operation would involve only a few men, men who knew exactly what to do and what to expect. Timing was crucial; it always was. Any delays could put the operation in danger, which would mean putting people in danger. Rushed jobs seldom ended well.

Satisfied, Hans motioned the young man to follow him. They inspected the barn-cum-warehouse minutely before walking round the outside, Hans indicating a couple of small improvements to be made. He didn't like blind spots, nor did he like too many trees, that one in the corner especially. He was assured that the alterations would be made. Finally, he stressed the importance of keeping communication to a minimum. He hated the use of phones on operations, with radios being even worse. If everyone knew their job, these gadgets shouldn't be needed. The young man nodded patiently, inwardly sighing in relief when his guest indicated it was time to get back. He was proud that he had kept his cool and calm despite being treated like a child. Who did this idiot think he was? A beginner.

As the 4 × 4 swung back onto the lane, none of the passengers noticed the black car parked among the trees. The two men waited a few seconds before gunning the engine and slowly pulling out. The passenger pulled out his phone, and a few minutes later the helicopter appeared behind them. It kept at a discreet distance and danced about, circling as if searching for something. As the lead car neared the outskirts of Belfast, the aircraft disappeared. The trailing car took over.

The journey back was as silent as the one out, both Hans and the young man remaining with their own thoughts. It was only when the latter pulled out his phone that the Dutchman spoke. Perhaps a bit harshly, he thought; he hadn't meant to be so abrupt. "Who are you calling? I thought I made it clear earlier that I do not like my partners communicating in that way."

His comments were received with a withering look and a shrug. The man ignored the request and continued dialling. Who the hell did this guy think he was, talking to him like that? He may have been older and may have been his ultimate employer, but there was no reason for such manners. He, Micky O'Doyle, was the head and brains of the largest and most lethal gang in Northern Ireland, and he didn't like the way he was being spoken to. Nothing could be done at present, but once this latest shipment had been dealt with and he had been paid, then, well, he would seriously consider teaching this foreigner whom he was dealing with. They parted company at the hotel, Hans mounting the steps and entering the lobby without looking back. The dislike was mutual, and still, despite the meticulous questioning, he didn't trust the young man.

As the 4 × 4 took drove off, the man in the passenger seat of the black car phoned in to his superior. The two had a brief chat before it was time to head for the house in Argyll Street and meet up with their colleagues. A day in their business was never over. It was not a nine-to-five job.

———◆◆◆———

Charly Flynn took a few notes and asked a couple of questions before thanking the caller and hanging up. He turned to Sean and Peter Hollins. "Well, we know where the warehouse is and the approximate date the shipment is due to arrive, so I suggest, Peter, that you get yourself down there first thing in the morning and start a recon. Sean, your man is flying back to Amsterdam on the first flight tomorrow morning. I will get you on it. I'll have one of my chaps drive you to the airport."

Peter was a happy man. He loved doing reconnaissance, planning, and plotting; that was what he was good at, apart from a whole lot of other things. He picked up a map and opened it up on the table, asking Charly to show him where he was heading. They discussed various points before agreeing that he would leave first thing in the morning. No, he didn't want or need an escort; he preferred to be on his own. Sean was also happy, feeling that things were fast moving to a conclusion. And with men such as Charly and Peter, he had no doubt about the outcome. It had been two long years since he had started the operation, and now the finishing line was in sight.

After the two men had gone to bed, Charly decided to call DI O'Grady and put him in the picture. After a short conversation, they agreed to meet the next day on the bench in Victoria Park.

Day was just breaking when Peter let himself out. He crossed the road to the rented car, where earlier he had loaded his gear, before going back and joining the other two for breakfast. The clock had struck seven when he made his way out and jumped into the driver's seat. He opened the map, following Charly's precise instructions on how to get onto the A24. Making good progress, and with traffic being light, he enjoyed driving through the lush countryside. A watery sun was peeking through the clouds. Finding the turn-off into the narrow road, he soon came across the farm and large warehouse-cum-barn. He may have struggled to find his way from the ferry port, but not now. He slowly drove past the lane leading up to the building and parked a few hundred yards further on, leaving the car in a small lay-by. After throwing the rucksack over his shoulder, and with map in hand, he proceeded back down the narrow road. He stopped and watched the building for a long time before walking up the track. It looked deserted. Making his way up to the old farm building, he knocked on the door before peering through one of the windows, seeing the place was empty. He walked round the back, checking the rear entrance to the lean-to kitchen, before forcing open a window. Slipping in, he made a quick tour of the cottage; a rickety table with two chairs was all that was there. He climbed back out of the window, closing it, and circled the vast barn. The large double doors were locked with a thick chain and a couple of padlocks, making it impossible to open. He then went to the back, where he found a small door, but that too was firmly bolted. Making his way down one side, he spotted a loose panel, which he carefully prised open. Squeezing himself through the narrow crack, he entered the warehouse. The vast building was empty except for a few unused stalls, three or four bales of straw, and an impressive forklift truck. At the far side was a modern set of scales with a table and a couple of chairs. He walked round the building and memorised the layout before leaving through the narrow entrance. Managing to loosen a few more bolts, he carefully closed the opening. He made one final tour of the exterior, pacing distance, before finally making a third circuit to ensure he hadn't missed anything. Checking if the way was clear, he headed back to the road.

Peter then crossed the road and headed into the wood, following an overgrown path before branching off and climbing the hill. He stopped several times to take his bearings and to look back down at the farm. He spent a couple of hours prowling the wood, getting to know its layout and getting a feel for the surroundings. He noted where several paths led and the precise location where they crossed, he ignorer nothing. By the time he had returned to his car, he had a perfect picture, having learned everything he needed to know, he started to formulate a plan. The following couple of hours were spent driving round the area noting where the various roads led to. He checked out the small hamlet on the west side of the hill, home to a half dozen cottages, most of which were holiday homes. One large farm dominated the area. Peter watched as the owner or tenant worked tirelessly, tending his sheep in the fields. As dusk started to fall, he decided to head back to Belfast, passing the farm building one last time. He was a happy man.

Sean had been collected shortly after Peter had left and had made his way to the airport. He was early, but after checking in, he'd sat in the hall, where he watched the early morning travellers start to trickle in. Just after 8.30, Mr Hans van der Brawn appeared and breezed towards the check-in desk. Although Sean had known his target would come, a wave of relief came over him when he spotted the tall figure of the Dutchman. He followed him through security and to the gate. Charly had worked wonders, getting Sean a seat two rows behind the man he was following. Prior to boarding, Sean had phoned the head of operations in Amsterdam to warn him that their man was travelling back, although it had been assumed he would be flying direct to the South of France. As the plane was rolling towards the runway, Sean's phoned pinged with a message: "Target booked on KLM flight leaving for Nice at 13.20. We will take over."

Charly Flynn was sitting on the bench in Victoria Park when the unmistakable figure of DI O'Grady appeared from the gate to his left. The two men greeted one another warmly before strolling down one of the paths. Charly did not waste any time in bringing the policeman up to speed. He was open about Peter and said that what they had decided was the best course of action. O'Grady was appalled and cringed at the thought of a spy and an SAS officer being let loose on such a sensitive and potentially explosive case. Charly patted the man on the shoulder. "Relax, Detective Inspector. All will be fine, trust me. I can assure you; we have everything well under control."

The DI was not convinced. Quite the contrary. Here were two men who, he was sure, were going to create mayhem on his patch, and it would be he, Patrick O'Grady, who would have to clear up the mess and answer to his superiors; he did not like it one little bit. He was about to open his mouth in protestation when Charly headed him off at the pass. "All will be well. I know we're not following protocol, but protocol goes out the window in operations like these. If we followed the rules, we would have our hands tied, with the result that the baddies would get off scot-free. I have asked you here for your help. I know we're great, but even we need help sometimes." He laughed at his own light-heartedness. They went to sit down on a bench, where Charly explained what he wanted and what his idea was.

O'Grady listened without interrupting. The more he heard, the more he was troubled—but excited at the same time. Here was an operation which, if all went well, would certainly help his flagging career. It was fraught with danger, and he was not sure his men would be up to it, nor was he certain that his boss would agree. He put these points to the man sitting next to him.

Charly understood the man's dilemma. He had seen many times before that same kind of person with that same kind of mentality; they feared sticking their necks out, afraid to take risks. Better keep a low profile, stay out of the limelight, and ensure a boring routine future, rather than use the brains they had. He was saddened each time to think so many thought that way, their having such limited ambition. He normally turned his back on such people, but not this time: he needed the man as well as the manpower, so he took a deep breath and turned on the charm. Forty-five minutes later they shook hands, both happy men—well, one happier than the other. Charly was relieved that he had not lost his art of persuasion, and O'Grady was relieved at the thought that maybe, if all went as well as he had been promised, he was on the cusp of a major career promotion. He had listened to the spy setting out his ideas and was impressed by the meticulous planning and professionalism of the operation; he, DI Patrick O'Grady, would never have dreamt up such a scenario.

As the DI strode away, his mind was racing. How would he tell his boss? *Would* he tell his boss? By the time he arrived back at the station, he will have made up his mind.

Charly watched the policeman make his way back down the path, head slightly bent. He was pleased he had managed to enrol his man and organise backup, but he was still hesitant as to whether his new ally would prove his worth. Time would tell. The police were now involved, for better or for worse. He needed them. He had no choice.

CHAPTER 25

Back in London, Ron Stokes was fretting big time. The accident which had happened to part of the first shipment was causing him major concerns, and it seemed to him that he was the only one to worry. No one had yet found the wrecked container; the French police were supposed to be looking but had found nothing. They had the entire area cordoned off, ensuring that none of his contacts had access. All enquiries were met with a stony silence. Ron was beginning to wonder whether they had found the cargo and decided to play a waiting game. Who knew what the cops were thinking? The remainder of the shipment had eventually arrived in the UK and was now being processed. The containers had sailed through customs with no one asking any questions. In fact, it had never been so easy. He wondered what the thousands of border control and customs officials were doing and what the Home Office was spending their money on. He smiled to himself. Well, it certainly didn't concern him. He was delighted with the apathy; it made life easier.

Ron was brought out of his dream by his phone ringing. Picking up the device, he saw it was Hans. "Just to let you know, boss, I have visited both locations and spoken to the creeps. All is in place and ready."

Ron congratulated his partner. They chatted awhile longer before Hans told him he had to go; his flight was boarding. "I will call you once I get back from the South of France, probably in four-or five-days' time. Should I send Jane your love?" he asked sarcastically. A grunt from Ron told him he could do whatever he pleased.

The mention of his estranged wife reminded Ron that he had to call his lawyer, which he did immediately. It was time to get rid of the woman, to go it alone; he didn't need her. He instructed his solicitor to do what was necessary and to keep the payment to a minimum, but most important of all she had to sign a document swearing to silence. If she did not, then the man had orders to impress on her that if any of Ron's business dealings were to come to light, she would pay with her life. No mincing of words, no pussyfooting around; empty threats never worked. No, she had to realise that if she wanted to enjoy a long and comfortable life, living till old age, she should keep her mouth firmly shut.

Turning his mind back to France, Ron wondered what had happened. The driver's story was vague. He, with the others, had stopped for a short rest and to check the cargo as was the norm. On opening the rear doors, he noticed immediately something was wrong, at which point chaos reigned. He tried to contact his other two colleagues, but they had driven off and did not respond. Taking matters into his own hands, he decided to move the truck out of sight, edging his way down a small forest lane until he got to a large clearing well hidden from the road. He had then unhitched the trailer before sprinkling it with the contents of the spare fuel canisters and setting it ablaze. It was night-time and miles from the nearest hamlet, with most people being asleep, so the fire went unnoticed. After checking the flames had taken well, he crept back to the main road then drove another dozen miles before running the truck into a deep gulley and abandoning it. No one had seen or heard from him since; no sightings had been reported. A local postman had spotted the vehicle on his way to work and had reported his findings to the local gendarmerie.

The other two drivers had been interrogated by their boss, but neither of them had an explanation. The man had made his way down to the scene to try to find out what had happened but was confronted by a police cordon, who told him to move on. He had decided to let Hans know—after all, the Dutchman was his main contact—and was unsurprised by the reaction he received. Hans had then phoned Ron to give him the news. Ron had exploded, Hans never having heard his boss shout and scream in such a way. Listening to the rant, Hans was pleased he had taken the decision to cut loose and take early retirement. He did not need all this, all the hassle, and mostly he was fed up with being blamed for everything.

Once Ron had calmed down, he called his associate back and apologised. He knew he had gone too far; it was certainly not the man's fault. An idiot of a minion had put the whole operation in danger and had potentially cost them a huge amount of money, but worst of all, Ron knew his reputation was in danger of taking a huge dive. Without one's reputation, one could never make the sort of cash Ron was commanding or dreaming of. To be the king in this dark and dubious world, a man had to prove his worth and trustworthiness. There and then, Ron decided that the French contact was doomed. Once the second load had safely arrived on UK soil, the man and his organisation had to be taught a lesson. Ron would instruct Hans to do the necessary, and then the murky underworld would get the message: Don't mess up. Don't play games with Ron Stokes.

After some thought, Ron decided to take a trip over and meet with his French contact. He was nervous and worried about the second shipment and needed reassurance. He would have sent Hans, but the Dutchman had insisted that he was going to the Côte d'Azur for a few days. Ron had tried to dissuade him, but to no avail. Well, he would have to make the trip himself and leave their contact in no doubt about his displeasure, sure to impress upon the slimy, devious toad that this was his last chance, although it was already decided in Ron's mind that the man was living on borrowed time.

Ron sat in his chair staring out the window. He could not fathom people, never having understood how their minds worked. There he was, Ron Stokes, a man who always thought of business, the next deal, how to advance in life, and how to make more money. He had learned a long time ago that cash was king; it brought power, obedience, and contacts. The wealthier you were, the more people looked up at you and were ready to forget their morals. They could be bought, hired, and treated like dirt, only to think you were doing them a favour. Stupid idiots! He didn't understand Hans, a man he had taught and taken under his wing, a good man, a trustworthy friend and ally. Hans was a ruthless operator who had understood that to be at the top of the pile, you had to show no pity, have no heart. Yet, after so many years together, Ron still didn't really understand the man. There they were, in the middle of two huge deals, and his associate was hell-bent on spending time in his villa in the South of France, probably fucking his boss's wife. If it were Ron, he would have waited until everything was finished before taking time off and enjoying the fruits of their labour. He shook his head. People! A weird bunch of animals, with even the best having moments of weakness or, in this case, madness. He couldn't care two hoots about his associate's having an affair with his estranged wife. Good luck to them. But to do it now? He despaired.

The phone rang, and Ron jumped at the sudden sound. He looked at the number but didn't recognise it, so ignored it. The phone rang again a few seconds later, the same number, but this time Ron answered, immediately wishing he had not. The foreign voice at the other end was smooth and smarmy, trying to be friendly but failing miserably. "Mr Stokes, it has been a long time since we last spoke. You are a busy man and difficult to get hold of." Ron shuddered and closed his eyes. His gut twisted in knots; he felt sick. "Mr Stokes, we have not heard from you and how you are getting on with our deal— you remember, the one we discussed in Boston."

Ron's mouth was dry as sandpaper and he gulped silently. He had hoped by not thinking of the problem, it would go away. He had deliberately not done anything and avoided contacting the snake at the other end of the line. Now, he tried to speak, but nothing came out. Clearing his throat, he managed to croak, "No, sorry, we've been very busy with a couple of deals at present and wanted to get those out of the way before concentrating fully on your proposition." He prayed he sounded all right. "Please rest assured that the deal is very high up on my list of priorities and hugely important to us. But, as I said, I and my associate want to finalise what we are doing now before getting back to you."

The voice at the other end remained slimy and aloof. "Mr Stokes, we understand, but I must stress that this matter is of the utmost importance. How long before you can concentrate on our business? My partners are getting restless and impatient. I wouldn't want to have to persuade you of the urgency of the matter."

Ron winced, and his stomach tensed even more; there was no doubt about the undertone. He paused a second before replying. "I would say that we'll be able to give your matter our full attention in just under three weeks from now. I am very aware of the importance and urgency; you can rest assured that we are taking the deal extremely seriously and are fully committed."

"Not good enough, Mr Stokes. My superiors and partners can't wait that long. Let us agree we will hear from you in two weeks at the most. After that, I cannot promise what decision my superiors and partners will take."

The phone went dead. There was no doubt in Ron's mind that the threat was real and very serious. His palms were sweaty, and his hands shook. How the hell had he ever gotten into this one? The vision of being followed returned, and he began breathing heavily. He recalled the look in the man's eyes as he sat across the table from him in Boston—those cold, dead eyes—and again, he was in no doubt that his threats were real. If he, Ron Stokes, were to live a happy life, he would have to pull out all the stops. The problem was that he knew nothing of the world he had been thrown into; it was totally unlike what he was used to. Yes, he knew where he could buy a modern, up-to-date pistol, even a rifle, but a whole shipment of arms and chemicals? That was different. How and why had they chosen him? What made them so confident he could procure everything they wanted? He did not understand, and the more he thought about it, the more panic set in. He tried to pull himself together, to refocus on the matter at hand, but his mind kept wandering back to the phone conversation.

He had slept soundly and had awoken early; it was still dark outside when he jumped into a taxi and headed for the train station. The journey to Calais was slow with several delays, and his mood was dark when he eventually landed on French soil. His patience was tried again when the train to Amiens was late, finally pulling into the city just after lunchtime. His contact was waiting in the main hall. Although

Ron had met him only once before, he recognised him instantly. A short tubby man dressed in jeans and a sweater stepped forward and greeted his English visitor with a nod and a limp handshake. The two men made their way across the square and down a busy street before entering a smoky bistro. The patron smiled and welcomed his guests, showing them to a table at the back of the restaurant, well away from any other customers. By the way the owner spoke and acted, it was clear that the little man was a regular. Conversation was difficult and stunted, but at last Ron got round to asking his host what really had happened on that fateful night. The man shrugged and went into a long discourse, giving various explanations, none of which made sense or helped Ron.

Over coffee, Ron grabbed the bull by the horns and came to the point of his visit. Looking the man in the eye, he calmly impressed upon him that there was no room for any further errors or cockups, saying that the second shipment, now leaving Bari, had better arrive on time and in one piece. Although he did not say it, he strongly hinted that if there were any further problems, there would be severe consequences. The Frenchman sat impassively across the table smoking his Gauloises. He did not like this jumped-up Englishman, but he swallowed his pride, only because the payment received was more than he could have ever hoped for. Having not missed the underlying threat, his mind was already making contingency plans.

On the way home, Ron made a call to his Italian contact and was delighted to hear that the new convoy was about to leave the port and start making its way up to Italy. He followed that up by letting the little Frenchman know the precise day and time to have his drivers be at the rendezvous outside Lyon. Once he was home, he let out a deep sigh, closed his eyes, and fell into a deep sleep.

CHAPTER 26

As the plane came to a halt in Amsterdam, Sean was quick to ensure he got off before Hans. At the top of the gangway, he spotted his Dutch counterpart. They made eye contact and nodded briefly. From now on it was up to the local secret service to take over.

Hans, having three hours to kill, fleetingly considered going back home, but quickly put that thought out of his mind. No, he would wander around the shops and have a decent beer. He took a long time deciding what to buy Jane. After all, he hadn't seen her in a while and they were about to emigrate to the Caribbean and live to together, so he wanted to buy her something really special. He hesitated, trying to decide between a watch and a fine diamond bracelet, eventually choosing the timepiece. It would be far more useful, and she had been making noises about wanting to buy a new one. He was pleased with his choice.

Having made his way to the KLM executive lounge, Hans found a comfortable seat and settled down to an ice-cold beer. He had barely started reading his paper when a young woman came and sat across from him. Over his newspaper, he studied the woman as she settled in and relaxed. She was attractive enough, a bit too much make-up for his liking, but what caught his eye was the long, never-ending legs. She was obviously proud of them and made the most of showing them off, using them as a major asset. He reckoned she was in her early thirties, with waist-long hair and fine features. A model possibly, or one of the numerous young women who spent their time on yachts entertaining rich entrepreneurs. His uncertainty cleared when he heard her speak to the waiter; she was Eastern Bloc, probably Russian and probably, or rather certainly, a tart. What is it about them? he wondered. They all look the same, are made up the same, and dress the same as if it were a uniform. Well, everyone is entitled to make a living. She had chosen the oldest trade in the world just as he had chosen his career. He went back to his paper.

The flight to Nice was delayed for almost two hours because of the late arrival of the incoming aircraft. Hans texted Jane and told her he was going to be late, saying she should come over to his place about 3 p.m. the next day. He apologised but said he had some business matters to attend to in the morning. Her reply was a sad face; she understood. She signed off with several hearts and kisses.

At last, the flight was called. Hans was happily surprised, and, in some ways delighted, when he reached his seat to find that the young woman was sitting by the window. She looked up at him and smiled sweetly, a smile that would hook any man. Her long hair fell loosely over her shoulders and partly covered the front of her low-buttoned blouse, her short skirt showing off those slender and shapely legs, which were mesmerising. Conversation was easy, and the time passed by quickly. They shared a bottle of champagne and talked about everything and nothing, with no mention of what either did for a living, which suited Hans just fine. He had a story for such occasions but didn't want to go there. He would have liked to have confirmation of his suspicions about the young woman's job, but being a gentleman, he kept his mouth shut.

———————◆◆◆———————

Jane awoke early and spent a long time in the bathroom beautifying herself, doing things that women did when they were going to meet the love of their life. She hesitated and swithered about what to wear, finally deciding on a light print dress. Although it was October, the weather was still warm. She liked the way the dress clung to her body, showing off her curvaceous figure. She busied herself until it was time to go, not wanting to be late, but not wanting to be too early either. If Hans was working, then she knew him well enough not to disturb him.

Jane swung the car through the open gates into the large drive, making sure she parked in the way Hans liked; he was a stickler for things like that. She smiled as she recalled the first time she had pulled into his place and the lecture he gave her: "always park facing the gate and under the tree," he had told her. "That way, if you're in a hurry, you won't have to make the two-point turn, and the car will be cool from the shade." It must have been his Dutch or Germanic upbringing which dictated everything he did in life, always methodical, always precise.

She got out and mounted the steps, letting herself in; he had told her the door would be open. In the entrance lobby, she took off her shoes before making a quick visit to the toilet. She was shaking, her excitement at seeing him again making her feel like a little girl. In the bathroom, she freshened up then took her knickers off, wanting to feel sexy and excite him. Considering taking a sniff of white powder to relax, she hesitated, she did not like using the stuff and only ever took it if she were really stressed or needed to let go. She hated it even more since she had found out that Ron made a living out of supplying it. She had to admit it did have its uses if taken seldom and with care. If not, it was a killer, a wrecker of lives, careers, and marriages. She looked at the small packet and decided to take a small pinch, sniffing it in deeply. Then she flushed the remainder down the toilet and went out to the hallway, where she placed her purse on the table along with her car keys.

Making her way through to the large living area, Jane enjoyed the sensation of the cold marble on her bare feet. Entering the bright, two-tiered room with its sunken lounge flanked by huge panoramic windows offering a superb view of the Mediterranean and the coast, she felt butterflies in her stomach. Looking around, she recalled the first time he had brought there: the fun, the lovemaking on those soft sofas dotted around the room.

Reaching the double doors that led to the patio and pool, Jane froze in horror at the scene she witnessed, clamping both hands to

136

her mouth to stifle the cry of shock. There in front of her, by the side of the pool, his back to her, was Hans, naked and making love to a fair-haired woman. She was kneeling on all fours, her hair covering her face, her breasts swaying with every hard thrust of his firm buttocks. The moans and animalistic grunts coming from both of them clearly indicated that things were moving fast to a climax. Jane stood rooted, mesmerised, tears welling up, her legs trembling at the scene before her. She blinked and just stood, her eyes glued to the coupling naked bodies, unable to tear herself away. Finally, she turned and ran back to the front door. Picking up her purse and keys, she practically leapt down the five steps leading to the drive. She put her foot hard on the accelerator and raced through the gates onto the main street, closely missing an oncoming van.

Through her tears, she sped along the twisting mountain road, her tyres screeching until, a few miles on, she pulled into a lay-by. She sat in the car sobbing, her anger rapidly building up. She screamed and thumped the steering wheel. The only other couple at the viewpoint were standing looking at the scenery and taking photos, ignoring her. She sat a long while, trying to calm down. Had she seen right? Had she imagined what she had come across? Was it a dream? No, none of that. She had just witnessed the man she loved, the man who had promised her a new life in a new country, making love to an unknown woman. Why? What was he thinking? The creepy, slimy bastard; how dare he? Her anger grew the more she reran the event she had just witnessed through her mind.

Wiping her eyes, she took several deep breaths before driving away. Dusk was falling with the first twinkling lights appearing in the harbour when she pulled into the apartment garage. She had been driving aimlessly for hours, trying to make sense of what she had seen, the images and groans now firmly etched in her mind. Tears had given way to anger and hatred; she didn't know what she was going to do or where she was going to go, but she was finished with men. They were all unreliable, devious, cheating bastards. At first, she had thought that Hans was different from Ron and the other men she knew, but no, they were all the same. Greed and self-satisfaction were all they cared about.

Jane went over to the drink cabinet and poured herself a stiff one, tossing it down in one gulp before helping herself to another. Night had fallen, the sea reflecting the pale moon, giving the water a ghostly look. She made her way to the bedroom and slipped out of her dress, then stood under the shower for a long time, trying to wash away the images and her thoughts, enjoying the feel of the cold-water biting into her skin.

Going to lie on the bed, Jane felt that her anger had abated slightly, but her sadness and pain were still deep and raw. Unable to get the picture of the couple out of her mind, she closed her eyes.

She felt his breath on her neck, his naked body pressing against hers. His lips travelled down to her nipples, and then his tongue made its way over her belly. With his hand, he gently caressed the area between her legs, sending shivers and a tingling feeling down her spine. She sighed deeply and arched her back. Upon feeling him entering her, his lips kissing her passionately, she let out a low moan of pleasure as her body spasmed uncontrollably. Her hands clasped firmly between her thighs, she turned onto her side in the foetal position, twitching; soon, darkness swept over her.

She awoke the next morning with a start, feeling clammy and sweaty, and lay there for a while. Had she dreamt everything? She walked through to the lounge, expecting to see Hans, and soon realised the whole, horrid scene, had happened. She picked up her phone and saw she had six missed calls and a couple of text messages. She did not open the texts, nor did she check who had phoned: she knew, and there was no way she was going to speak to him. Going through to the bathroom, she had another long shower, still trying to wash away the memories of the previous day.

Feeling refreshed, Jane went through to the kitchen and made a strong cup of coffee. The feeling of sadness and anger had not gone away. Going over to the phone, she noticed there had been a couple more calls. She picked up her mobile and scrawled through the messages. They were all from Hans, enquiring where she was, asking if she was all right, and requesting that she call him back immediately. A couple of messages later, he told her needed to see her and explain. He didn't know where the apartment was; Ron didn't want anyone to know for some reason. She went over to make another coffee as the phone buzzed again. She picked up. The relief in Hans's voice was palpable as he asked where she had been and if she was all right. Jane listened without answering, her anger deepening at the sound of his voice. She killed the call.

The phone rang several times more before Jane answered and told Hans to get lost. He talked over her, apologising, saying that he had not meant to upset her or hurt her and that what she'd witnessed wasn't what it seemed. Jane listened in silence to the excuses. He continued, saying, "Look, it really isn't what it seemed. I wanted our time together to be special, something unforgettable, and thinking you would enjoy a new experience, I decided it was going to be a surprise."

She closed her eyes and clenched her teeth. "Well, you certainly showed me something I hadn't expected, and it was certainly a bloody surprise, you cheating, bastard."

"Look, she means nothing to me. She's a Russian hostess working in one of the local clubs. I thought you would enjoy the experience of a threesome, something you haven't ever done. I really didn't mean to hurt you." There was a long pause. As Jane remained silent, he continued, saying, "It kind of got out of hand. She came onto me big time, that's all. I really didn't mean for it to happen."

Jane continued to remain silent, enjoying in a way his squirming and hearing the ever more pathetic and wild excuses. He needed to see her, wanted to talk to her and had something to give her to make up for what he had done.

"Please let me see you one last time. I understand. I want to say sorry," he pleaded. "I must go back to Amsterdam tonight. Things are moving fast, and I need to be back to help Ron. I don't want our relationship to end this way. I want to make it up to you. Please, can we meet? We do have a future together. I love you."

So, that was it, he never had intended staying a week, just a quick one- or two-night stand where they'd have sex and he'd keep her quiet for a while, then go back to help Ron with his dirty business. Where were all the promises of going to the Caribbean and making a life together? Although Jane didn't want to see the man again, she wanted, in a perverse way, to meet him and to confront him face to face, to look him in the eyes and tell him exactly what she thought of him. She agreed to meet him later that afternoon outside the train station and drive him to the airport.

CHAPTER 27

The chief customs officer stood at his office window watching the convoy leave the port gate. He was satisfied he had played his part to the full. True, he had been paid handsomely and was happy that he had stood firm in the negotiations. He didn't know the contents of the containers, nor did he want to—better not to know. And yes, he was fully aware that what he did was illegal. To take bribes could lead him into big trouble and prison, but on his miserly wage, with three young children, a wife, and a demanding mistress, what else could a man do? The past month had padded his pocket considerably and he had gladly taken the risk. As the trucks trundled out onto the open road, he turned and slipped the thick brown envelope into his breast pocket before making his way back to his family.

The drivers knew the way well, taking the back roads to a prearranged stopping place to check on their loads. They all knew of the disastrous problems of the last job and had been warned to be extra vigilant. Over the next day and a half, they made their way up the spine of Italy, slower than usual because of the more frequent stops and checks. Finally, the border was only an hour or so away. The lead driver gave his last orders to the following vehicles, took a deep breath, and headed to the frontier. His boss had assured him the usual customs officers would be on duty, men he knew well from the numerous trips he had made. He just hoped they would be as relaxed as they had been in the past. Normally he made the crossing by himself or maybe accompanied by one or two others, but never as many as today.

He stopped one last time and checked to see that everyone was following, and all was in order. Next time, they'd be well into France at the changeover point. He took a deep breath and pulled out of the lay-by. They were waved through the first barriers and slowly drove to the French side, when the driver spotted the two douaniers stepping out of their booth. The older of the two came up to the cab's window and started chatting. He looked back at the convoy and asked if they were all together and what was being transported. "Veg as usual," the driver replied. "This is a big order for one of your supermarkets in Lyon. They must have had a supply problem by the looks of it." He chuckled. The customs official smiled, made a few sarcastic comments, bade them a safe journey, and waved them on. Silently the driver let out a low sigh of relief. He checked in his rear-view mirror that the others had all cleared the barrier before putting his foot down, subconsciously wanting to leave the border quicker than normal. He couldn't put his finger on the reason he was feeling so anxious, figuring it must have been the thought of the threats his boss had made as they parted. Or was it the size of the shipment? Something niggled, and he became annoyed with himself. Pull yourself together. It's just a normal job, something you've been doing for three years, once or twice a month.

They turned into a deserted lay-by and checked the containers. Seeing that all was well, the lead driver called his men over and offered them each a cigarette. They all stood and chatted for a few minutes. Just as they were getting back into their cabs, a car pulled up and a man jumped out, and went to relieve himself.

They arrived at the rendezvous point on the outskirts of Lyon by 11 a.m. The front driver, spotting the battered minibus parked in the usual place, relaxed.

He was greeted by a short man smoking a Gauloises and was informed he was the "patron" of the French contingent. After meeting Ron, the Frenchman had decided to take command of his end of the operation, show leadership, and ensure there were no further problems. Having to rely on his regular drivers, he opted to ride with his head man as he, himself, did not have a heavy goods vehicle licence. Why should he? He was, after all, the brains and the boss.

As the trucks pulled out of the service area, a silver-grey car parked up not far away. The head driver from Italy had just settled in the back of the minibus and was looking out the window when he noticed the vehicle stop. He looked at it hard and long, blinking several times; he was sure he had seen it somewhere. Or was he imagining it? He shook his head and scratched his chin. No, he must be dreaming; tiredness can make the mind work in funny ways. As they drove out of the parking lot, he looked back but could no longer see the car. He drifted off into a deep sleep.

The convoy made good time. By nightfall, they were circling Paris before heading north. The patron was relaxed, making nonstop conversation with his driver, who was praying the man would shut up. He had never heard him talk so much and was driving him to distraction. Once past the capital, the convoy pulled off and stopped to make their regular check; all was fine. As they continued their trip, the boss became more tense, starting to smoke more and more. He asked the driver if they could change route and bypass the location of the previous shipment disaster. The man shook his head; he didn't have a map and had no idea where they could stop for their next container inspection, as it would need to be discreet and off the beaten track. The boss was not happy and fell into deep thought. They drove through the forest, the driver pointing out the general area of the fire and, a little farther on, the ravine where the cab had been dumped. Seeing no sign of police or what had happened, both men fell silent, lost in their own thoughts.

By early morning, the trucks stopped for the last time in a secluded spot before rumbling through the harbour gates. The initial plan had been to split the convoy into three, but all that had changed. Ron had insisted they travel as one and boarded the ferry as one. He didn't trust the group to be splintered, not after last time. Both men got out and stretched, breathing in the sea air mixed with diesel fumes.

As the last of the lorries parked alongside the others, no one noticed the silver car pull up behind the office building. Two men,

French and a Dutch Secret Service officer, got out and hurried in by a back door. Both were exhausted by the long journey and the tenseness of trailing a convoy. Figuring out how not to be noticed on such a long trip was always stressful. But they were professionals, and a job was a job however tired they felt.

The little man, accompanied by the driver, made his way across the lorry park and entered the brightly lit booking office of the ferry company. They were greeted by a young man in his early thirties, smartly dressed in his company's uniform. He listened to his customers and nodded before inspecting the paperwork they had laid down on the counter. "Gentlemen, I regret to advise you that due to a go-slow and work-to-rule by the crews, there will be a two-day delay," he said apologetically. "Of course, your bookings will be honoured. I understand you have perishable goods on board, so we will do our best to get you on your way as soon as possible."

The two men looked horrified and tried to pressure the young employee into helping them jump the queue. The young man stood firm. "As I said, it's out of our hands, and we can't guarantee anything. You know what the unions are like; they are stubborn and unhelpful. We could try to split you up, and possibly that way one or two of you could board tomorrow at the earliest."

The boss stuck a cigarette in his mouth and was about to light it when the attendant stopped him, pointing at the No Smoking sign behind him. The little man was getting irritated and began cursing and swearing. Why was it things never seemed to go smoothly? What was it with this country, no backbone, letting the unions rule the economy? The driver laid a hand on his boss's shoulder and tried to calm him down. "Boss, it's not the boy's fault; he is not to blame. It's up to you, but we don't have much choice. In my opinion, we should take the offer of splitting up and taking any spaces we are offered."

The little man turned, his face red, apoplectic with rage. "Shut up. Who asked for your opinion? You have no idea about anything!" he yelled. "This shit country and its shitty unions are going to cost us a fortune. Do you think the government will help? Not on your life." He paced around like a caged lion before snarling at the clerk. "Where is your boss? I want to see him, now."

"I'm afraid he's unavailable. I believe that currently he's in Boulogne with one of our directors, negotiating with the workers and union. I'm the senior member of staff here."

The answer enraged the little man even more, causing him to explode. "We will wait no more than two days. You make very sure we get all these trucks onto one of your damned ferries by then or I will have you reported for incompetence!" A thought suddenly struck him. He fished out his wallet and took out a large wad of cash, which he placed on the counter. "Here is five hundred euros. You'll get the same if you get us all out of here by tomorrow afternoon at the latest." He looked the man in the eyes. "Bet that will come in handy. So, get on with it. Take it; it's yours."

The young man stared back at the two customers before turning and heading back to his office, leaving the pile of notes where they were. Before closing the door, he turned. "I have your details. I'll let you know as soon as we have space available." Then he was gone.

The little man was seething and spat out some obscenities. Turning to the driver, he nodded towards the door. "Come, we'd better get these trucks back to base. We don't want any more disasters. Just hope the little jumped-up squirt gets back quickly or he will have me to answer to."

Back in the office, the two men had been watching developments on the TV screen. They beamed as the young man returned. "Excellent! You did a wonderful job. I congratulate you for keeping so cool. I doubt if I would have."

The second man rose stiffly from his chair. "Yes, young man, very well handled. I suggest you keep our friend sweating until Friday, and then ensure all the trucks get on the same ferry. Please keep us informed, give us a few hours' warning." They left by the rear door and were making their way to the car just as the first truck started to roll.

The boss barked his orders before getting in the front truck. The convoy slowly rumbled out of the compound. The short journey to the yard didn't take long. They swung in through the heavily guarded gates and headed for a huge warehouse, into which they were disappearing just as the silver car drove past slowly. The driver pulled over a hundred yards farther on, and his friend made a phone call. Not long after, a battered blue van appeared and parked behind them. It was time for the passengers of the car to go home and get some rest.

CHAPTER 28

Jane phoned her mother and asked her to get her room ready, saying she would be coming to stay a few days but was not sure when; she was going to be busy. Her mother picked up the vibe that not all was well, as mothers do. Jane then followed up that call by ringing the office to tell them she had urgent business to see to and would be probably away for some time. She then rang British Airways and booked herself on the evening flight to London. It was perfect timing as her flight would depart an hour after Hans's.

She went to pack a few belongings and tidy the apartment before going to the safe. Rummaging through the papers, she found her passports. Yes, she had two. Ron had no knowledge, although it was his idea. Not long after they had gotten married, he suggested it may be good if he were to get her a second passport, a Swiss one. He had a contact who could arrange it. Horrified, she had declined. Then came the discovery that her husband was not all he was made out to be, and she changed her mind. She had managed to find out who the counterfeiter was and went to him directly, not wanting to tell Ron. It was expensive business. She probably would have gotten a better price had she told the man who her husband was, but she decided it would be better for her if no one knew, not even Hans. She looked at the photo, which was true to her looks apart from the tied-up hair, and then at the name, Greta Bauman. Why she had chosen that name, she didn't know; it was the first thing that had come to her. She sieved through various envelopes and retrieved all the cash that Ron had stashed away, much of which had come from some dirty deals he had done locally. Stuffing the large wad in her purse and closing the door, she noticed a package, which she retrieved and opened carefully. Smiling, she rewrapped it, taking great care, before checking the safe one last time, then locking it.

One last glance round the flat before letting herself out. She liked the place but wouldn't miss it. There were too many bad memories, too many arguments and disappointments.

She drove down to the town centre and made her way to the bank, requesting to see the manager. A young woman appeared and ushered her in to a small but neat office. Half an hour later, Jane was shown out of the office. After a warm handshake, she made her way out into the bright sunlight. She smiled to herself, happy that everything had gone so smoothly, not having expected the closing of an account to be so easy. The young woman had taken everything in her stride, making several suggestions, which Jane had accepted. If ever she wanted to come back here to live, she would certainly use this bank.

As Jane drove up to the station square, she immediately spotted Hans. Her mood darkened. Taking a deep breath, she put on her charming smile and pulled up in front of him. He was travelling light, she noted, with a large holdall and a captain's briefcase, which he threw in the rear seat. As he jumped in beside her, he leant over to give her a kiss, but she pulled back. The thought of him touching her gave her the creeps. How things had changed. Thirty-six hours earlier she would have done anything to be in his arms, to be kissed by him, and to make love to him.

The drive to the airport was difficult, the conversation stilted. Hans tried to make small talk, also trying to apologise and to explain, but Jane would have none of it. No matter what he said, she did not believe him. She listened to all his lies and squirming excuses, but the more he carried on, the more she despised him. He asked her what she was going to do. He pleaded with her to change her mind and to forgive him, to come out to the Caribbean with him; he would prove to her he really loved her, they would live a happy and fulfilled life together. It all fell on deaf ears.

She parked the car in the main parking lot and paid with Ron's credit card. As she and Hans made their way over to the terminal, he noticed her bags for the first time. "Where are you going?" he enquired, a surprised look on his face.

"Back to London. I'm staying with my parents for a while until I sort somewhere to live." She looked at him before continuing. "I'm leaving Ron. He doesn't love me, and now that you and I are finished, I must make a fresh start." Hans was about to speak, but she continued. "You can tell Ron if you like, although I suspect he knows and doesn't really care; our love died many years ago." Turning and looking at Hans for the first time, she said, "I loved you, you know? I would have done anything for you, gone anywhere with you." She turned away abruptly as she felt tears welling up in her eyes.

Hans accompanied her to the check-in desk and helped her with the luggage, then they made their way to the KLM self-check-in machine, where he got his boarding pass. She told him to go through security and to meet her at the bar, as she had to go to the women's room urgently. She watched him go through passport control before making her way to the EasyJet desk, where she purchased a ticket in the name of Greta Bauman. The assistant was not too happy when she insisted on paying in cash, explaining that credit card was the preferred method. Jane, or rather Greta, explained that she had experienced problems with her card and was currently waiting for a new one. The young man reluctantly accepted the notes and handed over her boarding pass.

She found Hans sitting at the bar sipping a beer, scrolling through his emails. He got up and pointed to a table as she came to sit down. She declined his offer of a drink, asking him what his plans were and how the deals were going, pretending to be interested. At least that way it would keep him from making more excuses. He answered vaguely before trying once again to persuade her to go with him. A few more weeks and they could fly out to a new life. Jane smiled sweetly, but her eyes remained cold, distant, something he picked up. He sighed. "You are a hard woman, Jane. Surely you understand it was a mistake. I truly love you." He took out a neatly wrapped parcel and handed it to her before taking a large gulp and ordering another drink. "It's for you, a token of my love. Hope you like it."

Jane took the parcel and turned it over several times. She was about to hand it back, but he insisted she open it. Reluctantly, she unwrapped the gift and gasped involuntarily at the sight of the watch. It was an expensive Swiss make, delicate and beautifully crafted; it must have cost a fortune. She thanked him but handed it back, saying she did not take bribes; if he thought he could buy himself out of trouble, he was sorely wrong.

If Hans was hurt, he didn't show it. He simply pressed the watch into her hands and told her he hoped it would remind her of the good times they'd had. He insisted. Not wishing to cause a scene, she smiled sweetly and thanked him, strapping it in on her wrist. She had to admit it was nice and that he had made a good choice.

Time was ticking by, and eventually Hans's flight was called. He got up and asked Jane to look after his bags whilst he nipped to the toilet. She watched him disappear, sadness filling her. She had really loved him.

They made their way over to the gate, and she watched him disappear down the gangway tunnel. Going to the nearby window, she followed his plane with her eyes as it rumbled down the runway and slowly faded away in the evening sky. She took out her phone and made a couple of calls, the second one to request a hotel reservation.

Once the plane was out of sight, Jane made her way to the women's washroom. Locking herself in a stall, she took the SIM card out of her phone and flushed it down the toilet. Her British Airways flight was being announced as she emerged into the hall. She watched the holidaymakers and families slowly disappear through the gate. Her name was called several times, but she ignored the announcement each time. Half an hour later, she boarded the EasyJet flight to Zurich, but not before discreetly tossing the watch into a nearby trash bin.

Hans was glum as he sat sipping a glass of champagne. He could not understand why Jane had gotten so mad and why she couldn't see or understand that he meant no harm, that he still loved her. Women, he would never understand them, one minute they were all in love, and the next you could do no right. Yes, perhaps it had been a mistake to invite the leggy hooker back to his place. Yes, it was probably not a good idea to expect Jane to accept sharing him with her. Her cossetted suburban life would never have given her the inquisitiveness to try out a threesome or to accept that Hans could still love her after his dalliance; it was all black or white with Jane, never any flexibility. She was a jealous little cow. He took another swig and closed his eyes. Now what? Would he still go to the Caribbean? Probably yes. He'd had enough of the dirty lifestyle he was leading, the blood, the scum, and the looking over his shoulder. Ron had changed, had gotten harder with age and success; Hans was no longer sure if he wanted the same as his boss. He had sufficient money to keep himself in a very comfortable way for the rest of his life, and he need no more, not from the job he was doing anyway. He just did not like the thought of being alone with no one to love or to love him. He got out his wallet and pulled out a folded piece of paper. Well, he could always ask. She was good-looking, she spoke well, she seemed intelligent, and she could certainly look after him sexually; and those legs, they were a true turn-on. He pondered the idea for a long time before taking his decision. Once these two deals were done and dusted, he would make a new life for himself with Natasha. Feeling better, he asked the steward for another glass of champagne.

He made his way through passport control and was about to pass through the green zone when two customs officials stepped out in front of him. They respectfully asked him to go to the counter and open his holdall. Slightly irritated, he obeyed. He had been taken aback by their appearance but recovered and turned on the charm. After all, they were only doing their job. He stood watching as the two men started rummaging through his bag. Suddenly his world turned upside down. He stood, mouth gaping, as one of the officers pulled out a brown paper package he had never seen before. They looked at him questioningly. "What is in the parcel?" one of them enquired. Recovering quickly, Hans spurted out that it was a present for a friend. The man eyed him closely and asked for it to be unwrapped. Hans was about to reveal the contents when the second officer produced another, smaller and similarly wrapped, package. Hans was dumfounded.

The two officials marched him into a back office and ordered him to sit down. They waited until a third man, who was clearly their superior, entered the room. He looked at Hans in disgust and ordered his two juniors to finish opening the packages. Hans sat stunned as the bags came into view, each containing what seemed to be white powder. He knew instantly what they were, having seen something similar many times. In a total daze, he sat, his mouth gaping, his mind numb. The next hour passed in a haze. People came and left; they checked his belongings minutely before taking them away. His passport and mobile had been scrutinised and confiscated.

Sitting in the bland room guarded by the two police officers, Hans's mind was beginning to work again when a couple of plain-clothes men walked in. The first one introduced himself as the head of narcotics squad at the airport. He then turned to the man next to him, announcing that his name was De Boers, the duty lawyer who had been assigned to him. Hans was then arrested and taken away in cuffs, closely shadowed by the new arrivals. He was bundled into a waiting van and driven off.

Hours of interrogation followed. Hans was advised to cooperate fully and to tell them where he had gotten the drugs and whom they were going to. He repeated that he had no idea how they'd gotten into his bag, that it was all a big mistake, that he had been set up. And no, he was not a dealer or a mule. His request to call his lawyer or a friend was denied. Daylight was breaking when, eventually, he was led to a cell and unceremoniously dumped there. The door slammed shut with a loud metallic clang, and he was left on his own.

He lay on the hard bed, exhausted and confused; his mouth dry from too much champagne. He tried to focus, to think back to what had happened on the plane. His bags had been in the bin above him, and he couldn't recall anyone getting up during the flight or, for that matter, having used the same compartment, unless of course he had fallen asleep and missed it. He discarded that thought immediately, as he had not slept; that he was sure of. No one had approached him after he'd left the plane. He always kept well apart from people because he hated the smell of sweaty passengers and disliked being bumped into. Wracking his mind, he thought that it had to be someone somewhere before he'd boarded.

Natasha had left at nine o'clock that morning. After he had waved her off, he had gone to the lounge and made a couple of calls; then we went to have a shower, get dressed, and pack his bag. His bag had been empty, he knew for certain, as he always made sure he unpacked everything. He hated not putting things away, even for an overnight stay. He had then gone to the kitchen, made a mug of coffee, and phoned Jane.

Hans rubbed his hands over his face. Damn, he was tired. He closed his eyes, but sleep would not come. As he lay there, he continued to retrace his movements.

The taxi had come to pick him up, and he had placed his bag and briefcase beside him on the back seat. At the station, he had not let either item out of his sight. Same at the airport. He had helped Jane check in and then had gone through passport control and security. Now, there was a thing: had he had these parcels at that time then, surely, they would have been spotted. But no, nothing unusual had occurred.

He and Jane had sat at the bar, where he had given her the watch and he had gone to the toilet. He suddenly sat bolt upright, his heart thumping. The bitch! The little vengeful bloody bitch! It was she who had slipped the packages into his bag whilst he was away for the those few minutes. But wait, no, it wasn't possible. Where would she have gotten the drugs from? OK, her ex-husband was a drug baron, but he hadn't been in the flat for weeks, months perhaps, and no self-respecting criminal of his calibre would risk keeping stuff in his home—well, not that quantity. The dope found in Hans's case would have cost her a fortune, and he doubted very much if she had the first idea where to get that quantity from. No, it couldn't have been Jane. And anyway, how did the local customs know? Thinking back at the initial approach by the two officials, Hans felt it certainly seemed that they were waiting for him. Who would know his movements, and who wanted him put away? Whoever it was would have had to place the gear in his bag and then tip off the police. He sat there rubbing his eyes. Nothing made sense.

Ron? Was it Ron? Had he found out about Hans's plans to leave and retire? Hans knew the man was ruthless, but no, it couldn't have been him. Ron didn't, know and even if he did suspect something, it was certainly not in his interests to have his trusted associate thrown into jail a week, no days, before the culmination of two massive deals.

A sudden thought came to Hans. Was it to do with those people Ron had met in Boston? By the sound of things, they were a truly nasty bunch. Perhaps it was a warning. He had to speak to Ron, and soon. Feeling that he had to get out of this place, he went to the door and started shouting and banging, demanding his lawyer come to see him. He was ignored.

Hans must have drifted off to sleep. He was awakened by the rattling sound of keys in the door. The duty lawyer appeared, flanked by a policeman who placed a tray in front of Hans. Hans looked at the unappetising food and at the weak, watery coffee. Although not hungry, he took a few bites and winced as he sipped the burning, tasteless drink. Before the lawyer had time to say anything, Hans verbally laid into him, demanding to make a phone call to his proper lawyer and requesting the man contact Ron. The brief looked at him with a bored look and asked several questions, which Hans answered. The man then rose, promising to follow up on his client's request for his lawyer but saying he could not call his boss in England; it was out of his hands and outside the scope of his duties. He left, leaving Hans alone, staring at the food in front of him.

Night was falling when Hans heard keys rattling in the door once again. He sighed in relief as he saw the tall, black-haired figure of his lawyer enter the cell. The man stuck his hand out, shook Hans's hand, pulled up a chair, and laid his briefcase on the small table. He enquired how his client was doing before announcing that he had managed to secure a temporary release. It wouldn't be until early the next morning since the officials had already gone home for the night. He would be back first thing. Hans was not amused and resisted making any comments. The man had done his best, but officialdom prevailed. Hans was about to tell his brief what had happened when the man held up his hand. "Not now, Mr van der Brawn. You can tell me everything in the privacy of my office. Try to get some sleep; you look as if you need it. I'll be back first thing tomorrow." He smiled and rose to leave.

<hr />

Hans had slept badly. His tiny cell was hot and stuffy, and he couldn't stop thinking about who could have planted the drugs in his bag. The more he thought, the more he concluded it had to be Jane. But how? He rose from his hard bed; his back was hurting. He walked around the tiny room and, as he did so, got a strong whiff of his body odour; God, he needed a shower. It was daylight, a weak sun peeping through the clouds. He had no idea what time it was; they had taken away his watch, tie, shoes, and jacket. He was impatient. His lawyer had said he would be round first thing: *It must be 9 a.m. now, surely.* The door suddenly opened, and a tray was shoved on the floor. Hans's heart sank, breakfast, meaning it was only 6.30 a.m. He looked at the food in disgust and sipped the tasteless brown liquid, taking it back to his bed. He just lay there in a trance, devoid of any ideas or answers. He had never felt so lonely or so miserable.

At last, he heard the deep voice of his brief outside in the corridor, and soon afterwards the tall figure entered the cell, seemingly taking over the entire space. "Very sorry to be late. I did intend getting here first thing, but I was delayed." He looked at his dishevelled client and continued, saying, "You're free to come along with me to my office, but you'll have to always remain in my sight. Do you understand? I will explain outside." He looked at Hans intently, then nodded and led his client down to the hall, where papers were signed before Hans was reunited with his belongings.

Once in the car, the lawyer turned and looked at Hans. "I got a phone call this morning saying that you are under investigation for money laundering. They don't have sufficient evidence to keep you in for now. That's why I was late."

Hans remained slumped in his seat, incapable of saying anything, not understanding what was happening to him. Looking up wearily, he said, "I need a shower and some clean clothes. Take me home."

The lawyer shook his head. "Not possible. Your flat has been sealed by the police, and you, like me, aren't allowed anywhere near it. What the hell have you done, Hans? I will get my secretary to go out and buy some clothes, and you can have a shower at my office. Then, we must talk and talk seriously."

A couple of hours later, Hans was sitting across the large partners' desk, feeling refreshed after a good wash and dressed in clean clothes. He asked for a second strong cup of coffee and started to feel a little more human.

His lawyer watched him carefully. "Right, I think it's time you tell me everything from the start; don't leave anything out. I want just the facts, nothing else. You'd better start from the time you left Amsterdam a few days ago. Understand?"

Hans nodded, took a deep breath, and started telling the man everything—well, nearly everything. He omitted to mention the true nature of his visit to Liverpool and Belfast, just saying it was for routine business and meetings with his clients. He briefly thought about skipping over his encounter with Natasha and the sad error he had made the day of Jane's visit but decided to come clean.

The brief sat silently, listening intently, making copious notes. When Hans had finished, there was a long silence as the man sat back, his hands clasped under his chin, deep in thought. At last, he looked up. "Do you have any suspicions? Any idea who would want you out of the way or do this to you?"

Hans had lots of ideas and gave the man his thoughts.

"In a way, I agree with you, but it doesn't really stack up and doesn't explain this latest accusation of money laundering. Did Mrs Stokes have any idea, or did she have any involvement in your financial affairs?"

Hans shook his head. "No, no one has access to my bank details, certainly not Jane, so I don't understand who made this false accusation or why it has been made."

The lawyer pursed his lips. "The fact is that someone has, and the sooner we know who, the sooner we can get you out. As for the drugs in your case, I have strong feeling it is the doing of Mrs Stokes. You know the saying—a spurned woman ..." He left the phrase unfinished. "You say Mrs Stokes was booked on the London flight leaving a short while after yours. However, initial enquiries indicate that she did not get on the plane. Her luggage was off-loaded and remains unclaimed."

Hans looked shocked. He was incredulous. "You must be mistaken. She was most definitely booked on that flight. I was with her and helped her check in."

The man across the desk shrugged. "I'm only telling you what my assistant and the police have found out. Do you have any idea where she could be or where she could have gone? We need to speak to her, preferably before the cops do."

Hans's mind was whirling, and he was dazed. He quickly came round and suggested the lawyer speak with his boss and ask Ron if he had heard from Jane. The part he was not looking forward to, was when it was mentioned that he had been arrested for drug smuggling. Hans winced at the thought.

The lawyer agreed and got his secretary to ring the number Hans was writing down. The phone on the desk suddenly came to life. The lawyer answered, explaining who he was, then handed the receiver to Hans. With a trembling hand and a dry mouth, Hans managed to croak a few words. He found it difficult to speak and to explain the situation he was in; he could hear Ron's frustration and feel the man's annoyance. He handed the received back to the lawyer, asking him to explain what had happened. Hans sat listening and heard Ron's voice as it got louder and louder, swearing and cursing. Hans was impressed at the man across from him, at his calmness and patience, and felt a whole lot better thinking he had him on his side. At last, it was agreed that Ron should make the trip over to Amsterdam to meet the two of them face to face; matters like this were better not discussed over the phone. Before hanging up, Ron was asked to contact his wife and find out where she was.

CHAPTER 29

Ron Stokes was not a happy man. His day had started badly after a sleepless night. All he could think of was that call from those creeps in Boston. He hadn't like what he had heard and certainly did not like the threatening tone. Then came the call from that useless Frenchman telling him about the ferry delay, saying that no one knew when the shipments would be able to make their way over to the UK, although they were expected sometime within the next three to four days. It all meant more hassle, more reorganising, and certainly more possibility for disasters. This deal was proving to be a major headache and costly. Ron decided there and then that it would be the last of that kind. He hoped he could believe the little man that everything was safe and that he was guarding the shipments in his warehouse with his life. Well, time would tell. Ron just prayed the ferries would resume service very soon.

He had been mulling over this last turn of events when he had received the call dropping the bombshell that Hans, his closest and most trusted associate, a man he had nurtured and taught, had been arrested at Amsterdam airport for smuggling drugs. He could not believe what he'd heard; the stupid idiot seemed to have been set up, by all accounts by that silly tart of a wife of Ron's. What was going on? He knew Hans and his estranged wife were having an affair and was happy with that, had no problem with it. In fact, he admired his friend for having the nerve to openly screw his wife. OK, the story was that he was keeping Jane happy, out of harm's way; Ron was fine with that, but now, what the hell was going on? His whole world was falling in. Without Hans, he would be hard-pressed to see the two deals through, especially the Irish one. Hans had the contacts and the know-how and had planned everything. This was a deal that just had to be saved and seen through to the end. It was too big and too dangerous to walk away from.

Gulping down the last mouthful of his tea, Ron threw the mug at the floor in a rage, shattering the cup to smithereens. He stormed through to the bedroom, where he collected a few items, which he tossed in his overnight bag. Grabbing his briefcase, he hurried out the door. Just in time to catch the train to Heathrow, he sat glaring out the window as the rain beat down.

Feeling nausea coming on as he went through customs at Schiphol, Ron wondered whether he would be targeted as well. He shook himself down: Stupid, dumb idiot, how the hell would anybody know you were associated with a Dutch trafficker anyway? He got cross with himself for feeling weakness. Now was not the time for it; now was the time to show leadership and resolve and to ensure he got his man out of trouble fast.

On the way into Amsterdam, Ron called his lawyer. An abrupt voice came on, demanding to know who was calling and the purpose of the call, then immediately softened upon recognising the caller. A few seconds later, Ron was talking to his brief, a man he knew well and trusted implicitly. After a few banal exchanges, Ron came to the point. "Have you contacted Jane?" he demanded outright.

There was a slight pause before the reply. "Yes and no. I sent a letter, as you instructed, to her office and her flat, and a copy was sent to your place in France. I also tried to call her yesterday to make sure she had received it, but there was no reply, so I left a message both with her secretary and on her answering machine. I also tried her mobile but couldn't get through."

Ron grunted. What was she playing at? Probably just buying time, but it was odd she hadn't answered her mobile, as she was endlessly on the thing. He thanked his lawyer and hung up.

The taxi dropped him off outside a fine old building, typical of Amsterdam, and he marched through the heavy carved doors, making his way across to the reception desk. He was immediately shown to a lift and was taken to the fourth floor before being ushered into a large office. There he was greeted by a tall, dark-haired man dressed in in a well-cut suit and a crisp pink shirt with a matching tie. He came striding across the room, hand outstretched, and welcomed Ron like a long-lost friend. Introductions completed, he showed his visitor to an adjoining room, where his client was seated, hunched up and looking haggard. Hans glanced up at his boss but remained in his chair. To Ron, the man he had known so well looked as if he had aged ten years; hair dishevelled, with a two-day stubble and sunken eyes, he looked a broken man. Ron nodded and sat himself across the low coffee table, the lawyer seating himself between them. There was an awkward silence before the brief decided to speak.

"Mr Stokes, very good of you to come so quickly. As you are aware, your friend and associate Mr van der Brawn is in some bother, and I will not mince my words: it's big trouble. I have managed, giving my personal assurances, to secure bail for Mr van der Brawn for now, but I must warn you that your friend will be arrested again very soon." He looked over to Hans.

Ron was silent, clenching his jaw and twisting his hands. He wanted to yell at Hans, ask him what the hell he was playing at; he could have easily hit the man, but he knew that would not solve anything. "What do you mean by 'arrested again'? On what grounds? And why was he arrested in the first place?"

The lawyer looked between the two men before answering. "It seems, as you have been made aware, that Mr van der Brawn was caught entering the country with a large amount of illegal substance. How it got into your friend's bag is not clear. My assistant is currently on the case. We're making our own enquiries. From all accounts, it is extremely likely that your wife placed the packages in the bag, but this will be difficult to prove. We have only Hans's version of events. We urgently need to talk to your wife."

Ron glowered at his friend and took a deep breath. "You'd better tell me the story, your version, in full, without missing a single point. Start from the time you left Belfast, going right up to the minute you were stopped. I know you've already told our friend here, but I want to hear it from you, in full. Never thought you would be such a stupid idiot; thought I had taught you to always think of consequences and never to let your guard down. Now, start."

It took Hans awhile before he eventually started relating the story. As requested, he told Ron everything, from meeting Natasha at the airport, to Jane walking in and getting the wrong impression, to the argument he'd had with Jane and how she had agreed to take him to the airport. He explained that he had helped her check in for the London flight before they met up for a drink, where he gave her the watch, which she accepted. Everything. The only thing he did not mention was his plan to leave Ron and make a new life for himself and Jane abroad. The whole time he was telling his story, the lawyer made more notes, jotting things down and underlining various words. Hans wondered why he was doing this; it was the third time he had told his story, and each time the man had done the same.

Exhausted by the time he had finished, Hans slumped back into his chair. With his eyes glazed, he watched Ron's jaw tighten even more and the colour in his cheeks brighten. To his surprise, his boss did not erupt but merely turned to the lawyer.

"You are telling me Hans is going to be arrested again. Why?"

The man looked at his guest straight in the eye. "The police have notified me that they are also looking into money laundering allegations. It seems that on checking my client's accounts, they noticed some transactions involving banks in Switzerland and the Bahamas."

Ron said nothing. Now was not the time to quiz his friend about such matters, not with a stranger in the room, even if he was a lawyer. "I'm sure that's totally false. Hans would never do anything like that, just as he would not knowingly carry drugs. As his partner and associate, I can vouch that our business deals are all above board."

The lawyer looked at his guest and nodded. He didn't believe a word but didn't show it.

They discussed various options and possibilities for the next hour before Ron was shown to the door. "Please rest assured, Mr Stokes, I will do everything within my power to help our friend. Like you, I am sure he is innocent on both counts. We will win." He stopped before reaching the main lobby. "We do need to speak to your wife, urgently, so if you could help track her down, that would be of great help. I am willing to fly to London at any time to talk to her, but I stress, it is crucial we speak to her before the police do."

Sean and his Dutch counterpart were sitting in a car across the street from the lawyer's office. The operation had moved from the surveillance of Hans's flat, once the news had been received that he had been arrested, to keeping tabs on the man and his lawyer. They had watched as a well-dressed man had entered the office a couple of hours earlier; they'd managed to get a few photos. Whilst he was inside, they sent the pictures to head office and to London. An identification came back within thirty minutes which confirmed Sean's suspicions. He thought he had recognised the man but couldn't be sure. Ronald G. Stokes, a well-known and clever criminal who had been on their radar for some time, was suspected of drug trafficking, extortion, and possibly arms dealing. He was a clever professional crook who'd always covered his tracks well. They had known he had an associate in Holland but up to now couldn't pin anyone down. It was that suspicion which had made Sean go to his counterparts in Amsterdam. Thanks to their keen and eager chief, it wasn't long before they had identified Hans van der Brawn as the man. He also was well known to them, and like Sean, they knew he had an associate in England. Now things were coming together. The two men in the car were excited.

They watched as Ron came out and got into a waiting cab. A second car pulled out and followed the taxi to the airport. From that moment, Ron Stokes would be under surveillance 24/7; every move, every call, would be monitored. The net was closing in.

On his way back, Ron called his lawyer in London and reported on his recent meeting. "I can smell big trouble. This whole affair is no good. I need you to find Jane quickly. Get her to meet both of us. Use any excuse you have to but find her." There was a grunt from the other end. It wasn't going to be easy, especially after the divorce notice he had sent.

Ron thought for a long time. Things were not looking good. He'd had no news from the Frenchman or of when the ferry strike would end; his main man had been arrested and bailed, but it was very likely he would be charged, and that meant he would no longer be involved. Everything was going pear-shaped at the wrong moment. Ron had no backup plan and no one capable of taking over from Hans. He decided there and then to look for a couple of new associates, to take time and train them up to his standards, teaching them his way of thinking and how he operated. The only problem was that he hadn't the time for it, nor did he think any of his contacts were good enough or trustworthy enough. It wasn't going to be easy; he would have to take over and see the two current operations through himself, then start looking. He suddenly felt tired; did he really need all this, all the hassle? Yes, he certainly did. The thought of the millions he was going to make, the prestige he would have, and all the effort and hard work he had put in to get this far—now was not the time to get cold feet or feel sorry for himself.

He had to get hold of Jane, to scare her into admitting she had placed the drugs in Hans's bag and probably tipped off the police. No, she couldn't have done it, not Jane on her own. She didn't have the brains or the nous; she may have had a friend or someone else do it and paid them. Well, in that case she would tell him, he would make sure of that. Once she admitted to it and all this mess was cleared up, he would deal with her and whoever. Forget divorce, payments, and settlements; the only thing she or they would get would be a trip to the other side. And that, he would do himself if he had to.

CHAPTER 30

Sean was sitting at his desk back in London staring out the window, his mind miles away. He had returned the day after Ron had flown back. There was little he could do in Amsterdam; the Dutch were monitoring things and would report back on any progress the police were making. He liked and trusted the people over there, as they were extremely professional and methodical, and he had built up an instant working relationship with them. They thought as he did; they operated as he did; and they in turn realised he was a sharp and tenacious ally: the friendship was reciprocal.

He got up and made himself a mug of strong coffee, which always helped his brain cells to work, and was about to call Charly Flynn when the phone rang. He picked up. The strong Dutch-accented voice immediately came to the point. "We have just had a call from the French police. They have found a burnt-out truck container in the wood not far from the dumped lorry cab—you remember, the one I told you about. Well, it's not nice, not nice at all. Not sure why it has taken them so long, but there you are; that's the French for you."

Sean had not taken much notice of the story; the Dutch had told him about a tip-off they had had and how some truck had been found dumped in a ravine. Nothing else was said, and he had put it out of his mind. "What was in it?" he asked absently minded, his thoughts on the conversation he would have with Charly.

"Bodies, lots of them. About thirty-five from what they could make out."

Sean sat stunned, horrified at what he had heard. "What kind of bodies?" he asked, immediately feeling stupid.

"Human. Some may have died in the fire—others possibly before—or because of the smoke. The French are working on it right now. You realise what that means, don't you?"

Sean shook his head. "Not really, no." He remembered his friend telling him about an operation being carried out in France, but he hadn't taken much interest at the time.

"Well, we decided to follow the convoy from the Italian French border right up to Calais last week. We had been told it may have been carrying drugs and decided to shadow it. Luckily, I managed to persuade a French colleague I knew to join us. After discussion with his boss, we set up a joint operation and he decided to let the trucks through the frontier. One of my guys teamed up with one of theirs and followed the trucks to their destination. The eight trucks, all from the same transport company as the one found, passed close by to where the burnt-out wreck was lying and ended up in Calais. I was going to tell you but got diverted when van der Brawn got picked up at the airport. Anyway, the trucks were booked on a ferry to Folkestone but have been delayed by the go-slow."

Sean was horrified again. "Does that mean they're transporting people?" he asked.

"Not sure. Our sources indicated that they thought it was drugs. That's why we got involved. Anyway, it seems whatever is in them is UK-bound."

Sean cursed silently to himself. How could he have missed that one? He had found out about the Afghan shipment to Ireland but hadn't heard anything about other shipments by road. It would have been very risky to transport so much stuff by lorry all the way up from Italy; border checks were tight. He hesitated before asking, "Are you sure it's not human trafficking? If it's the same trucks as this other one, the likelihood of it being the same is high in my opinion. I think I know about every drug shipment in the world just now. I could be wrong, but my bet is that it's not dope. Where are the trucks now?"

The Dutchman thought a short while. "It makes sense. I tend to agree with you. These operators usually specialise in one or the other. The convoy left the docks after the ferry agent on duty turned down a bribe. The man in charge requested he be notified as soon as they had space for the entire convoy. Our men followed them to a warehouse on the outskirts of town. The place is under twenty-four-seven surveillance."

Sean grunted. It was not like him to be hesitant; normally he planned and made up his mind in an instant, but this was different. His instincts told him to allow the trucks to board the ferry and then follow them to their destination before swooping and arresting the gang. Again, this was different. If this involved humans, who had no doubt have suffered during the long voyage, he certainly didn't want to prolong their agony. "If it was me, I would order the place to be raided now, immediately; that way at least lives could be saved, and we could put those people out of their misery."

"I agree. However, our counterparts and the police in Calais don't want to do that. They say it would be too dangerous and that they don't have sufficient resources. My feeling is that they want to wash their hands of all this. Politically, there is no gain, and they can point the finger of blame at you lot. If it was drugs or arms, well, that would be different—big headlines on how they've saved the world et cetera, et cetera."

"That sounds very cynical. Never thought you were like that." Sean chuckled. "What do you want to do?"

The two men discussed what to do at length. Sean agreed to warn UK border control and the police. They would let the trucks into the UK unhindered and follow them to their destination or destinations before swooping and, hopefully, arresting the entire gang. It was risky, but there was no other real alternative since the French were unwilling to do anything. "We must make sure there is no more bloodshed."

Sean watched the office workers in the building across the small street beavering away, unaware of the nastiness of greedy traffickers who made a living out of other people's suffering. He felt disgusted. He loved his job but never could get used to how low people would or could stoop in order to make money. The thought of all the suffering caused by this scum spurred him on.

He picked up the phone and called Charly. After the usual opening banter, he told his friend of the latest news involving the presumed human shipment, before moving on to bring the man up to speed on their case. He was relieved that Charly had agreed that he had made the right call on the latest load, although it did little to relieve Sean's concerns and disgust. Before hanging up, they arranged to meet up in Belfast at the end of the week to finalise a reception plan for the forthcoming drug shipment. Sean would make his way up to Liverpool and board the same ferry as the container and be met by Charly. "Looking forward to a bit of fun and games." He chuckled.

Sean sat for a long time staring into space, his mind working overtime as it mulled over what to do and how best to act. He had lost track of time and was brought out of his trance by the ringing of the phone on his desk. He stretched and rubbed his eyes before picking up, noting that everyone had by now deserted the office across the street.

The Dutch voice sounded calm as usual. "My friend, you sound as if I have awakened you. Sorry."

Sean shook his head. "No, not asleep. Just thinking, going over everything. With so much going on, I needed to sort my mind out and plan. I was in a different world."

"Sorry to bring you back to reality. This may throw some of your plans out slightly. I have spoken to my boss, and he agrees with you: we need to move to save these poor people. Like you and me, he is convinced it's not drugs. Luckily, the union came to an agreement a few hours ago; sailing will resume by tomorrow evening. I have instructed our agent to ensure all the trucks are loaded on the first ferry the following day and to notify the transport company accordingly. My agents will board the same boat and keep tabs on the drivers. I will text you all the trucks' registrations once we know them, as well as our men's details. The rest I will leave to you."

Sean liked the idea and was relieved that the saga would soon be ending. He thanked his friend and immediately called his boss and brought him up to speed. He was promised everything would be ready and that both border control and the police would be waiting.

———◆———

Ron's day was going from bad to worse; he was in a foul mood. First thing in the morning, his lawyer had called to say that Jane's parents had suddenly left, the neighbour believed for Scotland. Nothing had been heard of Jane, and she had not responded. All his attempts had been met by the same message—the number was unavailable. Ron fumed. Where is the bloody woman? She couldn't have disappeared into thin air. And her parents, why leave suddenly, why now?? He instructed his brief to keep trying and to pull out all the stops to locate the parents.

After that, he had called the Dutch lawyer and was told Hans was being arrested again, this time for money laundering. The process could take a while, and he couldn't promise an early release for his client.

By two o'clock, Ron had had a third call, this one from the French contact, who told him the shipment would be leaving the next day. He was anything but a happy man when Ron instructed him to be on the trip and take full responsibility, right up to final delivery. The Frenchman pointed out that this was not in the agreement, that if he had to do the journey, he needed a bigger bonus; he was a boss, not one of his gophers. After some haggling, Ron had no choice but to offer the man a bigger cut. It stuck in his gullet; he hated being in such a position, and he swore loudly. That damned fool Hans, it was all his fault. Had he not got himself arrested, he would have met the convoy and escorted it to its destination, taking control and overseeing that everything went smoothly. Ron had decided not to go himself; he couldn't be in two places at a time, and he chose to attend to the bigger, more lucrative deal, the Irish one.

Ron picked up the phone and called a trusted thug whom he'd often used on his human-smuggling operations; the man knew what to do as his warehouse was the convoy's destination. Once the trucks had been parked inside that vast hanger, the migrants would be sorted, given clean clothes and some cash, allocated to a van or minibus, and be driven away by whomever had bought them. The man took it all in his stride and accepted the extra payment.

The two deals were turning into a nightmare. The first one had cost Ron a large compensation sum for the shortage due to the accident; for the ones who had died in the fire. His client was not happy and insisted he get a discount on shipment number two. On top of that, the extra payment to the French agent and this latest one meant that Ron's profit had been halved. All Hans's fault, the bastard; his stupidity had cost Ron hundreds of thousands of pounds. The man would pay—and pay dearly.

Sean was about to leave the office when he suddenly remembered something; he rummaged through his wallet and pulled out a crumpled piece of paper. Smiling, he picked up the phone and dialled the number. A man with a slight Welsh accent came on, giving his name and asking who was calling. Sean put on his best and smoothest voice. "Alwyn, you don't know me, but you met my friend Major Hollins a month or so ago at John Jackson's funeral, the man who was killed in Belfast."

The reporter immediately perked up and pricked his ears. Yes, of course he remembered, a very nice man who had offered to help his friend track down his brother's killer. He and his friend had been chasing their tails for the past two and half weeks down on the South Coast. His friend had got wind of some smuggling deal and persuaded him to come along, but despite their best efforts, they hadn't discovered anything. They had decided enough was enough and had planned to return north the following day. "Yes, I recall. You're a policeman or investigator, aren't you?"

Sean ignored the question. "I think I have a tip-off for you. In fact, I know I have, but you must promise me something." He paused until he heard a grunt. "Is that a yes or a no? What I'm going to tell you is

169

very sensitive and delicate, so I need to have your full assurance that you will do exactly as I instruct you."

Although a small reporter for a local paper, Alwyn Jones was not slow or stupid; his instincts immediately told him that what he was about to hear was special, something that could change his life and probably save his local rag. It was not every day that some top brass cop, or whatever this man was, called and promised him insider information. He saw no choice but to go along with whatever the conditions were, but he had to pretend to put up a fight. He gulped. "OK, I promise. But first, what are the conditions? I can't promise if I don't know what I'm getting myself into."

Sean smiled to himself. "We're on to a big smuggling case. It will be coming to a head tomorrow. A large shipment of eight trucks will be landing at Folkestone first thing in the morning. The plan is to follow the convoy to its destination, and once it's there, the police will swoop. Now, I'm giving you the chance of a lifetime, a chance to put yourself and your paper in the limelight, but you must do exactly as I say. Any deviation or change on your part could jeopardise the whole operation. And I will hold you solely responsible, do you hear? You have a choice, fame or oblivion and a life in jail," he said, stressing the last few words.

The reporter's hands started to tremble; his breathing became slightly ragged. He nodded and croaked his agreement. He listened carefully to what his caller was telling him, making a few notes as he went along. He swore not to tell anyone and accepted the conditions he was given.

After hanging up, Alwyn sat for a long time, his hands shaking, excitement mounting, perspiration trickling down his face. He could not believe what he had heard. If all went to plan, his life would change. It was going to be difficult to persuade his friend to go home alone and not to tell him—he would lose a good buddy—but he had sworn on his mother's head, so no going back. He picked up a bottle of beer and gulped it down. *Cheers to a new life.*

CHAPTER 31

There was a flurry of activity in the warehouse situated on the outskirts of Calais. Men came and went. A couple of vans drove in and were waved in before the shutter door closed.

The two men sitting in the clapped-out van just up the road noted every movement, photographed every vehicle and person entering and leaving the premises, and scribbled down reg numbers. It wasn't easy as daylight had not yet broken, but with the help of modern technology and cameras, they missed nothing. It was just before 8 a.m. when the first truck came rumbling out of the gates, closely followed by seven others. The two men in the van hung back and radioed their colleagues, who picked up the tail and followed the convoy to the ferry port.

As with the night watch, the new group recorded every movement. Boarding was prompt, and thanks to the office manager, the trucks were shown in first and placed at the front of the ship. As instructed, the crew made sure they were all close together. Satisfied all lorries and drivers were on board, the surveillance team sent all registration numbers to their English contact. They waited until the ferry had departed.

Sean's phone pinged, and he immediately forwarded the message to Folkestone. He had considered going down there himself but decided it was not necessary. His boss had confirmed that everything was in place, and everyone was on red alert. The gang would not be left unwatched for a second, and a series of checkpoints and tails had been organised along the way. More than a hundred men and women had been mobilised, and all possibilities had been covered. The net was tightening.

The French contact made his way up on deck and pulled out a packet of his favourite cigarettes; he dragged deeply as he watched the coastline slowly get smaller. Despite the extra cash he had managed to negotiate, he was not a happy man. He did not like ferries, did not like "les English", and certainly did not like waking up so early. Why the hell had that Ron man changed the plans? He didn't know, but clients were clients, and this one paid well. Still, he didn't like having to get involved directly; the thought of spending two days in England with their rotten food and warm beer did not appeal to him. Perhaps he could try his luck and wrangle a few more euros out of the man. He flicked his stub over the side and decided against the idea. No, better still, this would be the last of such deals. He never liked them in the first place, not that he cared what cargo he transported, just that with all the problems they'd had lately, it was time to cut ties with the Englishman.

The Frenchman was joined by his lead driver. They chatted about football. The man was a fanatic. As the boat approached the coast, the white cliffs looming ever closer, they made their way belowdecks and joined the other drivers.

The first car to leave the ferry was a white Audi with Dutch registration. It was followed by a procession of eight trucks, all bearing the same name and logo. They headed for customs and queued patiently until the officials were happy and waved them on. Once past the port authority gates, they pulled up in a lay-by until they all had been let through. The white car had vanished, and soon a stream of vehicles were heading for the motorway. Once the last truck came into view, the little Frenchman nodded to his driver and the convoy trundled off towards their destination, making the short journey to the small village. Not too much longer now and it would be all over.

Heading north, they made their way up the A260 for a short while before turning off onto small, narrow roads meandering their way through the hills; the drivers were not best pleased. A small private plane flew overhead, heading to Canterbury, the noise of

172

its single engine echoing through the countryside. The Frenchman's stomach started to churn. For some reason he was nervous. It was understandable, this was the first time he had accompanied his men on such a journey. He looked over at the driver, who was whistling silently to himself; he felt like asking him to stop but desisted.

As the light aircraft past overhead the convoy, the crew radioed to their colleagues on the ground. Soon afterwards, a police helicopter took off. It wasn't long before a couple of motorcycles came up and began following the convoy, unable to overtake the trucks because of the windy road, trailing the trucks patiently.

Alwyn Jones was following instructions. He had previously checked in with police headquarters in Folkestone as instructed and gotten his orders, which were to accompany the chief of police and to watch, but on no account to get in the way or deviate from his instructions. As he sat in the back seat of the chief's car listening to the crackle of radio conversation, his apprehension and excitement grew. In all his years as a reporter, he had never been part of such an operation—hadn't ever dreamt he even would be. With every mile, they were getting closer to the rendezvous point. The circling helicopter up ahead relayed up-to-date information as more vans and outriders converged upon the unsuspecting tranquil village from various directions. All roads were monitored and patrolled. From what Alwyn could gather, there were dozens of men and vehicles heading for a small village some ten miles away.

The lead truck driver looked up to the sky as he heard the loud thud of a helicopter; in the distance he spotted a yellow dot circling low over the rolling hills. "Looks like a rescue copter. Must have been an accident on the main road." He pointed in the direction of the noise. His boss peered into the same direction, a deep frown crossing his brow, his anxiety growing even more.

He grunted and wiped a bead of perspiration from his brow. "What does that mean for us? Are we heading that way?" He looked over nervously to his man.

"No, nothing to worry about. We're just ten minutes away, there over the far brow." The lead driver sniffed and looked at his side mirror. Everyone was following comfortably, keeping a couple of car lengths between them as ordered. Behind the last truck, the two motorbikes had been joined by a car and a white van. He briefly thought about pulling over to let any traffic pass but decided against it; way too complicated—and it would cause mayhem on these narrow roads.

As the convoy approached the small village of Eltham, neatly nestled among the rolling hills, the lead driver turned to his boss. "Two minutes and we're there, boss." His passenger sat up and glanced out his side window, no longer able to see the helicopter. They passed a large sign pointing to Eltham vineyard; the boss inwardly snorted and shook his head. What did the English know about winemaking? What a bunch of arrogant idiots, thinking they could make wine. He involuntarily screwed up his nose. Just before entering the village, the driver indicated left and turned in to a narrow lane. A hundred yards further on, they were confronted by a huge warehouse in the middle of a yard surrounded by a tall fence with razor-sharp wire at the top. As they drove through the gate, the driver gave a blast of his horn and, as if by magic, the huge, shuttered door slowly opened. They entered the cavernous depot and parked at the far end. Once the last truck had stopped and all engines had been turned off, the giant door closed, and the drivers got out.

They were immediately met by half a dozen men in overalls and balaclavas who waved and pointed to a door leading into a shabby office which doubled as a canteen. The French boss followed his drivers and immediately asked to speak with the head man. He was ignored. He looked round the room in disgust as his drivers immediately went to the toilet or made themselves comfortable, some of them chatting among themselves in low voices. The little man turned to his driver. "What now? Where is the man in charge? What's happening?"

The man looked at his boss, an expression of half surprise and half pity on his face. "The chap in charge was the one who greeted us, the one with the blue mask. They are now checking the contents and sorting the consignment. You saw the vans parked at the far end. Well, the migrants will be split into prearranged groups depending on who has bid for what, then they'll be loaded on to the various vehicles and driven to wherever. We wait here until they have left, and we get the all clear."

"How long does it take? How long before we can leave?"

"Normally a couple of hours if all goes well. The boys need a rest anyway. The cops here are very strict and check tachometers, especially if the trucks are foreign." He sat down with a cup of tea and offered one to his boss.

The operation seemed to take forever. The little Frenchman paced the hot, stuffy room relentlessly, sweat pouring from his brow. His driver had difficulty stopping him from leaving the room to see what was happening. The man looked like a caged lion.

The wait dragged on until the boss could no longer hold back his impatience. Striding over to the door, he threw it open and marched into the vast warehouse, where he was confronted with sudden chaos. The large shutter door had been barely opened halfway when all hell was let loose. Dozens of voices were yelling orders; the sound of gunfire echoed; flares burst into flames; and smoke quickly filled the area. Stunned, he stood, frozen, unable to comprehend what was happening. He was suddenly knocked to the floor and felt a knee pushing deep into his back. His hands were cuffed behind his back, his head covered with a sack. He lay there trembling, too scared to make a noise. All around him the deafening noise continued, a gunshot followed by a scream. He heard and sensed other bodies being told to lie flat beside him and trembled as they did so, he had no idea who anyone was or what was happening. The choking smoke of the flares made him gag.

After what seemed an eternity, the shouting ceased, replaced by a cold voice giving orders. Footsteps echoed all around the Frenchman. He smelt the fear from the man beside him and heard someone loudly groaning in pain but was too scared to whisper and ask who it was. He was suffocating under the hood. A feeling of nausea came over him, and then the unthinkable happened; he wet himself in fear.

Suddenly, unexpectedly, someone hauled him up off the ground and took off his hood. Blinking as the light hit his eyes, he took in the scene around him. Dozens of police officers, armed to the teeth, were escorting groups of men and women towards police buses. Others were rounding up men who were handcuffed and hooded, leading them to a fleet of vans. A couple of paramedics were covering a corpse.

The Frenchman looked down at his drivers, who were still lying flat on the ground. He went to bend down to the groaning man but was immediately stopped, the vicelike grip on his arm tightening. He watched as one by one they were unceremoniously lifted from the floor and marched off to a couple of waiting police vans. Then it was his turn. Half dragged, half frogmarched, he was thrown into the back of a waiting cell truck. The door slammed shut, leaving him once again in the dark.

Alwyn Jones had been watching from his seat in the back of the police car as the raid was happening. His orders were to stay there until signalled. He scribbled notes and cursed himself for not having brought his camera, then remembered his phone. Slipping it out, he filmed discreetly from his vantage point. Things had calmed down by the time a young bobby came over and waved him to join him. As the two made their way to the warehouse, Alwyn asked a few questions but was met by a stony silence. They joined a heavily armed policeman, who nodded and indicated to Alwyn to follow him. The scene was something out of a film. Dozens of armed officers were rounding up hooded and cuffed men. Others were escorting women and young men to a fleet of minibuses. A couple of medics were patching someone up, whilst two more were standing over a corpse. The reporter shook his head in disbelief.

Alwyn was about to walk over to one of the medics and ask some questions when the chief waved him over. The chief looked around, surveying the operation, and smiled. "A job well done wouldn't you say?" He continued watching his men. "A total of two hundred and eighty illegal immigrants saved with only one minor casualty. Pretty good effort from my boys."

Alwyn nodded, initially speechless. Then he asked, "Who are those men, the hooded ones?"

The policeman wrinkled his nose. "Those are the bastards who are involved in organising this racket, bloody scum. Those sitting on the floor, they're the ones who have 'bought' the poor sods and will no doubt have used them as slaves or forced labour. Not sure yet who they're working for, but you can rest assured we'll find out in no time. None of them will taste a free life ever again."

The chief turned away and ordered his men to wrap up the operation. "Well done, men. First-class job. Now, impound the trucks, seal the whole area, and get all this crowd back to base. Move it!"

The reporter watched as the vehicles moved out in a long column, motorbike outriders and police cars leading the way whilst others followed close behind. Overhead, two helicopters hovered, shadowing the convoy's every move. He turned to the chief. "How much can I write about? Should I leave parts out?"

The man looked puzzled. "You are a hack, are you not? When did you become all coy and soft? Write as much as you want. Tell the people the truth of what you have seen; let them know how low people can stoop. Just two things: don't mention the names of any of my men, which must be kept secret for their sakes, and don't say anything to anyone or print anything until you hear from me. Understood? This is an ongoing investigation, so for your career's sake, do as I say. Apart from that, feel free."

Back at the car, the chief turned and surveyed the scene one last time. Watching as several officers secured the premises, he was a happy man. Satisfied that everything was being done as ordered, he fished out his phone and called Sean.

CHAPTER 32

Ron had decided to fly over to Holland and talk to Hans; he had to find out what the man had arranged and get all the details. Now that the idiot was bunged up, it was he, Ron, who had to take control and oversee the operation. He didn't like the idea very much and would have much preferred to let his aide-de-camp get on with the dirty work but needs must; he would show everyone why he was the boss.

He had managed to secure through the efforts of the Dutch lawyer a visit. It had taken the man most of his skills of persuasion to get the interview, but after lengthy discussions with the police and the local drug enforcement agency, he had managed to arrange a meeting for the following day. Conditions were strict: the prisoner was to remain in his cell, and the lawyer had had to vouch for his client and had always to remain with both. No phones, tapes, or writing implements would be allowed, and checks would be severe.

Ron had taken a plane the evening before. The visit was scheduled for eleven o'clock the next morning. He certainly didn't want to be late. Sitting in his hotel bedroom nursing a large whisky, his mind turned to the current operation which had taken place that day. Reports from the French contact indicated that they were to board the first ferry that morning, which meant that by 3 p.m. GMT time at the latest, everything should have been settled and dusted. Ron was not overly concerned that no one had contacted him; delays happened, and his orders were to call once all the shipment had been split up and had safely left. Knowing the lads, they'd probably be tidying up, ensuring no tell-tale traces were left. The Frenchman would only call once he and his men had returned to Calais; only then would Ron transfer the extra payment.

Ron switched on the TV and found the BBC just in time to catch the ten o'clock news. The usual boring stuff, a long report about climate change, followed by speculation the ferries would strike again next week in support of their Eurotunnel workers. His mind wandered to the meeting with Hans the next day. He would need to keep calm, and not show his frustration as he had a couple of days ago. He would need to stay focussed and ask as many questions as he could, needing to know every minute detail. The ship was due to arrive in Liverpool in three days' time. Currently knowing very few of the details, he starting to get worried. When the weather forecast came on, he switched the TV off.

Ron was met the next morning by the lawyer and the two of them made their way to the detention centre. He had slept fitfully, awaking early. He was disturbed that he had still not received a call from his man in Eltham and was even more surprised at the silence from France. Having tried to ring both, with no success, he started to feel uneasy, he didn't like it. What the hell was going on? Their silence boded ill. Having no time to dwell on the matter, he decided that he'd get to work on that once back in England.

The cell was small and dingy with a metal bed tucked along one side and a small table with three chairs placed in the centre. A couple of LED bulbs provided a harsh light. The room smelled of sweat and needed a good airing.

Security had been tight with both men being searched before passing through a scanner. The lawyer's briefcase had been emptied before being handed back to him. Only a few legal papers had been allowed to be taken in. A guard escorted them to the cell and ushered them in, telling them he would be back in fifty minutes.

Hans was sitting in one of the chairs, dressed in joggers and a T-shirt, his sunken eyes and unshaven look ageing him considerably. He did not get up but just pointed to the two remaining seats. He was not looking forward to Ron's visit, he just wanted to be left alone. When he'd first been told about the proposed visit, he had asked his brief not to pursue the matter, but as expected, Ron had insisted—and what Ron wanted, Ron usually got. Hans, knowing precisely why his boss had come, had mentally prepared all the information. Conversation began with Ron asking what exactly Hans had been re-arrested for. He was told it was money laundering and that, unlike with the drugs, the police had sufficient evidence to send his client down for a very long time. With that, Ron immediately came to the point. He quizzed his aide thoroughly and demanded clear answers to every question. The lawyer sat silently, squirming inwardly at what had been planned. Now that he knew the real reason for the visit, he wasn't sure that it was a good idea. The entire conversation would be a death knell for his client should any of it be overheard or come out. He tried several times to warn Hans not to reply, not to incriminate himself further, but each time Ron cut him short and threw him a withering look.

The allotted time was up faster than Ron would have liked. He tried to have it extended, but to no avail. He rose and tapped Hans on the shoulder. "Keep smiling. I promise, we'll get you out of here sooner than you think." With that, he made for the door, closely followed by the lawyer. Once outside, Ron inhaled the fresh air and tried to blow away the heat and stuffiness of the cell. He turned to the Dutchman, who was standing at the other side of the car. "You breathe or whisper the slightest thing about what you heard, and I guarantee it will not be long before you find yourself at the bottom of a canal." He threw the man a withering look.

The lawyer was about to answer but thought better of it. Not that he was afraid; he had had plenty of threats in his career. No, being duty-bound to defend his client, he would do the best he could to get him off. He would work hard to get the man freed. Only then, and once he had been paid, would he consider going to the police.

Back at the airport, Ron tried to phone his man in Eltham but got the message that the recipient was currently unavailable. The first serious doubts started to take seed in his mind, causing him to feel uneasy. It had now been twenty-four hours since the operation should have been wrapped up, and still no contact from anyone. On the plane, somewhere over the Channel, he decided to go down and check things out. His plan had been to go home, have a quiet evening, and prepare for the upcoming operation. His flight to Belfast was booked for 1 p.m. the next day.

The traffic on the M25 was, as usual, heavy and progress was slow. As Ron approached the exit for the M20, his phone rang. Glancing down, he saw it was from his English lawyer and was disappointed. It could wait. His apprehension grew with every mile, and the sense of ill-boding intensified. With his stomach twisted into knots, he began to breathe heavily. The closer he got, the more certain he felt that something had happened. He cursed and swore to himself, promising to wreak retribution on all those useless bastard associates, especially that little toad of a Frenchman. He had never trusted the man and was now surer than ever that he had pulled a fast one. Ron promised himself that once the Irish deal was complete, he would personally go over to Calais and dispatch the man, sending him to where he belonged.

As Ron drove through Eltham, he started to feel nauseous and to shake nervously. He had to control his breathing. Turning into the lane, he looked anxiously towards the warehouse. No sooner than he had come into view of the gates, all his worst fears were confirmed. He stopped the car and stared at the compound and at the blue and white police tape surrounding it. Slowly, in a daze, he got out and made his way over to the gate. He stood there for a long time, trying to make sense of what he was seeing. Making his way round to the back of the compound and out of sight of prying eyes, he scaled the fence. Everywhere he looked were signs the police had posted warning people to keep out. Ron made his way to a small door, but it was locked. Not to worry, he knew the hiding place and went over to retrieve the key. It wasn't very safe, but who cared? There was never anything in the warehouse; it was used as a triage centre for his special shipments and sat empty between times.

Ron entered the large, cavernous space and looked around; it was empty, as it should be. As he walked over to the small office, he noticed a dark red patch on the floor and quickly realised it was blood. The office had been left in a mess. Half-empty mugs lay on the table;

crumpled-up paper, wrappings, bags, and scraps of food littered the floor. There were no signs of a struggle. He sat down heavily on one of the wooden chairs and his eyes welled up. He slammed his fist on the table in rage and yelled obscenities, his voice echoing through the warehouse. Calmer, he got up and made his way through to the empty building, every inch of which he slowly scrutinised. Apart from the bloodstain, there was no indication of what had happened.

Ron shook his head, thinking. What could have happened? Clearly the police had raided the place and probably caught everyone red-handed, but how the hell had they known? Who had betrayed Ron and his team? His rage swelled up again. He would find out, would make it mission in life to find out who he, or they, were and mete out the punishment. Whoever had grassed on him would regret their decision and wished they had never been born.

Back at the car, Ron checked his phone, but there were no messages or voice mails. He tried to call the Frenchman, but his phone rang out. Ron decided it was better not to try to call anyone else in case the cops were checking the phones; it would lead back to him. He sighed deeply. First Hans had gotten himself arrested—twice—and now this. What other disaster would befall on him? Life was not being kind to him, and he didn't understand why.

It was late evening when Ron got back to the flat. He was exhausted. On the drive back up to London, he had tried to understand, but nothing made sense to him. Surely, if someone had betrayed the organisation, why were the police not after that person? And why hadn't Ron gotten a call demanding a ransom or payment or making threats? No, it just didn't make sense. Someone somewhere had planned all this, but for what reason? Ron had paid all his suppliers, had sent the bonus to the Egyptian, and had even transferred Hans's share to the man's Swiss bank account, not that that would be of any use now. The Frenchman still had to be paid, but it couldn't have been him. It would have been completely daft. Or was it him? Perhaps he had cut a deal with the French authorities. Not possible; he had been part of the escort. OK, Ron had insisted that the Frenchman accompany his men to see how it all worked and to ensure no further losses occurred. Was that why the little frog had put up such an argument not to go?

Things went round and round in Ron's mind until he gave up, too tired to continue. He needed rest and a clear head for the next few days, and once those were over, he would go to the apartment in the South of France and think things through.

He had slept badly. Wild dreams mixed with anxiety about what was to come had made for a long night. He rose soon after 6 a.m. and took a long, hot shower. Over a cup of coffee, he trolled through the online papers but could find nothing on any police raid anywhere. He was abruptly jolted out of his world by the ringing of his mobile. He looked down at the number with trepidation.

Ron's English lawyer was a middle-aged man with a gravelly voice. He never gave any signs of emotion, whether giving good news or bad news.

"Ron, I phoned you yesterday, but you must have been busy. Don't have much good news, I'm afraid. It seems Jane has vanished from the face of the earth. No sign of her anywhere. I had my colleague in Marseille check out the flat. Neighbours seem to think she left about a week ago. Enquiries at the airport found that she had a ticket for London but never showed up at the gate."

Ron's mood darkened once again. "Have you tried the office here and checked her parents' house?" he enquired tetchily.

"Yes. No one at the office has heard from her since the day before she disappeared. I went down to the parents' house myself; it's all locked up. It seems they've gone to visit friends in Scotland. Nobody seems to know who, where, or for how long."

Ron sighed heavily. "She can't have just disappeared into thin air. You haven't been looking properly or in the right place. Unless she fell or has been pushed over a cliff, someone must know."

The lawyer remained silent for a while, then began to speak. "The only thing I can suggest is that we alert the authorities and ask both the French and British police to look into her disappearance."

"No, no, we can't do that. Must not do that at all." Ron realised he had uttered the words too quickly and in a panicky voice. The last thing he wanted at this time was for the police to start snooping around. "Sorry, didn't mean to be so sharp. Not sure if getting the cops involved just yet is a good idea. I will ask my brief in Holland to ask Hans if he knows anything. You make further enquiries. Go back to the office, ask more questions, then try to find out where the parents went and whom they're visiting. One of Jane's weaknesses is that she's devoted to her parents. And her father is not well. They can't have gone far. She's bound to be in contact with them sooner or later."

The lawyer agreed to continue his investigations and promised to call back as soon as he had any further news. After they had hung up, Ron swore once more. What the hell is happening to me? Why the hell is everything going so wrong? A thought of inspiration flashed through his mind. Yes, of course, the raid. Who else could it be but Jane, the cheating, vengeful little tart? She must have somehow got the information from Hans, probably as they were making love or whatever else they were doing and used the information to get to him. Well, she would regret her decision to cross me. Who does she think she is? He picked up the phone and dialled.

"Yeah, it's Ron. I want you to pull out all the stops and find out where that conniving little bitch of a wife of mine is, and fast. She has just wrecked a deal I had going, and I'll be damned if I'll allow her to do it again. I will pay you double, understand? Find her!" He killed the call, leaving his lawyer speechless.

CHAPTER 33

Jane Stokes, now Greta Bauman, had rented a small two-bedroom flat on the outskirts of Zurich. She had not been fussy about the location, just requested the place be in a quiet area and, above all, be clean. She had told the agent that she was flying in from abroad and requested the contract be signed electronically prior to her arrival. Having paid the deposit and three months' rent up front, she picked up the keys from the concierge and settled into her new home.

It was pleasant enough—clean, bright, and away from the bustle of the nearby main street. She had chosen the Swiss city for its central location and for its banking. Her schoolgirl German was rather rusty, but she had been listening to tapes for a couple of months and could get by, not that she intended on staying in the area for long. On arrival, the first thing she did was to cut and dye her hair. Donning a pair of oversized sunglasses, she made her way into town, where she purchased a few essentials, some trendy clothes, and a pair of dashing boots she couldn't resist. Happy with her morning's work, she entered a branch of Credit Suisse and requested to see the manager. She was about to leave when a young man, dressed immaculately and sporting a bushy moustache, appeared and greeted her. He apologised profusely for having kept her waiting and showed her into his office.

Miss Bauman explained that a few days ago she had requested her branch in Nice, not Credit Suisse, to arrange an account be opened for her here in Zurich and said that she had now come in to sign the necessary papers. Rummaging about in her new oversized tote bag, she pulled out her passport and driving licence and passed them over to the young banker. Returning from photocopying the documents, and in reply to his new client's question, he confirmed that a large amount had been received and credited to her. After the various papers had been signed, she asked if she could withdraw a rather large sum of cash. Half an hour later she walked out into the street, happy and relieved that everything had gone smoothly. She was also happy that she had asked the counterfeiter to produce a new driving licence as well as her passport, although it had cost her an arm and a leg.

Back at the small apartment, she pulled out her new mobile phone, inserted a SIM card, and dialled her mother. The voice at the other end clearly perked up upon hearing her daughter's voice. She listened carefully to the instructions given, memorising every single word, not interrupting. After they had said their goodbyes, Jane's mother sat for a long time making sure she had understood everything. She was excited and intrigued.

The next day, Jane's mother timed her visit to the post office cum village store just in time to catch her neighbour collecting her daily paper. The two chatted awhile. Jane's mother announced in a loud voice that she and her husband were off to Scotland to meet some long-lost friends. No, they didn't know how long they would be away; it depended on her husband's health. She was rather vague as to where the friends lived, having been told to take the train to Glasgow and assured that they'd be picked up. Yes, strange how they didn't know where the friends were living, but they had lost touch and had been contacted out of the blue a few weeks ago, which was when they'd been invited. They would be leaving the next day. Turning to the postmaster, she paid a small outstanding bill and asked him to cancel the *Telegraph* until further notice.

Twenty-four hours later, Jane's parents were sitting on a train bound for Southampton, where they got out and boarded a cruise liner heading for the Greek Islands. Jane had done things well, having reserved a comfortable cabin with a view and in a peaceful section of the monster liner. She had paid for all this from the bonus she had paid herself from her profitable business. Her father was impressed;

his respect for his daughter increased greatly, although, sadly, he had forgotten everything a few hours later. The one thing he couldn't understand was why they were going away; he was happy in his home and felt confused when out of familiar surroundings. He was sometimes frustrated; his mind was playing tricks; and he could hardly remember what he'd had for lunch the day before. The name Greta Bauman seemed familiar, but he was hard pushed to recall anything these days.

Jane's mother watched her failing husband with sadness. Long gone were the days of having fun and laughing, taking caravan trips around Britain together. It seemed to her that he was getting worse by the day, a mere shadow of the man she had married half a century ago. She knew he didn't understand where they were or what they were doing; he had accepted the news that they were going on holiday to see their daughter and asked the reason for all this turmoil. She doubted very much he would remember in a few hours. She had to keep repeating everything continuously, and lately she'd had to tell him who she was after returning home from the shops. The only person he seemed to remember was Jane; there seemed a slight flicker of remembrance when she showed him her photo. It wasn't easy, but she loved him. She watched him stare out towards the open sea and wondered what was going on in his mind.

The week went fast; they had stopped off in Malta, and it wasn't long before they were docking in Genoa. Jane had arranged for them to be met and escorted to one of the top hotels. As they entered the vast marbled hall, she greeted them with open arms. They hadn't seen her since her last whirlwind visit a few weeks back, and she was shocked to see her father's rapid deterioration. With her changed looks, there was no way for her father to recognise her. He just stared and repeatedly asked who this woman was. He tried to remember the name Greta Bauman. Jane's mother was equally shocked at seeing her daughter looking so different and wanted to know the reason. She was told that Jane would explain everything another day when they were alone.

Jane and her parents spent a couple of days resting and shopping before Jane drove them to Tuscany, where she had rented a small house halfway between Florence and Siena with wonderful views of the rolling hills. She had explained to her mother that she had chosen this place as there was a first-class retirement home close by where her father would be well cared for.

Her mother fell in love with the place at first sight. She appreciated everything her daughter had done and was even more ecstatic when she learned that Jane was planning to move in by the end of the month. What about her job? her flat in Zurich? Over dinner on the second night, Jane told her mother everything, explaining what had happened in France with Hans, and that Ron had become more and more aggressive and that they were now living separate lives. That explained the change in her looks and all the secrecy. Jane had also told her mother about her plans for the future. Her mother was sad to think of her daughter's problems but smiled happily, hugging her tightly.

CHAPTER 34

Sean, who had been kept informed of developments in Eltham, grinned broadly when he heard that the gangs had all been rounded up. He was worried, however, that Ron would suspect or guess what had happened and go into hiding, but he doubted his man would flee from the lure of the upcoming Belfast deal. The total press and media blackout of the raid was impressive and would make the task of coming to a full understanding of what had happened difficult for Ron.

Sean was at the airport when he was advised that the target had left his flat and was heading for Heathrow. The young MI6 officer tailed his man, sitting across the table from him on the Heathrow Express and following him into the vast hall of Terminal 5. The young man picked out Sean immediately, seeing him standing under one of the large screens, and nodded in the direction of the target before turning away and making his way back to the station.

Sean followed at a distance but never let Ron out of his sights. They made their way through security and along the endless corridor to the designated gate. Looking like just another businessman, Sean managed to get a seat a few rows behind Ron. He settled down for the short flight.

Ron, at first, had decided to go to Liverpool and make sure the containers arrived and were transferred to the ferry, but after his meeting with Hans, he had opted to skip that part and meet the ship in Belfast. He knew none of the gang in Merseyside, and after what had happened in Kent, he decided that it would be wise to stay well away. Although he had spoken often to his Liverpool contact, he had never met the man. The fewer people who knew his face, the better.

As they crossed the arrivals hall an hour later, Sean spotted Charly Flynn loitering under the large clock. The handover was easy. The big man kept an eye on Ron before a fresh agent, a female operative, took over.

Charly joined up with his friend. As they made their way into town, he spoke for the first time. "Sounds as if the first sting went well. Everyone rounded up, and not a peep from the press or media. Amazing."

Sean replied, "Yeah, the boys did well. Took them completely by surprise, with the added bonus of nabbing the French contact. He is not a happy bunny, nor is our friend Mr Stokes. He went down to the warehouse yesterday and spent some time snooping about, but the lads left no clues. He must be wondering what has hit him. First his head henchman, Hans, gets caught for carrying drugs and money laundering, and now his entire people-smuggling operation has been shut down." He paused and sniffed. "It's interesting how little loyalty these guys have. By the time the last of the thugs had been processed, we knew who all the intermediary scum, or clients as our friend Stokes likes to call them, were and where they are based. Last night in a secret operation, eighteen different organisations across England and Wales were raided, and a total of ninety-eight people have been rounded up. Not bad, eh?"

"Impressive, but it will only create a void for only a short while, until someone else gets in on the act. Then, I guess we'll have to start all over again."

Sean sighed. "You're right, although taking out our friend will leave a big hole. It'll take time for a new man to get established. Sadly, it may have put a stop to our home-grown lowlife, but there are plenty left out there who are ready to fill the gap, especially the Middle Eastern and North African mafia."

"Ach, don't get depressed. Just think, thanks to all these bastards, we still have a job. Without them and all the drug gangs, what would we do?" He chuckled. "I can't see you tending your plot or going to coffee mornings. You'd die of boredom."

They drove into town in silence, both deep in thought. Charly was the first to speak again, saying, "Where shall we go to celebrate tonight? Anywhere you fancy."

"No time for that yet. We need to go over our plan and prepare. Are you sure that girl is up to the job? Now is not the time to mess up and lose our man. When is Peter flying in?"

"Peter is already here. Never left. He gave me a list as long as my arm of his 'requirements'. They should be at my house by tonight. As for that girl, her name is Katherine. By the way, Kath is one of the most capable and reliable agents we have on this side of the Irish Sea. Mr Stokes will be hard put to lose her or hide anything from her. She has eyes like a hawk and is sharper than you or me. Now, have you decided what you want to eat, or shall I decide?"

They were sitting at a table in the corner of a small restaurant, a couple beers in front of them, when Charly's phone buzzed; he looked down and smiled. "Seems our man has bunked down for the night, so Kath is coming over to meet you." Noticing the shock on Sean's face, he quickly added, "Don't fret. We have a guy in the hotel lobby. Stokes's room is bugged and monitored. And we have another man at each exit. He can't blink or pick his nose without us knowing."

A few minutes later, a young woman dressed in jeans and a jumper came through the door. She looked round briefly before spotting the two men and making her way over to them. She introduced herself to Sean and ordered three more Guinness. Sean was taken with her immediately, and it wasn't only her fine features and her curly red hair; it was also her warm, relaxed personality, which was immediately contagious. Her smiling eyes darted between the two men as she reported that Ron had checked into his hotel, made his way up to his room, and ordered a chicken and ham salad for his meal before going for a shower. She confirmed that his every move was being watched and that any phone calls would be recorded and monitored. Sean liked her—a lot.

After the main course had been cleared, the two men sat chatting for a long time, reminiscing, and swapping old stories. Kath listened politely and made the occasional comment or asked a question, enjoying their banter and the dry sense of humour. She had been recruited three years earlier when she was serving in the office of a special ops. unit based in the south. The request had come as a surprise to her. She had accepted immediately as there was little sign of the promised action or promotion ever happening. Educated in Dublin, she excelled in maths; was an excellent athlete, especially in martial arts; and liked rifle shooting. Her sharp brain and steely nerve caused her to stand out from the others in her unit, and it soon became apparent that her skills were being underused. Her observant and interested commander wrote to a friend saying that he had the ideal candidate for a move into the secret service. Two months later, she was in England undergoing rigorous training and learning the art of spying.

It was midnight when Charly let himself and Sean in, leading them towards the kitchen. Kath had left them to go back to the hotel, where she was to take over for the man on hall duty. Peter was sitting at the table nursing a steaming cup of coffee whilst poring over a map covered in scribbled notes. He looked up and greeted his host. He had difficulty hiding his excitement. "The delivery arrived late afternoon as you said it would. Thanks. I like it. And all looks good, just as I asked."

Peter had just returned from a run when the doorbell had rung. Several boxes were handed to him by a man who did not look like a driver. He asked Peter to identify himself and confirm that Charly Flynn lived at the premises; after checking Peter's ID and comparing it to the photo on his phone, he nodded, indicating he was happy. Peter wasted no time in taking the boxes up to his room and spent the next few hours going through each item with a fine-tooth comb. He checked every minute detail of each piece of kit and equipment, taking it apart before carefully reassembling it. He tested everything from buttons to switches, from bolts to nuts; nothing was left untouched or taken for granted. Finally satisfied, he went to have a shower before returning, at which time he wrapped and precisely packed the two kit bags with all the items.

"You certainly pulled out all the stops, Charly. Really first-class pieces of kit. I'm impressed."

Charly nodded appreciatively and pointed at the map on the table. "What are you doing? I thought you had done all that last week."

Sean butted in, "doing what Peter does best, going over and redoing what he just checked, just to make sure he had everything right the first time. Is that not so?"

"You can never be too sure. I'm trying to memorise the layout and come up with a cunning plan. When am I going to meet your colleague, the one you're insisting comes with me? I really would prefer to work on my own. I no longer need a chaperone."

"You'll like her. She's good. Promise."

Peter's eye popped wide open as he exclaimed, "SHE! What do you mean, she? You never told me I was having a nursemaid. I don't want one, and I certainly don't need the hassle of looking after a bimbo."

"Now, now, now, you can't talk like that." Sean turned to Charly with a quizzical look. "Do you think that's wise? I know you hold her in high esteem, but don't you think you should have asked Peter first?"

Charly shrugged his shoulders and sniffed loudly. "No. I'm in charge of this operation. I feel confident Kath can be of great help. We need as many people as possible; a lone SAS soldier is not enough. Think about it; you and I will be in the background monitoring movements and making sure the coppers do their jobs. We anticipate at least ten to a dozen bad guys, perhaps more. What can one man do on his own? No, Kath will be very useful. And I'm sure Peter will get on with her just fine."

There was a silence before Peter spoke, saying, "and when am I due to meet my Cinderella who will save my life?"

"Tomorrow morning. She's coming here at eight o'clock for a briefing and to meet you. You can work on a plan together and bond." He smiled ruefully.

Seeing that it was getting late and that they were all going to have a very hard few days ahead of them, Sean decided to go to bed.

It was just before eight o'clock when the doorbell rang, and Kath was let in. She was dressed in joggers with her hair tied back. Even at that time of morning, after a long night with little sleep, she looked fantastic. Her sparkling hazel eyes darted between the three men as she was led into the kitchen. Both Sean and Peter were mesmerised and just sat there, speechless. Peter was the first to recover. He stood up to introduce himself using his full military title. They shook hands, and Kath was handed a steaming cup of coffee. Conversation was awkward at first but got more relaxed as the young woman answered Peter's interrogating questions. Half an hour later, he suggested they go for a run, saying he liked to jog every morning. On their return, he would explain in detail his plan.

To his surprise and delight, Kath kept up with him on the run, matching his pace and not seeming to suffer. And he didn't stop, which didn't seem to bother her one little bit. The two of them chatted about their respective pasts and how they'd gotten involved with the current operation. By the time they returned to the house, Peter had changed his mind and was as happy as he would ever be when working with a new partner for the first time. In his business, trust was everything, and that was something that came only from working together over a long period of time and under different sorts of circumstances. He was certain Kath, in theory, was very capable and excellent at her job, but all that had to be proved in the field. Partnerships bonded and understanding came only with experience, which was where he had concerns. He was confident of his abilities under pressure, but what about hers? It was obvious it was her first major operation, very different from her usual task of stakeouts.

Over another mug of strong brew, Kath and Peter sat down, and he spelt out his plan in detail. They pored over the map and covered the different scenarios he had imagined could happen. She questioned and put in a few ideas of her own, some of which he liked, others of which he discarded after explaining his reasons. They went up to his room and he showed her the gear Charly had organised

194

for him, totally dismayed to learn she was unequipped. He bounded down the stairs and burst into the lounge, where Charly and Sean were discussing their plans.

"What the hell are you thinking of! How do you expect the poor girl to be of any help to me when she has no kit? I'm not giving up one little piece of mine, so if you want her included in this mission, you'd better get your finger out and equip her." He shook his head in exasperation. "I thought you were intelligent and organised!"

Charly held up his hands. "Sorry. I wasn't sure you'd be happy having her to help or what she would need."

"I don't seem to have much choice. Yes, she seems good enough and a nice lass; only time will tell. If she's on, then I suggest you make sure of kitting her out fully. We're moving out tonight." He turned and stormed out.

Sean winked. "Think he likes her. Better get to work and organise those things. I'll go over the plan again and make those calls. We can finalise all the details later this afternoon."

He had just about finished talking when Peter returned. "Any news on the shipment? Where is it? Kath wants to get back to the hotel and get an update before she joins me."

"All in hand. We have a couple of men keeping track of the load. They have just set sail. Same at the hotel; they'll report immediately on any developments, so no need to panic. I suggest Kath goes home and gets some rest. You do what you want but leave me in peace if you expect me to sort the equipment."

He was silent whilst he scribbled a note and handed it to Peter. "Get Kath to meet us there, 5.30 p.m. sharp. You also."

———◆◆◆———

The seven men and the woman were sitting silently round a table in an unoccupied office building not far from the docks, watching a young, longhaired man dressed in jeans and a T-shirt finish sweeping the room for bugs. They had all been carefully searched upon entering. Once the young man had left the room, DI Crawley questioned why all the checks. He had been summoned by Sean earlier that day, having been told to drop everything and get himself to Belfast on the next plane.

"Just precautions. We've rented the room from the port authorities, and as we are about to discuss some extremely sensitive matters …" He left the sentence unfinished. "Now, let's begin."

As his eyes moved round the table, they came to rest on the reporter Alwyn Jones. "Mr Jones, glad you made it. Just wanted to thank you for keeping everything under wraps. Once tomorrow's operation is finished, you will be famous and in big demand. Keep your mouth shut, do as I say, and all will be good, understand? I, and only I, will tell you when you can release the stories."

———◆◆◆———

Peter and Kath finished packing the gear and got into the dark green van. It was 2.30 a.m. when they started to head south, soon making progress through the countryside. Peter was, by now, familiar with the road, having made the trip a couple of times in the past week. He turned off and drove along the narrow road that led towards the farm and massive barn. As they approached the farm entrance, he switched off the car lights and crawled past. Everything was in darkness with no sign of life. He stopped and looked through his night vision glasses, then handed them to Kath. Peering through the binoculars, she whispered, "can't see any sign of activity. The farm looks deserted."

Peter agreed. He flicked the headlights back on and continued along the road for a mile or so. Reaching a small lay-by, he turned off and carefully made his way along a rough, rutted track until he reached his destination and parked the van under a bushy tree. He and Kath quickly gathered their kit before covering the vehicle with a camouflage net. Kath watched her partner cut a few branches from a fir tree and make his way along the track, brushing any tyre traces. Task completed, he returned and attached the branches to the net.

Happy that all was as he wanted, Peter nodded to Kath to follow.

They found a prominent rock covered with moss and hid the van keys. They had just taken a couple of steps when Kath turned on her torch; she collided with Peter as he froze and turned on her. "What the hell are you doing? Turn the thing off!" He snatched the light from her and flicked the switched before she knew it.

"It's pitch-black. How are we going to find our way?" Her voice was louder than she had wanted.

Peter gave her a withering look. "Keep your voice down. Do you want everyone in the county to know we're here?" he hissed. "I know the way; I don't need any light, and we certainly don't need to advertise our presence. If you're unhappy, then go and wait in the van. Thought you were highly trained. What did they teach you?" He sounded exasperated. Starting to walk off, he stopped suddenly after a few paces. "Look, I'm sure you're great, but I'm in charge, OK? I've spent my entire career fighting people in daylight and in the dark, and I have killed more people than you have eaten hot meals. Just do as I tell you and we'll get on fine. Obey my every order, and we'll have a good chance of finishing off this bunch of scumbags." He turned and set off at a marching pace.

Kath tried to follow but kept tripping. As hard as she tried, she was unable to avoid stepping on branches which snapped with a crack. How on earth did this man walk so fast and silently in the dark? She was annoyed with herself for not thinking clearly and was annoyed with him for being so intolerant. She fell several times, but not once did he look back or slow down. Trying to keep up, her legs were hurting. She was tired and breathing heavily, certainly not used to carrying a heavy rucksack full of equipment.

Finally, Peter stopped. He put his kit on the ground and took out his night vision glasses, scouring the length of the dark forest.

Kath was lost, having no idea where they were. Once he'd finished, she whispered, "where are we? Can you see anything?" still trying to catch her breath.

"This is where we set up camp. The farm is just there, through that gap." He pointed towards it and handed her the binoculars. She took her time and, as her breathing slowed, picked out the outline of the buildings. They were much closer than she'd imagined. Peter started to unpack his bag and took out a foldable spade. Kath watched as he started to dig a trench-like hole. When he was finished, he turned and whispered, "A bit tight, but it'll have to do."

She looked at him quizzically, frightened to ask what it was for. Guessing she had no idea, he explained, "our home for the next day or so. We get in there and watch. If you need the toilet, better do it now. From now on, we don't move until I say." She looked at him in disbelief; she had read stories about this sort of stuff but always thought it was fiction.

CHAPTER 35

Ron Stokes had yet another fitful night and not slept well. The excitement and worries of the next day, coupled with his unease, had made for a bad night. He had finally dozed off by 5.30 a.m., but a wild dream woke him up soon thereafter, and now he was soaking. Returning to his bedroom after a long shower, he sat on the bed and went over his plan for the day.

Timing was going to be crucial; he didn't want the container staying in Belfast any longer than necessary after the ferry had docked. He had given instructions to the driver to always remain with the truck once he had landed and to set off for the farm in time to arrive by 10.30 at the latest. It was unfortunate the sailing arrived in early evening, but the logistics of securing the four vans, three of which were coming from the south, gave him no other choice but to keep the truck at the docks. He wanted no delays or late arrivals; the clients had to be at the barn between 11.30 a.m. and 12 noon, roughly an hour after the container arrived. The load would be quickly split between the buyers, with Ron supervising to ensure that no one cheated or claimed a bigger share. After they had left, the truck would return to Belfast ferry port and board the sailing to Liverpool. The vans were given specific instructions as to the route they should take when leaving. Ron didn't want anyone following one anyone else as four plain white vans simply did not do such thing.

Ron's local contact and his men would stand guard, one outside, the other two helping their boss inside whilst the shipment was divided. After the vans had departed, they would tidy up, all tell-tale signs erased; only then would his man be allowed to leave—and Ron would return to the city a much, much wealthier man.

His thoughts were interrupted by the buzz of his phone; it was the Egyptian. What did the crook want now? Ron knew but asked the question anyway. As suspected, the caller wanted to know why his bonus for the second shipment had not been remitted, as he had completed his side of the deal. He was surprised his associate and ally hadn't seen to the necessary in his usual timely fashion.

Ron thought about telling him about the Eltham fiasco but quickly discarded the idea. No one knew what had happened, not even he, and he sure wasn't going to admit that his whole team, along with many of his clients, had most probably been arrested. Having not forgotten, he apologised profusely, explaining he was currently in the midst of another highly complicated deal; once this had been completed in a day or two, he would get his bank to make the transfer. The Egyptian, mollified, agreed to wait for the sake of their long-standing friendship. He wished Ron success and hung up.

Ron had barely put the phone down when it rang again; this time it was his lawyer in London. The man sounded gloomier than ever. There was still no trace of Jane. He and his contact in Glasgow had come up with nothing, no trace, and no one had seen the parents, who had not yet returned, no one knew when they were due back. Ron pacified the man and told him not to worry, saying they would discuss the matter when he got back. Then came the bombshell.

"We have a problem, a big problem," came the gloomy voice. "I had a call from Barclays Bank. They want to talk to you urgently. It seems Jane's company needs funds; it has reached the agreed overdraft limit. Her deputy has tried to contact her, but unsurprisingly, she has been unable to find her. I called the office and spoke to the woman; she says that a week ago a very large payment was made by Jane to some foreign outfit. The woman had never heard of the company or of any deal. She was shocked that the payment had left the business with no funds to pay wages, suppliers, or the quarterly VAT bill. She too has been trying to contact Jane, but nothing."

Ron slumped on the bed; his hands were shaking, and he felt

weak, rage building up inside. What had the devious little woman been up to? He had never thought she could have planned all this. Had she been instrumental in Hans's arrest, tipping off the police about Eltham, and now was clearing her company's account? No, she didn't have the brains or the know-how. She loved Hans. OK, she had caught him banging a Russian tart, so probably she had set him up—women were like that—but Eltham! Ron doubted she knew anything about the ins and outs of any of his deals, unless of course Hans had blabbed when the two of them were in bed. Ron didn't doubt the man was an idiot, but he didn't see him as that much of a fool. As for the business account, Jane lacked the nous to arrange some transfer to a ghost company, and she hadn't the faintest idea Ron had financed her and had guaranteed the bank. He shook his head. How much had he signed for, half a million? How can anyone make such a transfer without the bank questioning it? Well, they were at fault; it was their problem now. Ron told his lawyer just that. The man disagreed. "Ron, if you don't pay them something soon, they will foreclose, and the business will go belly-up. No, you must sort this out today." There was a slight pause before he continued. "Think of it: you'll have to make the staff redundant and put the company into liquidation, never mind having to fight HMRC. No, your name and your reputation is at stake."

Ron's rage was increasing by the second. He felt his temple thumping. His heart was ready to explode, just like his temper. He certainly did not need this hassle, not today of all days. Controlling himself and his voice, he agreed with the lawyer and asked him to let the bank know he would sort the mess out as soon as he got back to London the day after next. The man agreed, but before hanging up he suggested, once again, that they notify the police about Jane's disappearance. He also suggested they ask them to start a criminal investigation into fraud. It took all of Ron's skill to persuade the lawyer not to go down that route, not now at least; he said they could discuss it as soon as he got back.

Ron sat staring at the floor for a long time. His head was spinning with everything the lawyer had said. How and why was everything going so wrong suddenly? Ever since he realised his wife had no interest or, to be frank, the brains to join him as a partner, he had been meticulously careful not to tell her anything. He took even more precautions since she had found out what he did for a living. OK, things had turned sour. No longer loving her or caring for her, he had offered her a divorce with very favourable terms, which she had turned down. Why would she want to ruin him, ruin everything he had worked for? He kicked the bedside table in frustration. Now was not the time to think about all that. Tomorrow was going to be one of the biggest days of his life, so he needed to concentrate, make sure everything went smoothly and to plan. When it was all over, he would have more than enough to plug the hole with the bank and to pay off the staff and HMRC before closing the business. Even after paying his and Hans's lawyers astronomical fees, Ron would be a multimillionaire and he would retire to some far-flung corner of the world and enjoy the fruits of his labour.

The two men drove in and were directed to park behind a truck loaded with an unmarked container. The previous afternoon they had demanded to speak to the duty manager of the ferry company, showing their credentials. They briefly explained what they needed and made it clear that their request was of the utmost importance. There was no discussion; the official confirmed that things would be done as they required.

Having locked the car, they proceeded past the truck, which was in the process of being lashed down, and followed the driver and his companion. The truckers made a beeline for the cafeteria and installed themselves at a table, taking no notice of the couple of passengers who sat behind them. As the ferry slipped its moorings, the younger of the two passengers sent a message. It was short, simply confirming they were leaving Liverpool.

After what seemed an eternal crossing, the passengers glimpsed the first sight of the Irish coast; two hours later they were entering Belfast Bay and making their way up slowly to the pier. The passengers were asked to re-enter their vehicles. The truck trundled out into the open air, closely followed by the car. It continued its journey through the gates as the lorry pulled into a night parking bay, immediately making a U-turn after leaving the compound and parking up in a lay-by offering an uninterrupted view of the container.

CHAPTER 36

Dawn was breaking when Kate stirred. She had eventually drifted off into an uneasy sleep. Her body ached from the cramped position she had been in, she was cold, her fingers numb. Her stomach grumbled as she hadn't eaten anything since lunchtime the previous day. More urgent, she needed a pee. She looked over at Peter, who had not moved, and wondered whether he was still alive. In a whisper, she asked what time it was. He looked over and smiled. "Feel better?" he enquired. "You fell asleep in the middle of telling me about how you got involved with the Firm. At least you didn't snore." He grinned.

"I really need to go for a leak, then get a hot drink."

He shook his head and nodded towards a nearby bush. "You can go behind that clump, but mind to crawl and keep your head down. Don't be long."

With difficulty, she managed to get her stiff body moving and make her way over to the designated point. On her return, Peter presented her with a small cup of tepid brew and two biscuits. "Feel relieved?" He grinned. "Room service, madam." He handed her what he had fished out of his bag. She thanked him and asked if he had slept.

"No. Kept a lookout and made sure you didn't snore. I've trained myself to catnap; I can go two or three days without any proper shuteye." He asked her if her tea was warm enough.

"Thought an army lived and fought on its stomach."

"Some do, but in my business, we are taught hardship, how to survive on the bare minimum, and to eat whatever you can find. Go to sleep and you might wake up dead. Too much food makes you sleepy. Drink too much and you need to pee. When I was in Iraq, I was sent out on a mission with two men. We lived like this for just over ten days. By the time we returned, we had each lost well over a stone in weight and slept for forty-eight hours straight." He looked over to the farm. "They shouldn't be long now. I suggest you put your earphone in. Just had a message the guys in the truck are stirring." As he said that, he handed her a pot of shoe polish. "Smear this over your face, like this." He showed her how to do it. It took a superhuman effort on her part not to burst out laughing.

———◆◆◆———

Sean and Charly were down early. Both had slept lightly but well and were now looking forward to the day ahead. Sean switched on the mic and tested it. He called the stakeout car at the port and was told the lorry driver and his partner were stirring; he would be advised once the truck was moving. After confirming that the other cars were heading to their designated points, he checked in with Peter, making sure he and Kath were ensconced and all right. Charly had phoned O'Grady and confirmed the meeting time and location. It was all systems go.

———◆◆◆———

If Ron had slept badly the night before, then last night was worse. It was not so much what would be happening today but Jane. He turned all the problems of the past few days round and round in his head, analysing every possibility. Each time he came back to Jane; it must have been her. He couldn't understand how she had managed to grass Hans, to learn about Eltham, or to convince the bank to clear her business account. As for disappearing, she must have had help from that mother of hers. Ron tried to think if she could have found out about the present deal. That worried him. It worried him a lot.

Just after eight o'clock, he received a call from his local associate in Belfast advising him that his men were ready and that the truck would be moving on within the next twenty minutes. Did Ron have any last instructions and news of the vans? They should have left Dublin by now. Ron had checked and had called each of his three clients in the south. Yes, they were on their way and would be arriving on schedule; no, they, wouldn't be early and would take all necessary precautions.

Dressed in jeans and a T-shirt, Ron strode through the hotel lobby and made his way to the car park, not noticing the man who had followed him through the rotating door and stopped at the top of the steps, watching him. The man turned away and spoke into his lapel. As Ron got into his hired car and drove out of the parking lot, a white car fell in behind, following at a discreet distance.

Ron was just reaching the city limits when his phone rang. It was his associate calling to tell him that the lorry had now left the port and that he and his men were about fifteen minutes from the warehouse.

The container truck turned onto the main circular road and headed slowly south. The driver and his friend had been given strict instruction on the route they had to take and had been told to keep to the speed limit and not do anything to attract attention. They had been given a timeline that they had to adhere to.

Neither man noticed the blue Volvo following them, and even if they had, their suspicions would have evaporated when it turned left at a junction. A grey Honda fell in behind.

<hr />

Peter suddenly picked up his binoculars and trained them on the small country road. He had heard a car engine getting lounder as it approached. He nudged Kath beside him. "Someone's coming. Must be them." He nodded in the direction of the road. She had not heard anything. True, she had been listening to the chatter of their colleagues as they kept one another updated. Heart beating faster, she looked through her glasses. Suddenly she picked out the dark blue estate Mercedes, closely followed by a white Transit van; she watched as they came clear into view and turned into the farm lane. The van stopped and a man jumped out to open the gate before following the vehicle up to the farmhouse, parking beside the Mercedes. Three other men got out and stretched. Peter mumbled something into his mic and started relaying every movement.

The back door of the van was opened as one of them distributed high-viz jackets, which they all put on. A well-dressed man strode over to the large double doors of the barn and unlocked the heavy padlock, signalling his men to help him pull the doors open. The white Transit was then driven inside, and soon they all disappeared into the darkness. Ron had watched and kept an eye open whilst the men got ready before following the well-dressed man into the cavernous barn.

Kath's excitement and trepidation were growing by the second. She had been trained for such events, had staked out many buildings and had arrested countless people, but this was different. She had never really been involved in a such a large or complex operation, and the anticipation of what was to come made her nervous. Beside her, Peter calmly talked things through and kept everyone informed. He answered their questions clearly and concisely. She looked over to him and nudged him. "What are we going to do?" she asked in a hushed tone.

"Lie here and wait. Watch. Report every move. It's just beginning. Patience is key, trust me." He continued to look through the binoculars, which he had never put down.

A fleet of cars and unmarked police vehicles were reaching their various destinations. Patrick O'Grady oversaw the inner circle, placing his men strategically in and around the nearby village situated at the other side of the forest. They had learned from eavesdropping that the container truck and two of the vans would be passing through the hamlet whilst the other pickup vans would be using the small road. O'Grady had detailed half his force, under DI Crawley, to patrol the main road and that narrow lane. On no account should anyone be seen or arouse suspicion. He had only spoken to his English counterpart once and had met him for the first time the evening before, so he had no idea of his capabilities. The man seemed a good enough cop and no doubt was, but had he any experience of such operations? That was O'Grady's concern. He hoped so.

Sean had decided to stay with Crawley's party and had agreed that Charly would supervise O'Grady's men. Neither spook was confident. The only certainty was Peter.

<hr/>

The blue Mercedes had made its way swiftly down the road, followed at a distance by the grey Honda. As Ron turned into the lane, the shadowing vehicle continued its way unnoticed; the driver immediately radioed his superiors and made a U-turn.

Ron was feeling knots beginning to form in the pit of his stomach. So much depended on today. Success would bring wealth beyond his imagination, as well as respect in his field of business. Once all this was concluded, he could relax, enjoy the fruits of his labour, and plan how to get Jane out of his life once and for all. He knew what had to be done. She couldn't hide forever, not from him. Yes, it may take a while, but he was certain she didn't have the wit or the patience; she would want to boast of how she had tricked him, rub his nose in it. She would want to see her parents. Once she reappeared, her life would be short-lived.

Ron concentrated his mind on today's events as he followed the white Transit van and turned into the farm. He parked next to the old farmhouse and looked around. Everything was calm, and the air was still. The tops of the trees were being blown by a light breeze, and grey clouds hung nearly motionless in the sky. He walked over to the barn and was greeted by the suited man, his Belfast contact. They shook hands and chatted for a while; Ron had been updated on the progress of the various parties and passed on the messages. He was happy the plan he had put together was being followed, but he was unhappy that the instructions that Hans had given to remove the tree in the corner had not been followed. Why had that tree not been taken down? It hid the view of any oncoming vehicles. Unhappy with the lame excuse, Ron made his feelings clear. He then marched inside.

Shortly after, a man dressed in a high-viz jacket came out and stood guard. Whatever he was looking out for was unclear, but he was obeying orders given by the Englishman.

Sean's voice suddenly crackled over the airwaves. The truck was heading towards the village and had been spotted turning off the main road a couple of minutes ago. There was suddenly tension in the air. Various voices confirmed the sighting and gave the latest position. Not long after, Charly confirmed that the vehicle was trundling through the village.

Peter, binoculars glued to his eyes, acknowledged. He had not moved in half an hour, never letting down his glasses. Kath was amazed. She tried to make conversation, but he ignored her. Then he hissed his annoyance. It was no time for chitchat.

It was a few minutes before 10.30 when the truck appeared and slowly turned into the lane. It inched round the sharp entrance, just missing the gates. The guard watched as it drove towards him. He opened the giant barn door, waving the driver through. The doors were swiftly closed with a loud thud, the patrolling man taking up his position.

Once inside, the driver and his partner jumped out and were greeted by Ron, who questioned them about the journey. They had nothing to report; no one had followed them. They then went to unlock the rear doors and jumped inside. The operation was swift and smooth. The two newcomers, helped by the two local men in yellow jackets, unloaded the cargo and carefully arranged each crate in a line. The suited man, Mr X as Charly had labelled him, took a crowbar and cracked open each case and peered inside whilst Ron counted every box. Satisfied everything was in order, Ron ordered the driver and his partner to follow one of the two remaining guards outside and take some rest; he certainly didn't want their prying eyes seeing what the boxes contained.

The remaining men worked fast and efficiently. Each knew his job, two of them having done so many times before. Packages were taken out, bundled, counted, before carefully being replaced in new cartons but left open.

Each new box was marked with a symbol before being placed in a separate area of the barn.

———◆◆◆———

Sean's voice came over to announce that a couple of vans had just turned into the small road leading up to the farm. He had just finished when Charly cut in, announcing that a black one had come through the village.

Both men stressed the importance of not being seen by the new arrival. Orders would be given in due course, but until such time, radio silence had to be maintained. Only they and Peter would be allowed to talk from now on.

The hidden figures in the wood watched as the vans came into view. Through their binoculars, they followed them every inch of the way. Peter made a note of the number sitting in the front of each van, three in each. He doubted anyone would be in the back. He got Kath to jot down the registration number he whispered over to her. Just before the vans entered the barn, he managed to take a couple of photos of each vehicle.

———◆◆◆———

Inside the vast building was a hive of activity. The two truck drivers watched as the small fleet of vans drove in and disappeared into the barn where the main passengers were greeted by Ron.

CHAPTER 37

Having been greeted and shown to their section of the barn, each of the bosses were instructed to inspect the goods now neatly prepared and allotted to them. There was little talk between the members, most of whom were heads of rival gangs. Ron had selected the organisations carefully and ensured they did not overlap. The worst and most dangerous mob leader was the one from Cork, a nasty piece of work whom Ron had met a few times before. Despite his dislike of the man, Ron recognised he was a valuable customer and thus treated him with respect.

Once each man had checked his delivery and was satisfied, the various vans were loaded. Ron then took each boss aside and was paid the balance owed in cash. Trust, not being high on anyone's agenda, dictated that Ron had taken a 50 per cent prepayment when the shipment left Karachi. An additional 25 per cent had been paid when the shipment had left Liverpool, with the balance being remitted in cash on final delivery. Ron had been insistent from the very first deal that that was how he operated; if his clients were not happy, they could go and find another supplier. The clients had little choice but to go along with the demands. Wads of notes passed hands, neatly bundled in bags. Each one was checked meticulously. Mr X and his trusted henchman stood over, keeping a close watch.

Money counted, Ron gave a nod, and the drivers were called back. The giant doors were pulled back, the drivers started their engines, and in silence the bosses mounted their vehicles. The convoy drove out into the daylight, proceeding down the lane. The two leading vans turned left, retracing the route from which they had come; the others headed for the village. Ron handed a wad of cash to the truck driver and his companion before sending them back home. He watched, satisfied, as the truck rumbled out.

Peter had been watching intently and reported back. He carefully counted the passengers and checked the registration numbers. Nothing had changed; all occupants were accounted for, and vehicles still had the same registration plates. He radioed Sean and Charly and gave them the latest news.

Next to him, Kath's heart was thumping. Having never known such a feeling, she started to tremble. She hadn't wanted to ask, but it just came out, "what now?"

Peter put down the binoculars and turned, a smile on his lips. "Now the real fun begins." He turned back to look as one of the men came out to meet his fellow guard, the doors closing behind him. Peter watched for a few seconds more before speaking. "You see that bush over to your left, about fifty yards away? I want you to crawl over there and hide; make yourself invisible. On no account do you move, make a noise, or do anything until I tell you, understood?" Kath nodded and inched her aching body out of the hole. She was barely halfway out when Peter whispered, "Move slowly, flat on your belly and keep that bum down. Now hurry."

He watched her as she slithered and wriggled over the stony ground. Once she had reached her hiding place, he turned back, checking that the two men were still at their post. He took out a small torch and flicked it on a couple of times for a brief second. Watching the men, he noticed that one had seen something but was hesitant. He repeated the process a couple of times more until the guard pointed in his direction. He watched as they talked animatedly and as the one who had spotted the light pointed again in his direction, Peter flicked the light on for a split second. This time both men saw it. They ran across to the car and pulled out a couple of guns, speaking a few words before the first guard started to jog down the path towards the wood.

Peter moved stealthily to his right and hid behind a large fallen

212

tree trunk; he still had a good view of the farmyard and of the second man, now crouching by the car. He whispered a code into his mic and glanced to where Kath was hiding, checking she was well out of sight. It didn't take long for the man to reach the wood and start the short ascent towards the light, which by now was blinking more irregularly.

Fifty yards away, the guard slowed and called out. He looked around and moved closer, checking every few paces to his right and left. He called out again and ordered whoever was there to show himself. He half turned as he thought he heard a rustle of leaves, but he would never know. The last thing he felt was a hand over his mouth and the cold blade of a knife sliding across his throat. A couple of gurgles and he was slowly lowered to the ground. Only when Peter was sure the man was dead did he release his hand.

There was a slight crackle in Sean's ear: "Man 1 down. Man 1 down." Charly instantly heard the same.

Kath had been watching and couldn't believe what she had witnessed. She had closed her eyes as Peter slit the man's throat. On seeing the body, blood gushing from the wound she started to tremble uncontrollably, tears pouring down her face. She was quickly brought back to reality when she heard Peter's loud whisper telling her to keep down, shut up, and not move. Instinctively she obeyed, watching as he moved the body and hid it under a bush. Body hidden, Peter took up his binoculars and began watching the second guard. The man was certainly on edge. He had left his place by the car and was looking anxiously towards the wood. He was not happy, concerned his mate was taking so long; five minutes had passed and no sign of him. As he tried to locate his friend in the wood, a blinking light caught his eye. He peered intently. Yes, there it was again. He wondered what was taking his pal so long. Watching the light flicker a couple of times more, and forgetting his orders not to leave his post, he started for the wood. Following his friend's path, he made good progress. That light kept flickering. As he neared it, he called out for his mate. Moving slowly, searching, listening, he called out again, this time softly. Receiving no reply, he inched forward, his nerves on edge. He held his gun up in front of him, swinging it right to left, ready to shoot at any noise or movement. He had stopped to look down at what seemed like blood, when a firm hand was clamped over his mouth and nose. The sharp blade of a knife slit his throat, and eternal darkness descended on him.

"Number 2 down; number 2 down. Three to go. Three to go." Peter had just finished hiding the body when he heard a rustling sound behind him. Quick as a flash, he turned, blade at the ready, and just managed to stop his thrusting motion as he caught sight of Kath standing in front of him. "What the hell are you doing?" he hissed. "I nearly killed you. Thought I said to stay where you were until I told you otherwise. Now get down." He pulled her to the ground and put a hand over her mouth to stifle her voice. Looking deep into her tearful eyes, he slowly released the pressure. She was shaking uncontrollably.

As they sat in their hole, he tried to comfort her as best he could. He had never been married or had a proper girlfriend—never had time or the inclination, his nomadic lifestyle of fighting wars did not go hand in hand with a love life. Just like Sean, he was devoted to his profession and had little time for romance.

As the container truck came into sight of the village, the driver cursed; the road was blocked with dozens of police, who were swarming around. He slowed, and before he had time to fully stop, the cab was overrun by three armed officers. They quickly handcuffed the two men, tuned off the CB radio, and confiscated their phones. As the men were being marched towards a police car, they noticed a couple of the white vans that had been at the farm were coming into view. Quick as lightning, the police swarmed round the new arrivals. The passengers were handcuffed and were being pushed unceremoniously into one of the numerous police vans.

Charly was pleased at the swiftness of the operation. No one had gotten away, and all forms of communications had been switched off, with mobile phones impounded. He was inspecting one of the white vehicles with O'Grady when his phone rang. It was Sean.

"Any luck yet? We have just rounded up our little crowd. Looks as if the shipment was bigger than we first thought. Masses of stuff!" Charly agreed and briefly gave an estimate of the value they had found.

It had been a lightning strike, taking the three dealers by surprise. They had left the farm and were more than satisfied with their purchases when the driver of the lead van had slowed down; a car was in the ditch, blocking the narrow road. He cursed loudly. His boss looked up from his phone and ordered him to reverse immediately. The manoeuvre was impossible as the second and third van was now hard on their tail. Before they knew anything, dozens of armed police had surrounded the vehicles shouting orders and burst into the front cabs overpowering the occupants. The gang members were hauled out and were told to lie on the ground. They were swiftly handcuffed. Their phones were taken away and all form of communication disabled. The entire operation had taken less than a minute.

DI Crawley had been watching from a distance. His job was to keep an eye on the reporter Alwyn Jones and to ensure no traffic turned up into the narrow road. They had stationed a police car on the main A24 and erected a sign saying - Road Closed, Accident. He was impressed at the rapidity and smoothness of the operation. Sean had shot up in his estimation. Crawley had had his doubts the night before when they had the briefing and they had been told the plan, but no, he had to give the man and his pal Charly their due; they certainly knew what they were doing.

Both parties worked fast, gathering up the boxes, photographing the stacks of drugs and gathering vital evidence. The vans were put on low loaders and driven off to be searched for forensic evidence. Prisoners and cargo were taken away under heavy guard. A large number of officers remained in both locations. The operation was far from over; the main instigator, as well Mr X and his henchman, were still at the farm. They were the ones Sean and Charly really wanted.

Kath had calmed down slightly. The vision of Peter slitting the two men's throats was still vividly etched in her mind. She had served in the army, but in the office, she had never fired a gun in anger or seen active duty and had certainly never seen anyone being killed. She was shaken out of her dream by Peter crawling out of the hole. He turned to her. "So far, everything is going to plan. All those guys who left have been arrested. Now it is up to us." He handed her a rag, picked up his heavy rucksack, and signalled her to follow him.

On the way back to their van, he stopped at a small stream and told her to clean her face of the camouflage. As she was doing this, he explained what he wanted her to do next. She had to look natural, as if she were genuinely lost, to divert attention away from him. She asked why and what was going to happen.

"We need to try to get the third man out of the way, neutralise him. We need to isolate them as much as possible." He then pointed to a large tree between the road and the farm. "I want you to get yourself noticed. Get him to follow you. Once you're behind that tree, out of sight of the building, I'll take care of the rest." He looked at her. "I promise I'll try not to kill him."

They drove through the wood carefully and turned onto the narrow road; as they reached a bend just behind the big tree, Peter drove the van into the nearside ditch. He turned and smiled. "You are a bad driver!" He winked and smiled. "You were on your way back from birdwatching when you thought you saw a kite and lost concentration. After that, what you say is up to you. Look natural, act natural, a damsel in distress. That's what you've been taught to do, isn't it?"

They got out. "Wait here until I signal you. Don't forget the binoculars." He marched off at a brisk pace. Kath was not feeling confident. She waited for the signal before walking towards the farm.

———◆———

Ron and his local contact, helped by the latter's trusted henchman, were busy tidying up, making sure no signs were left. Ron turned to the third man and told him to join his friends, saying he and the boss would be out shortly. Neither he nor the suited dude wanted any witnesses to the handover of cash that was going to be made nor did Ron want anyone to hear about the next shipment. Ron had decided to pretend there were going to be further deals; he didn't want anyone knowing his real plans and was pretty sure that enthusiastic talk of another big payday would ensure the suited crook wouldn't try anything nasty. Left alone with his contact, Ron saw the thug's gleaming eyes count bundle after bundle he handed him wads of cash before they were stuffed in a bag.

The third guard, surprised not to see his pals, went over and looked by the cars. Seeing no one he strolled over and peered into the farmhouse. Still no one. He walked round the back of the building, all doors and windows were locked, so he retraced his steps, concern etched on his face. He was about to go and warn his boss when he spotted a woman walking up the farm lane. He hurried over to head her off and, in no uncertain terms, tell her to get lost.

Kath ignored his orders and introduced herself, saying she was driving home from a bird-watching session when something caught her eye, causing her to lose concentration and end up in the ditch. She now needed a strong man to help her and push her car out. The thug looked at her dubiously. She turned on the charm, smiling sweetly and tears welled up in her eyes. He looked at her silently, inwardly debating what he should do. He tried to imagine what sort of figure was under that camouflage jacket. She had turned and beckoned to him to follow. He quickly caught up with her and fell in step, a feeling of unease growing. Something was wrong, he knew it, but his curiosity got the better of him. As he walked towards the car, he tried to visualise her naked body. Yes, she had quite a figure. As they turned the bend and passed a large tree, he couldn't resist. Swinging round abruptly, he grabbed her and tried to forcibly kiss her. She resisted and fought hard. In a flash he realised that he had made a mistake; few women without serious training could put up such resistance. He renewed his effort, grabbing her by the throat and started to squeeze hard. Pinning her against the tree trunk, he asked her in a hissing voice who she was, what was she really wanting.

Kath felt the hands tightening round her throat. She had difficulty breathing and her eyes started to bulge. With the man's face just

217

inches from hers, he asked again and started to exert more pressure. She tried to shake her head and attempted to get her mouth to form words, but no sound came out; she started to feel faint, her legs weakening.

The man had lost all sense of control. He knew he was strangling the woman to death, but he didn't care, she has lying and was probably working for one those southern thugs he had seen earlier. She would be a decoy so that the bastards could gain access and probably kill his boss and the Englishman. She deserved everything that was coming to her. Once he had dispatched her, he would haste back and warn the two leaders, if it was not too late; this was for them. He suddenly felt a hand clamp over his nose and mouth and a blade slide into his neck, severing the jugular. With blood spurting everywhere, he slumped to the ground. Peter looked at the body at his feet and went through the man's jacket and trouser pockets before checking that Kath was all right. He took her shaking body in his arms and calmed her down. He could have done without this, but the poor woman was in a serious state. She looked down at the body and started to sob uncontrollably. "I thought you promised no more killing," she said, whimpering.

Peter shook her gently and looked her in the face. "I had no choice. It was either him or you. You're lucky I anticipated this might happen. Now, get yourself back to the car, lock the doors, and wait for me or one of our boys to return. Don't, under any circumstances, move, do you hear?"

She nodded and he let go of her, watching as she slowly make her way up the lane. He contacted Charly and Sean and reported back. Then he made his way to the farm, checking carefully as he went. He made for the access lane and moved himself closer, all the time keeping out of sight. Silently, he ran to the large double doors and noiselessly closed the large padlock, locking the occupant inside. He then made his way round the back of the farmhouse, along the side of the vast barn, stopping at the loose panel he had used when he first explored the place. Squatting, he put his ear to the crack. He heard distant voices and what sounded like someone sweeping the floor.

Ever so slowly, he prised open the panel sufficiently to let his body through. Once inside, he blinked and allowed his eyes to adjust to the semidarkness. Yes, Ron and Mr X were there. He smiled to himself.

Kath had returned to the van and locked herself inside. She rubbed her sore throat and tried to compose herself, drying her tears and sniffling. This was not for her. It had all sounded so exciting when she first started, but now, nothing resembled the exercises and practice raids she had enjoyed so much. The thought that she had witnessed three brutal killings in less than half an hour, all in the name of saving the country, was too much for her. She was sure it could have been handled differently. As much as she had enjoyed Peter's company when they first met and had admired his military dedication, she hated him for what she had just witnessed. She would have to report him for unnecessary brutality.

Kath was brought of her thoughts by the noise of a car approaching. She slid down into her seat and hoped the vehicle wouldn't stop. A few seconds later, Charly's face appeared at the window. She relaxed and opened the door. They spoke briefly, and he told her to get into his car. Once she was inside, she wondered why they weren't moving. "Why are we not going to the farm? The last two remaining dealers are still in there, and Peter was heading in that direction."

Charly told her they would be going in once Sean had made his way up from the other side and only when they had word from Peter. He listened to Kath relate the events of the past hour and tell him about Peter, her concerns, and her disgust at his inhuman actions. Charly didn't try to explain or justify his friend's actions, just nodded absent-mindedly, and stared intently at the nearby buildings.

Peter had taken cover behind a few large bales. Continuing to listen whilst watching the two men through a small crack, he was formulating a plan. Taking care not to make any noise, he retrieved a length of twine and quickly untangled it; he took out his knife, placing it in his belt. Peering through the small crack, he watched for another minute; the two men were busy clearing up. He picked up a couple of pebbles and tossed one. The noise of the stone skittling along the floor echoed round the building. The voices stopped, as did the sweeping. The two men looked round, unsure if they had heard anything. After a short pause, they resumed their work, until a second pebble stopped them in their tracks. The shorter, fairer man nodded to the suited man to go and investigate. As Mr X neared the bales, another noise, this time to his right, made him stop. He looked back at Ron, who signalled him to continue. Slowly, brandishing his broom, he edged forward. He was beginning to sweat, not liking being in this sort of position unarmed. It had been Ron's implicit instructions that they did not come equipped with shooters; the clients had been requested to leave any guns at the door, under surveillance of Ron's guard, before being allowed to proceed.

Mr X had reached the edge of the first bale and stopped to listen. Nothing. Not a sound yet. He knew that someone or something was close by. Tightening his grip on the broom, he crept forward and rounded the wall of straw. No one. Moving forward a few more steps, tension mounting, he was now gripping the broom so hard that his knuckles were turning white. Suddenly, out of nowhere, a hand came and covered his face. He tried to extract himself, but the grip around his neck tightened and he was dragged down to the floor. Lying face down, a rag was shoved in his mouth and, quick as a flash, his arms and ankles were bound tight. A hood was placed over his head and tied with a rope which went over his mouth, ensuring the gag did not come out. The entire scene had taken but a few seconds.

Ron looked at the bales with growing apprehension. He called for his accomplice when he heard what seemed to him to be a scuffle. He called again, louder, but still nothing. Deciding it was time for him to make an escape, he headed to the main sliding doors. He tried to open them, but they were locked. Shaking and rattling them, his frustration mounted when they refused to budge. Someone had locked them. Ron started to panic. Picking up the crowbar, he decided to confront the person or people. Surely it couldn't be one of his clients. They had all left, having been promised an even bigger and more lucrative deal in a month or so time. Was it the bastard who claimed to be his loyal local accomplice and his henchman being greedy? He had deliberately paid the man a bonus and equally promised him more for the next such deal. You could never tell with scum like that.

Ron walked steadily forward towards the rear of the warehouse; crowbar raised in front of him. Whoever the person or people were would cop a blow to the head the second they showed themselves; they didn't know Ron Stokes. Nearing the place where the muffled sounds of the scuffle had come from, he tensed slightly. Something fell on the floor behind him. He turned in a flash, his makeshift weapon raised above his head ready to strike. He cursed himself for not having a gun. He felt a hard blow to the side of his head and sank to the ground, unconscious.

***

Peter expertly searched Ron and retrieved the padlock key, then tied up the inert body before leaving it to get to work on the next part of his plan. He hauled the two men's bodies across the floor and got busy. Satisfied, he left the same way he had entered. Once outside, he radioed Sean and Charly and told them to meet him in the yard. The weather had not improved, but his mood was anything but grey or damp. He was standing at the main door when the cars turned in, followed by a fleet of police vehicles. He watched his two friends alight, followed by Kath, who was now looking calmer and more composed. She looked at him hard in the eye. "So, I suppose you're going to gloat over two more bodies," she said, brushing past him. He looked down guiltily and shrugged at Sean's questioning look. They were followed by the two detectives and the journalist.

Peter unlocked the doors and pulled them open. They all marched in and stopped. In the centre, hanging by their feet from a girder, were two trussed-up shapes; low muffled groans could be heard.

Peter turned to a couple of armed officers. "Better get these two bits of meat down from there. On the right is our friend Ron Stokes. The other, I'm not sure, but my guess is that he's the piece of dirt who's been causing most of your problems in Belfast, DI O'Grady."

CHAPTER 38

The three men were sitting at the bar, each with a pint of Guinness in front of him. Charly looked over his shoulder towards the door, then shot a glance at Sean. Rubbing his nose and clearing his throat, he turned to Peter. "We have a problem. I've had a complaint—"

Peter interrupted him, saying, "I thought you might." He sighed. "Nice girl, and probably excellent at desk work and stakeouts, but not cut out for rough action and war."

"Did you have to kill those three guards?" Sean asked.

Peter shrugged. "I had to eliminate the first two. Couldn't risk them shouting or giving our position away. The third guy, well, it was a case of either letting him strangle Kath to death or stopping him. I have no regrets. In my business, pretty much everything is allowed. It's not pretty. In most cases, it boils down to either you die or the enemy dies. There's no place for niceties. I was on my own, so I had few options. I don't regret what I did." He finished his drink and ordered another round.

Charly was about to speak when Kath walked in and went to sit at the far end next to Sean. She greeted Charly and Sean warmly but ignored Peter. Conversation was difficult, and they kept to mundane matters. "Where are DI O'Grady and Crawley? I thought they were joining us."

Sean explained that both were back at headquarters; they had piles of paperwork and had started to process and interrogate all the felons. Crawley had offered to help before catching the first flight back to Manchester. He was going to accompany the reporter and would give him the green light to tell his stories once they had landed.

"What about you, Sean? What are your plans?"

"Going down to the station with Charly in the morning to help, then I'm heading back to London—have my reports to file, and I need to tie up some loose ends." He looked over to Peter. "Pete is leaving in the morning. Aren't you?"

Peter nodded; he had not uttered a word since Kath had sat down. "Sorry if I upset you, but we, I, had little option, he said to Kath. "Deep down you know that." He paused. "I'm heading off to Leeds to visit my aunt for a few days before re-joining my boys in Afghanistan." He took a sip of his beer and licked his lips. "I know you have made a complaint; it's up to you if you want to pursue it. It will be a long, drawn-out process with loads of paperwork, and I'll have to be recalled from my posting. We're short-handed as it is, but if you feel I merit being hauled up in front of a court martial or a criminal court instead of fighting the Taliban and terrorists, then so be it. I will defend myself. It's up to you, but I'm happy with my actions given the circumstances. I will defend my name to the end." He finished his beer, ordered another three drinks, and excused himself; he was going back to Charly's house.

They watched him leave. Charly was the first to speak. "I haven't known him for very long, but from what I have seen and all the reports, he's a good man, professional and dedicated. The top brass in the army think very highly of him. It won't be easy to bring charges. Yes, I agree, perhaps he was a bit heavy-handed, but don't forget, he has experience in these sorts of situations."

There was a long silence before Kath spoke. "Perhaps I am not cut out for this kind of work. Back at training camp, it seemed easy; it was all pretend and fun. But I realised it is all very different when that man was trying to strangle me. I just froze, forgetting everything I had been taught." She knocked back her drink and accepted another. "I'm just not sure if my conscience can allow me to forgive. I know it's silly and even wrong ..." Her voice trailed off.

Sean laid a hand on her arm to reassure her. "Nothing wrong with having a conscience, but just think what it will do to his life. If your complaint is successful, it will mean the end of his career. He would lose any hope of serving in the army, not to mention losing his pension. I just ask you to think carefully before you take your final decision."

They were silent for a while, each deep in their troubled thoughts. Sean was the first to break the silence. "You seem to be a nice girl, bright, intelligent. Perhaps fieldwork isn't for you. Why don't you consider coming back to London with me? I need help. Office work has never been my strong point. You'll still be employed by the Firm, just a change of direction." He looked up at Charly. "What do think?"

"Sounds a great offer to me. Getting to spend time with one of the best spooks in town, keeping him under control. Wish I had that chance."

Kath smiled and thanked Sean, saying she would sleep on it.

———◆———

Back at police headquarters, DI O'Grady and DI Crawley were ploughing through piles of paperwork. The excitement of the operation and the arrests had been superseded by the tedious task of processing the criminals and writing the reports. O'Grady was pleased he had his colleague to help. The more he got to the know the man, the more he liked him. The feeling was mutual. Crawley had arrived in Belfast with apprehension, the recollection of their last phone conversation still vivid in his mind. Now, he had taken to this Irish detective, a man full of humour and wit, but at the same time, a serious and dedicated policeman. They got on like a house on fire.

A few doors down the corridor, O'Grady's team were interviewing the dealers, taking fingerprints and photographs, and completing the whole process of requirements. They took extra care when it came to Ron and his associate; these were two key players, and no one wanted them to wriggle through the net because of a technicality.

Patrick O'Grady sat back and stretched. He looked over at his colleague. "What do you think will happen to Stokes? I bet he'll be taken to London to stand trial, although I would dearly love to see him in front of the courts here."

DI Crawley stopped tapping on the keyboard of his computer. "One hundred per cent guaranteed he will be shipped to London; he seems also to have played a major part in organising shipments of illegals. The Old Bailey is beckoning, then a life in prison."

There was a knock on the door, then a young policeman popped his head round. "You are requested, boss. Your man Stokes will talk only to you. Says he wants to make a complaint." Both detectives looked at each other. Getting up, O'Grady signalled Crawley to follow.

<hr />

Ron Stokes was sitting, head bandaged, facing the door, a metal table in front of him and a duty solicitor by his side, with a policeman standing guard. The door swung open, and the two detectives marched in, accompanied by a second guard, a young man looking as if he had just come out of secondary school. They had barely sat down when Ron started making his complaint. The Irish detective held up his hand to silence the prisoner, but it did no good. Ron complained about having been physically assaulted by the authorities at the farm; he pointed to his head and demanded to make an official complaint. He had decided that attack was the best form of defence and his best chance of throwing a spanner in the works of officialdom. He was wrong; his tirade and accusations were dismissed. Firstly, the police had not been responsible for his injuries, as they weren't the ones who had hit him on the head. Secondly, even if they had been present, the mere fact that they found a handgun in his jacket with his prints on it, was sufficient for them to take any appropriate action. Finally, Ron was reminded that it was the police who had retrieved him from the girder and patched him up.

The duty solicitor nodded his agreement but did little to help his client, which enraged Ron even more. They were both assured that the police were actively looking for Ron's assailant, although the detectives hinted that they suspected it was one of the gangsters he had been dealing with. Ron's shoulders slumped; his brain started to work overtime. Which one of those devious crooks could it have been? There must have been an extra thug who never came in, someone he didn't see, an accomplice brought along for the purpose of getting him; they even planted the gun on him. Wait, that made no sense. What about his associate? He had been strung up too. No, there was more to this. Ron would have to think matters through.

After a fruitless hour of arguing, the interview was terminated, and Ron was taken back to his cell. Neither side had made any progress. Ron had steadfastly refused to say anything except for "No comment" to every question. In turn, the detectives had dismissed his repeated requests to make a complaint and to be appointed a new lawyer. He would be allowed a phone call to his solicitor in London sometime in the morning. The senior detectives sat and watched the prisoner being taken away. Crawley shook his head. "Arrogant bastard. The sooner we get him back to London, the better. Can't wait to see his face when he gets hit with all the other accusations."

———————◆◆◆———————

Alwyn Jones was lying on his hotel bed going over the events of the past twenty-four hours. He was miffed that the police had taken his tape recorder, notebook, and camera off him. They were keen to use him to their advantage, but they didn't trust him. Although he was a small-time reporter, he was a reporter nevertheless and couldn't be trusted to follow orders. He had been promised that once on the plane, all his work tools would be handed back. Having managed to scrounge a few sheets of paper from reception, he was now jotting notes on the events he had witnessed.

He had to admit that he was impressed at the smooth running of the operation and in awe at the speed at which it had been carried out. Deep down he knew the police had been playing backup to the three men and the woman, but even though he had sat in on the meeting the evening before last, he still didn't understand who the main players were. One was army or ex-army, that was for sure; it was the way he talked in a clipped, assured way. As for the two plain-clothes individuals, he had no idea. They could be police, but he doubted that, seeing as they spoke and acted differently from any cop he knew. As for the woman, no clue. She seemed to be shy and hardly spoke. He sucked on his pencil and made a few more notes.

CHAPTER 39

They parted company at the airport. Alwyn Jones, clutching his now returned equipment, made his way back to the office, whilst Peter headed for the station to catch a train. Before going to Leeds to see his aunt, he had one very important visit to make. He had mixed feelings at seeing his friend Brian Jackson. He couldn't report for certain that they had caught, or even found, his brother's killer or killers, but there was a good chance that Ron Stokes or one of his Belfast mobs was the culprit. From all accounts, it was probably a case of very bad luck and being in the wrong place at the wrong time, not that that was much solace to Brian or to his brother's widow.

They were sitting in the lounge where Peter related in detail the events of the past few days. When he had finished, Brian thanked him and announced he was going back to Kabul the following week. He was feeling restless and useless, as well as getting under Felicity's feet. Leave was fine for a short time, but boredom had soon set in. He had to get back to a normal life. That way, he would have things to think about apart from thoughts and memories. Felicity had suggested he went back, not that she didn't like having her brother-in-law around and having his support, but she knew from experience that a soldier needed action and to be among others of the same ilk.

The grey-haired editor glared at his young reporter; he was not amused and did not appreciate a junior's having been away for so long, especially without his blessing. He handed the man an envelope and told him to go by the accountant's office, where he would be given his P45 and severance pay. Alwyn stood at the door speechless. His first thought was to obey the old man, but quickly changed his mind and stepped forward. He placed his neatly written files, along with the tape recorder and camera, on his boss's desk and politely suggested he take a look.

An hour later, the small office was buzzing with activity. Any journalist present was ordered to drop whatever he or she was doing and to rally round. The old man was busy on the phone, talking to several national papers. At first, he was greeted with derision and laughter, his interlocutors asking how a small provincial rag had gotten a story like that. It was a joke. No, it was insulting.

Working until late, the team ensured the stories of both the Eltham raid and events outside Belfast were published the next day. It didn't take long for the major dailies and various TV stations to get wind of the events. Furious that they had been side lined and beaten to the post by a small-time provincial paper, they tried to muscle in on the act. Their phone calls and complaints to the police were skilfully fended off by the authorities, who told them to contact the editor of the *Daily Echo* for further information. By eleven o'clock in the morning, the phones were ringing continuously with financial offers streaming in. Alwyn was inundated with offers of interviews and appearing on TV chat shows; he had never dreamt he would be in such demand.

Ron Stokes was sitting on a plane to London, handcuffed to a policeman, when he saw the headlines and his picture on the front page of the paper. He managed to glimpse that the story was all about him and the arrest of a large gang of drug dealers a couple of days earlier at a farm outside Belfast. He asked the policeman if he could get a paper, but his request was refused.

He was sitting in his cell later that day when the door opened. A guard entered and told him he had a visitor. He was shown into a small room, where his lawyer was waiting. Ron and his lawyer waited until the guard closed the door before speaking.

"You have to get me out of here, and fast," Ron hissed. "It's all a terrible mistake. And I want to make a complaint: I was hit and injured by the police."

The lawyer listened patiently and asked a great many questions, noting everything Ron told him. When his client had finished, he was silent for a long time. When he did finally speak, he said, "I must be honest; although I believe everything you tell me, we will have a hard task persuading the court to grant you bail. As for proving your innocence, that will not be easy either. The fact that you were found at the farm at the time of the raid is not good. They have photo evidence of the vans entering and leaving the warehouse and of those same vans laden with drugs. As for your complaint, I feel we have very little hope getting that taken seriously. By the sounds of it, you were found tied and gagged by the police, so it couldn't have been them." He looked at his client before continuing. "You'd better start telling me what your involvement was in the Eltham raid."

The meeting went on for several hours. At last, the lawyer decided he had enough to go on. Before buzzing for a guard, he told Ron that they had not gotten any further with finding Jane whereabouts and strongly suggested they report her missing. Ron refused point-blank, pointing out that the police would probably assume he had bumped her off and pin her disappearance on him. The lawyer agreed and admitted that such could be a possibility. He left after promising to return on Monday.

The news of the farm raid was reported on television across Europe. Reporters were sent to London and Belfast. Speculation was rife that the drug gang was also involved in people smuggling, all run by a notorious Englishman named Ron Stokes. The police were not confirming anything, saying that their investigations were ongoing. The only thing the media had to go by was Alwyn's story.

Hans's lawyer sat glued to his screen, not believing what he had heard. This was his client's boss, the very man who, not so long ago, had threatened him. He did not like the implications one iota. The latest developments would certainly not help his client's case one little bit either; the link between the two would be easily made. The Dutch police would be in contact with their English counterparts imminently, if they hadn't been already. The lawyer guessed there were mobile phone calls that could be traced as well as, no doubt, a whole lot more. He grimaced; it wasn't going to be easy to have his man mixed up in all this. The money laundering, the large packages of drugs in his bag, the woman; it was a big web and getting bigger by the minute. He would have been happy to continue with the case but for one thing, money. He had pulled many strings, but even more than that, he had put in many long hours. Who would pay him, and how would he be paid? He would have to go and talk to his client, the sooner, the better.

Hans had been languishing in his cell for far too long and was anxious to get out. Bail had been refused and no date for his court case had been set. His only contact with the outside world was with his lawyer, whom, he noted, he hadn't seen in three days. He was pleasantly surprised when he was summoned to the visitors' room and found his man. Beaming and smiling broadly, he sat down across the table.

His elation soon disappeared when he was told about Ron and the raid in the countryside of Ulster. He realised immediately the consequences. His hopes of getting out of the hellhole he currently was in were seriously dented, if not completely gone. He quickly figured out that the police would add two and two together and come to the obvious conclusion that Hans van der Brawn and Ron Stokes worked together. Policemen were known to be thick, but not that stupid. Hans's thoughts were confirmed by the man sitting across from him. What to do? What was the best course of action? He was relying on some sound advice.

The two men talked for a long while. Hans opened up to his brief, telling him everything, every little detail in the vain hope it would help his cause. The man listened intently, taking copious notes. He didn't speak until he was about to leave, at which point he got up and looked at his client. "Hans. I can call you Hans, yes? How do you expect to pay me? My fees are already high and were going to be settled by Mr Stokes, but it is clear now this has changed. Your assets have been frozen. I am happy to continue defending you, but I have to live, I have bills to pay. My small firm cannot sustain not being paid. I suggest you think about it. We can discuss the matter next time." He smiled politely and left.

Back in his cell, Hans lay on his bunk deep in thought. He had much to consider. The more he tried to think, the more he became depressed. There was no happy ending that he could see. His mind drifted back to the Riviera, to Jane and to the Russian tart, whose name he tried to remember but couldn't. What had happened to Jane? Where had she gone, and where was she now? He would dearly love to know. It was all her fault he was in here.

Hans's lawyer sat behind his large desk, unable to see a way out of this mess. He saw no hope of winning, so he had no hope of getting paid. Ron had been his guarantor, and now that he too was in jail, there was little or no hope. The lawyer sucked on his pen for a long time before he picked up the phone and dialled police headquarters.

———◆———

Sean was sitting with his Dutch counterpart when the phone on the desk rang. A minute later the Dutchman looked over and beckoned Sean to follow him; they were off to police headquarters.

They were shown into the office of the head of police, where they were greeted by the man himself and a tall, dark haired individual who introduced himself as Hans van der Brawn's lawyer; he spoke good English. For the next couple of hours, they listened to what he had to say, interrupting only for clarification. What they heard was unbelievable. Well, not really; it all made perfect sense. It confirmed everything they had discovered and discussed. They sat back and thanked the lawyer profusely. Yes, he would gladly fly over to London and testify. In turn, Sean agreed he would do the same in Amsterdam. They parted very happy men.

———◆◆◆———

Ron's lawyer sat glum-faced across the table; he was in no mood for chitchat. Earlier that morning he had been invited to a meeting with the head of narcotics, one of the detectives involved in the Ulster raid, and two gentlemen unknown to him. He was not surprised to be told that the prosecutor's office had sufficient evidence of Ron's culpability. He would be charged with drug trafficking in a huge style, people smuggling, and money laundering. What really shook him was the news that the Dutch lawyer employed by Ron to defend his accomplice Hans van der Brawn would also testify that his client was Ron's right-hand man and accomplice in all operations. Hans, now languishing in an Amsterdam cell, had admitted to everything, and was prepared to sign a written affidavit.

Ron was shattered. His whole world had collapsed. His so-called friend had deserted him, but worst of all, the lawyer he had employed to defend Hans had turned against him. He looked at his brief in despair.

The man shrugged, suggesting that Ron should cooperate in the hope of getting a reduced sentence, saying there was no other solution. He had quickly dismissed any idea of getting paid by his client, knowing full well that most of the man's fortune had probably been embezzled by his ex-wife and what little was left had been frozen by the authorities. No, he would go through the motions of defending Ron. It was the least he could do after so many years.

"You have to find that bitch of a wife of mine. It's all her fault. She's the one responsible for all this, I know it," Ron hissed. "Once you have found her, come and tell me, and I will make sure she pays."

CHAPTER 40

The trial of Hans van der Brawn took place in Amsterdam six months after he had been arrested. His lawyer had deserted him and was now a witness for the prosecution. The young lawyer who had been appointed to him was nice enough but totally out of his depth. Dressed in joggers and a T-shirt with a week's worth of stubble, Hans looked a shadow of his former himself. Gone was the muscular body, the neat hair, and the sparkling blue eyes. As he sat in the dock listening to proceedings, he cast his mind back to that fateful day when Jane had caught him with the Russian tart. What was her name? Ah yes, Natasha. He doubted he would recognise her if she were to walk in. All he could recall were those long, endless legs.

Jane had a lot to answer for; there was no doubt in Hans's mind now that it was all her doing. He never dreamt she would be so vengeful or, for that matter, have the brains and the balls to set him up. Gone now were the dreams of a peaceful retirement, living a life of luxury in the Caribbean. There and then, he vowed that when he got out, if he ever got out, he would find Jane and make her pay dearly.

As proceedings droned on, Hans's thoughts turned to Ron, his mentor. He had a lot to thank the man for. Ron had taught the young Hans all he knew. He had looked up to the Englishman, had venerated him, and had done deeds he had never dreamt he was capable of. He, Hans, had learned fast and, through his dedication and hard work, had made his way up to the top. All that counted for nothing now that he knew the man he had idolised, was not what he had thought. No, just another lowlife gangster with big ideas and a big ego. Hans had been blinded by Ron's confidence, his bluster, and the promise of wealth; he never thought of the consequences. The stupid idiot of a man had proved he was no better than himself. Hans had spent weeks preparing the Irish deal, and within a few days of the boss taking over, the whole operation had crumbled. Thanks to Ron's incompetence and naivety, he, like Hans, was in prison.

Hans's lawyer had deserted him, the rat, and his chances of winning his freedom were minimal. No, Jane had a lot to answer for, but Hans blamed Ron even more. All their hard-earned cash had been frozen, and their assets impounded. No money and no proper lawyer equalled a long life in a cell. Hans doubted he could survive the ordeal for very long. He swore that if ever he got out, he would go after Ron and make him pay for putting him behind bars; Jane would be a close second.

Ron Stokes sat in the dock at the Old Bailey, surrounded by a couple of guards. Unlike Hans a week earlier in Amsterdam, he was dressed immaculately in a suit and tie; he had decided to keep up standards and appearances.

He listened to his lawyer intently and had to admit the man was good. Not only that, but he was also loyal. Fully aware that the chances of getting paid were minimal or non-existent, the man put on a great show. A real actor, he involved the jury fully and painted a picture of Ron as a hard-working businessman who had been stabbed in the back by a jealous and ungrateful associate. He dismissed the Eltham raid as police fabrication with no proof. Had his client been at the warehouse? Had the police found any concrete proof? It was all suppositions. As for the drug raid, well, it was unfortunate timing. His client had been duped to going along and had gotten caught up in something he knew nothing of. All was going well—the jury were wavering—until the Dutch lawyer took the stand and gave evidence. From that moment, Ron knew he was doomed.

Ron had asked his lawyer to bring Jane into it and blame her for using him as cover to organise her secret underworld deals, but the brief had dismissed that idea immediately. Jane was still missing with no one having seen or heard from her. He was worried that a further charge of abduction and murder would be pinned on Ron. No, best keep her out of it.

Back in his cell, waiting for sentencing day, Ron swore that if, and when, he was released, his first task would be to find his ex-wife and make her pay big time. He did not tolerate being crossed, especially by a dumb, brainless blonde. Who did she think she was, messing with Ron Stokes? No, she would pay with her life.

As for that useless, sexed-up Hans, whom he had once considered a friend, well, he would pay too for being so stupid. What a fool to have trusted him. All that time spent teaching him, nurturing him, and looking after him only to have all his efforts thrown back at him. Ron hadn't minded his aide's messing with Jane; in fact, it amused him and had given him more ammunition to use against her. What had possessed the man to choose a cheating lowlife lawyer? Ron would have to think of a suitable punishment for Hans.

He had never liked that lawyer—too polite, too cold, and always saying the right thing. Never had Ron heard the man come up with anything concrete or positive. He hadn't trusted the Dutchman since their last meeting, when Ron had to threaten him; it was something in the lawyer's eyes. Well, he was easy to deal with. Lots of people fell in canals and died. He would be one of them.

<hr/>

Only a few people, mostly the press, occupied the visitors' seats in the courtroom in Amsterdam. They watched Hans as he took his seat in the barred enclosure. He seemed to have aged even more during the past week. His grey stubble, dishevelled hair, and hollow cheeks made him look like a ghost.

He sat silently, oblivious of what was going on around him, only half listening to what the judge was saying. His mind was away on a sunny beach in the Caribbean when he felt a hand grip his arm and he was taken to a waiting minibus.

———◆◆———

The courtroom was packed with journalists and curious onlookers as Ron was marched in to hear the verdict. Still defiant to the end, he had instructed his brief to make an immediate appeal if things went against him. The lawyer had sighed and promised to do just that, knowing full well it would be instantly rejected, yet he had to go through the motions.

As the judge and everyone listened to the jury's verdict, Ron's shoulders slumped for the first time. He screwed up his eyes and shook his head in disbelief as he heard the sentence. A few members of the public cheered and clapped.

Alwyn Jones had watched the whole proceedings with interest and took copious notes that he would send back to his boss. He looked round but saw no one from the police he recognised, nor any of the men who had orchestrated the two raids. He watched Ron be taken away, head bowed, hands cuffed, and was proud, as well as grateful, to have played a part in putting away such a dangerous individual. He was thankful that he had taken the decision to go to the funeral that fateful day and was happy for his luck at finding Peter Hollins, a meeting and a decision that had shot him to fame and fortune.

CHAPTER 41

Kath turned up the volume on the television to listen to the news. Both she and Sean were eager to hear about the trial. He sat there nodding with satisfaction. His man Stokes had been sentenced to life with no hope of early release, as had his accomplice Hans in Amsterdam. Both trials had taken place within a week of one another, and sentencing had been organised, thanks to diplomatic discussions, to be on the same day. Sean looked over to his new assistant and nodded with satisfaction. "A job well done; wouldn't you say? Two big players taken out of circulation, along with numerous smaller criminals also behind bars. I know it's only a drop in the ocean, but hey, every little bit helps."

Kath was pleased for him; she knew how hard he had worked, with countless long days and sleepless nights. She knew he enjoyed his job—not so much the paperwork, but getting out there trying to outwit the lowlife, the enemy, as he called them.

She had moved down to London a week after he had left Belfast. It hadn't been a difficult decision. And with help from both Charly and Sean, her transfer was streamlined. They had provided her with a small one-bedroom flat for a couple of months until she had time to find something more permanent. At the same time as her move and to thank her two mentors, she had dropped the complaint against Peter. She wasn't comfortable doing so but had decided it wouldn't be worth all the aggravation or worth upsetting her new friendship with the two men.

Sean leapt out of his chair. "I think we should celebrate, don't you?

I know this little Chinese place in Soho. They serve the best chilli beef in town." Kath agreed instantly.

Before leaving the office, Sean decided to call Peter. It would be the middle of the night where he was, but that wouldn't upset his friend. A sleepy voice answered, soon turning to fully awake when he heard the news. "Yes, fantastic. Well done, guys. Really, really pleased you got them behind bars. Make sure to have a drink on me."

Sean related as much as he could and asked how things were going over in Afghanistan. "Oh, just the same old. Like you, I spend my days chasing blood, taking out baddies. Don't tell Kath I said that." He chuckled. "By the way, how is she, settled in OK and looking after you?" They said their goodbyes. Sean heard an elated whoop as the phone went dead.

Kath and Sean were walking down the busy street when he suddenly stopped. "I have been meaning to ask, what about you coming to live with me? The flat is large enough for two. What do you say?" She grinned broadly. "Never thought you'd ask," she said, kissing him tenderly.

<hr />

Charly Flynn had helped DI O'Grady close the case and was delighted when his new friend called to report that Mr X and the other gang members had all been sentence to long terms in prison. After much interrogating, Mr X had spilled the beans, admitting that the shooting of John Hollins had been an accident. A turf war had erupted between rival gangs instigated by himself and things had gotten nasty, which resulted in the numerous muggings and beatings in the city. The soldier had been inadvertently caught in the crossfire of one of these battles.

After Sean had left Belfast, Charly had called his boss and arranged for Kath to be transferred to London. He explained that Sean needed someone to assist him with all the paperwork and said that Kath was eager for a change. No questions were asked and the transfer came quicker than expected. The only condition Charly had requested of Kath was that she drop the charges against Peter.

She had little choice. It had taken her by surprise, but after Sean had left, she realised how much she liked him. She missed his cheeky banter, his happy nature, and his sense of humour. Unexpectedly, love had crept up on her, completely taking over her mind and her feelings. She was not sure if he felt the same way but decided to make it her task to ensure he did.

———◆◆———

Alwyn Jones's life had changed dramatically over the period of a few days. He was no longer the junior reporter spending time covering accidents or petty crimes, no longer the gopher and the butt of his colleagues' jokes. After his scoops, he was the centre of attention, a man in demand. He spent most of the ensuing weeks appearing on TV chat shows, giving radio interviews, and being asked his opinion on anything that happened in the world. He had been offered many lucrative job opportunities with larger national papers but declined them all. To the amazement of his boss, he remained loyal to the *Daily Echo*—and for that loyalty, he was promoted to assistant editor.

He had gone down to London for Ron Stokes's trial to ensure that his paper had good coverage of proceedings and the sentencing.

After the publication of his reports on Eltham and Belfast, Jones had been contacted by Charly Flynn, who reminded him that he had responsibilities and a duty not to divulge names or any sensitive information he may have learned about him or Sean. He, Charly Flynn, would be watching - any sign of indiscretion and the reporter would regret his error. Alwyn Jones was in no doubt as to the consequences, and the threats came to mind continuously.

———◆◆———

Jane nestled into the sofa and snuggled up to her mother. They had been to the home that afternoon, and the news was not good. Her father had suffered a stroke, and the doctor didn't expect him to live for much longer. She sipped on her wine and chatted about the future.

Her mother loved the place, including the countryside and the view over the valley and onto the village below. The house was surrounded by vineyards. It was peaceful. Jane decided to talk to the agents the next day and ask to either extend the lease or perhaps even buy. Her Italian was not good, but neither was her German—and she certainly preferred the small house they were in to the flat in the suburbs of Zurich.

Her mother was worried Jane would get bored. Could they afford it? What about Jane's business? And what to do with the house in England? Her daughter reassured her; she had already sorted the business out, and no, she would not get bored. As for money, she had made all the necessary arrangements; there were no worries. Just what to do with her parents' home, though—that was tricky. They could put it on the market, but too many awkward questions would be asked. She would have to use her real name, and she didn't want to do that. She also didn't want to put her mother through all the stress and complications, not now when her husband was dying. She would have to think about that one, all in good time.

Jane switched on the TV and flicked to Sky, nearly choking when the picture came on. There, in front of her, were photos of Ron and Hans. She turned up the volume. The presenter was telling viewers that these two notorious drug dealers, people traffickers, and money launderers had been sentenced to life with a minimum of twenty-five years behind bars for each offence. Coincidently, their trials had taken place within a week of each other in Amsterdam and London, and the judges had given their verdicts simultaneously earlier that day.

Jane's mother looked at her and raised her glass. "Good riddance. I never liked that man of yours, although your father thought he was great. He never saw through him like I did. He was impressed and envious of his so-called success and what he had given you." They continued to watch until the subject was changed.

"What are we going to do?"

Jane smiled. "Nothing. Just enjoy our new life together. No more bullying, no more crook of a husband or cheating lover and, more importantly, no more looking over my shoulder."

They laughed and clinked glasses.

ABOUT THE AUTHOR

Following forty years in the hospitality and retail industry, **Paul Stanley** retired in early 2019. During the pandemic and lockdown, he wrote his first novel, A *Devious War*, something he always wanted to do but never had the time. Widely travelled with many life experiences, he has brought his uncompromising business thinking to his writing and stories.

Printed and bound by CPI Group (UK) Ltd, Croydon, CR0 4YY